Hazards of the Game

A CEDAR HARBOR MYSTERY

HAZARDS OF THE GAME

NORMA TADLOCK JOHNSON

FIVE STAR
A part of Gale, Cengage Learning

GALE
CENGAGE Learning™

Detroit • New York • San Francisco • New Haven, Conn • Waterville, Maine • London

LIBRARY OF CONGRESS CATALOGING-IN-PUBLICATION DATA

Hazards of the game : a Cedar Harbor mystery / Norma Tadlock Johnson. — 1st ed.
    p. cm.
ISBN-13: 978-1-59414-881-1 (hardcover)
ISBN-10: 1-59414-881-3 (hardcover)
1. Widows—Fiction. 2. Murder—Investigation—Fiction. 3. Suburban life—Washington (State)—Fiction. 4. Washington (State)—Fiction. I. Title.
PS3560.O3819H39 2010
813'.54—dc22   2010013295

First Edition. First Printing: August 2010.
Published in 2010 in conjunction with Tekno Books and Ed Gorman.

Printed in the United States of America
1 2 3 4 5 6 7 14 13 12 11 10

ACKNOWLEDGMENTS

Thank you, Detective Eddie Rogge of the Burlington Police Department, for answering my questions about about police work and terminology. Anything non-factual is either my mistake or was altered to fit the plot.

Thanks to my editor, Alice Duncan, for making *Hazards of the Game* a better book.

CHAPTER ONE

Paula Madigan was a reserved sort of person. It wasn't that she disliked people; rather, she had always preferred observing to interacting. You didn't get hurt that way.

Fred never understood. Fred was a domineering man. So Paula dutifully attended parties, hosted guests and joined the golf club, where she found to her surprise that she rather enjoyed the game, all the while she assiduously avoided the committees. Let Fred do that. He thrived on gracious manipulation.

He was at his peak the year he was chosen president of the golf club. His business, cloning electronic components for the airline industry, was prospering. He'd been appointed to the board of the art museum the year previously. Paula attended the museum openings; Fred's name was prominent on all the fund-raising committees for needy charities. Paula often acted as secretary, quietly observing the progress as well as the infighting. Her husband was even approached about running for the State Senate. A Democrat had been inconsiderate enough to win the representation from their well-heeled district the previous election. "You're just what our party needs," he was told. Paula shuddered at the prospect.

All was well in Fred's life until that last time he played golf. The foursome, besides himself, consisted of two of his regular playing partners and a newcomer, Walt Graylock. Walt was one of those picky rule-followers. "Like the women," Fred commented in a quiet aside to his best friend Al.

All through the round Walt asserted his knowledge of the official rules. "You know that's against regulations," he'd said when Fred knocked a gob of mud off his ball on the soggy second fairway. He complained, albeit with a chuckle, "You're bending the rules as well as that branch," when Fred merely tried to make it more feasible to get his ball out from under a bush on the dogleg on the fifth. He tried to assess an extra stroke when Fred ticked the ball with a practice stroke on the eleventh green. Fred exploded. He also died on the eleventh green, his red face turning pale as he clutched his chest and then collapsed, beyond the help of the CPR administered by Walt.

Paula was bereft. She'd never pictured life without Fred upon whom to lean. But then she astounded even herself. She gathered together resources she hadn't known she possessed, dealt with a patronizing attorney and sold the business. With plenty of money, she settled back to decide what to do with the rest of her life.

She was in her early sixties, and alone. She and Fred had had only one child, born with difficulty after ten years of marriage. Her name was Jennifer, but Paula tried hard not to think of her. It had been years, sixteen years and three months to be exact, since she'd had any contact with her daughter. Most of the time she managed not to think of the dark, curly-haired youngster so like herself whom she had reared. Only occasionally, usually in the black of night in the bedroom, did the memories intrude.

Actually, Paula might have continued living the way she always had if it hadn't been for the well-meaning people of their suburb of Seattle—not to mention Fred's business associates and the busybody lawyer. They all seemed to think it was their duty to help Paula over her grief, to draw her out of her seclusion. Not one of them ever noticed that, given a choice, she had always preferred that seclusion. The phone calls and visits had become almost unbearable when a last one altered everything.

"I thought," Kay Morris said, leaning back in the leather chair, "that you might need a change about now." Her brown eyes twinkled understandingly over the Lenox teacup.

"I hadn't . . ." Paula began to answer, then, to her own surprise, said, "Maybe."

"I remember when my Charles died," Kay said. "The people, to be blunt, drove me crazy. They all thought they knew what I needed." She sipped her tea and waited.

Paula nodded in agreement.

"So," Kay continued, "I have this cousin who lives up north in that posh new development, you know, the Kamiak Hills thing, and they want to go to Europe for the summer. They're looking for someone to stay at their place, a house-sitter if you will. I know you have a house here you'd worry about, but at least you don't have any pets. They have two cats, obnoxious Siamese in my opinion, and they can't bear to leave them at a kennel. You don't mind animals?" She peered closely at Paula.

"No, I don't mind animals—that was Fred," Paula answered. She made up her mind quickly. "When did you say they're going?"

A month later, Paula drove up the freeway in her loaded car. It was new. It was a Toyota. Fred had never approved of small cars, especially Japanese ones. Paula had not been the least sorry to see the two Cadillacs go. She'd made arrangements with an agency that promised to care for her yard, change the lighting system electronically and oversee the house. She set the burglar alarm and departed, wondering a little if she really would ever want to live in the house again.

Paula was disconcerted momentarily when she drove into Kamiak Hills and discovered that the Pappas house was situated on the golf course. But then she shrugged and decided it was just as well. She hadn't been able to bring herself to play on the course on which Fred had died. She couldn't in her wildest imaginings picture what it would be like to putt on the very green where the unpleasant event had occurred. Still, she enjoyed the game, and this might be just what she needed. She certainly had to occupy her time with something. There was no question that life dragged, living by herself. Fred had kept things hopping when he was around, more than she ever had realized.

Paula pulled up in front of the sprawling, white-stuccoed home with urns and baskets of red geraniums that matched the house's tile roof. She had timed her arrival to meet the Pappases before they departed. Mrs. Pappas was a tiny brunette with flashing eyes. She welcomed Paula with enthusiasm and led her into the white-carpeted living room. "This is Mum-mum," Mrs. Pappas said, as she picked up a wary cream-and-brown cat and tried to cuddle it.

Mum-mum clearly knew something was afoot that wasn't to her liking. The glance she shot Paula was not friendly.

"And Carioca," Mrs. Pappas said. "Where are you, my dear?"

Carioca eyed the proceedings from the mantel of the white fireplace and ignored her.

"Oh, well, you'll have lots of time to get acquainted later." Mrs. Pappas glanced at her watch urgently. "I've left lists," she explained as she led the way through the immaculate house with the white carpet flowing from room to room. Paula was relieved to see that one of the lists had the name of the cleaning woman who came every Friday.

"This is probably the best room for you." Mrs. Pappas threw open the door to a bedroom that held a king-sized bed covered with a sprightly green-and-yellow flowered spread. Gauzy curtains hung over a sliding door that led to a side patio. "Although you're welcome to choose any you like, of course." There were five, Paula discovered. What did the Pappases use five bedrooms for? she wondered, since nothing was said about anyone else in the household.

With two quick hugs for the reluctant cats, Mrs. Pappas gathered the rest of her luggage, her purse, and her tall, silent husband and departed. Paula exhaled in relief and began to unwind.

For three days, she did nothing but enjoy her solitude. The larder was well-stocked; she didn't even have to leave to go to the grocery store. The weather was pleasant, and she sat on the deck much of the time reading the books she'd brought with her. She was relieved when Mum-mum and Carioca ignored her except when they wanted to be fed. She did like animals that at least pretended to like her in return, but so far, the two Siamese had not responded.

Living directly on a golf course was a new experience. Clumps of small trees more or less marked what she assumed was the boundary of the Pappas holdings, since an out-of-bounds marker was in line with them, but errant golfers regularly trespassed to retrieve their balls. Paula wasn't quite sure how to respond to their presence. Should she ignore them? Or should she smile in commiseration with their misfortune or maybe even start a conversation? At first she pretended to be so engrossed in her book that she didn't see them, but gradually, she began to acknowledge their presence with a nod and then, finally, by smiling and saying hello.

By the time the doorbell rang the fourth day, Paula was ready for a break. She opened the front door to find a blond woman standing on the doorstep holding a covered plate. The woman smiled tentatively, then said, "I'm Ellen Cogsdill. I live next door. I promised Lynn Pappas I'd come over and get acquainted, but the children had day camp . . ."

"Come in," Paula suggested, holding the door wider. "I'm delighted to meet you."

The gray eyes, which had held a touch of apprehension, widened in relief, and Ellen stepped inside. "I brought you some cookies," she said. "Although, I didn't know, in this day so many people are dieting . . ." She eyed Paula's trim figure.

Paula smiled, noting that Ellen, herself, evidently did not worry a great deal about restricting her food intake. "I love cookies. Shall we have coffee and enjoy some?" She led the way to the kitchen.

"Lynn was so happy to locate you," Ellen said, settling on a bar stool while Paula made the coffee. "She just didn't know what she was going to do with those cats, and I sure didn't want to take them on. They don't like kids much, and with mine . . ."

"You have several?" Paula inquired politely.

"Three. Josh is twelve, and Susan is eight and Mark is six. We'd always intended to have more, but . . ."

Paula was beginning to find that Ellen had a habit of not finishing her sentences. Perhaps in a busy household, she didn't get the chance. She also was a talker, and maybe, Paula surmised, she'd just gotten in the habit of interrupting herself. Ellen chattered while the two women drank their coffee, explaining who lived where and which ones were divorced. Paula listened politely, as was her habit.

Paula had almost tuned her out when she was startled at a sudden change of subject. "You don't play golf by any chance, do you?" Ellen asked. "My usual partner is on vacation."

"As a matter of fact, I do," Paula answered.

"Wonderful! How would you like to play tomorrow? The kids are staying over at my mother's tonight. We could get an early tee time. The weatherman says it's going to be hot . . . and we can have lunch afterwards at the clubhouse."

It was earlier than she liked to be out and about, but pleasant, Paula found the next morning as they drove up to the first tee in Ellen's cart. It was one of those rare June days that promised real warmth after the last of the humidity was burned from the air. June so often was cool and damp in the Pacific Northwest. Early dew still glistened like gems on the fairway. Pretty, but the balls would be difficult to find. Beyond the first green, Mount Baker rose, its massive white bulk dominating the skyline.

They were to play with a Mr. and Mrs. Griffin, she discovered. The Griffins were old acquaintances of Ellen's. "Call me Babs," the woman suggested when Ellen introduced them. "And this is Ben." She gestured at the heavy-set man with a pleasant face Ellen had informed her was a retired banker. He held out a hand, and Paula, taking it, gave her own first name.

"Welcome to our community," he said.

Ben, it quickly became evident, hit booming balls that were as likely as not to be out of bounds or on the next fairway, whereas Babs's timid shots remained precisely in the middle. Ellen's style, it developed, was more akin to Ben's. The only thing that saved her from real trouble was the fact that she didn't hit the ball as far.

Paula's handicap was barely respectable due to the erratic nature of her game, but she was pleased this morning to find that she at least had started with some of her better shots. Other than the predictable searches for Ben's missing ball and sometimes Ellen's, the four moved along at a good pace. The course was a difficult one, with deep sand hazards placed to trap the careless. "The next hole has a humungous water hole," Babs informed her. "I always lay up short."

Paula appreciated the advice when the glistening hazard came into view, although it had become evident that Babs gave suggestions a mite freely. Ben didn't always seem to appreciate it and Paula could see why. He had, presumably, played this course numerous times.

As they approached the fourth green, Ellen hit a chip that should have stayed nicely on the surface. Instead, it rolled slowly and disappeared over the edge. "Damn," Ellen swore. "That awful sand trap."

Paula smiled sympathetically. Her own ball was safely on the green, but she had just wasted two shots extricating herself from the deepest bunker she'd ever seen. Babs hit her orange ball carefully onto the putting surface, but short, and Ben missed his chip entirely. "You're peeking again, dear," Babs said. "If you'd just remember what that expensive pro told you, your score would be much better."

Ben glared, then took a handkerchief from his pocket and wiped his bald head. "It's beginning to get warm."

"I told you to wear a hat," Babs said primly. "You heard the weather report this morning. But you never do pay any attention, do you?"

Ben muttered under his breath, whether at his golf ball or Babs, Paula was too far away to determine. He swung again in the approved manner with a club that should have lifted the ball gently into the air, but instead, clipped its top, causing it to roll. It dropped into the cup. Ben laughed, but his expression was chagrined.

Ellen parked their cart to one side of the green and climbed out. Paula pulled her putter out of the bag and walked toward the hole to wait. Her footsteps showed in the dew, which still clung to the manicured putting surface. Ellen hesitated before choosing a club; then, mumbling to herself, trudged into the huge bunker that guarded the green like a moat. Her pink ball glowed damply where it rested on top of the sand.

To Paula, watching, Ellen disappeared entirely from view as she bent over in the monstrous trap. Her blond head reappeared as she straightened. "At least it's on a hump of some kind," she said. "I'm lucky. I don't remember a raised place the last time I was here."

"Maybe somebody buried treasure," Babs suggested with a wry smile.

Ellen grunted, then took a wild swing. No ball appeared on the green. Her face was flushed. She took another haphazard swing, looking as if she were attempting to kill a rattlesnake rather than attack a golf ball, Paula thought. In her usual fashion, however, she refrained from saying so. Ellen might not think it was funny. Not now, anyway.

Ellen swung again. "Oh, my *Gawd!*" She whirled and stepped backwards as if she had seen a snake. Her face was not red anymore. It was, in fact, white with blotchy purple spots. She threw one hand over her mouth and pointed dramatically with the sand wedge held in the other. Then, dropping her club, she staggered backwards out of the trap and plopped down on the grass, her eyes screwed shut.

"What in hell?" Ben strode rapidly forward.

Ellen buried her head between her knees. "Tell me I didn't see it. Tell me I didn't see it!"

Paula had been standing still, stunned by her partner's behavior, but now she, too, moved forward quickly and stared over the lip into the bunker. Ellen's fluorescent ball lay, untouched, next to something that protruded from the sand, something that definitely wasn't buried treasure.

Ben hurried around the edge of the bunker. Babs stood on top, sucking her fingers, her eyes wide. Paula followed Ben far enough to have a clearer view. That was enough.

Ellen obviously hadn't imagined anything. She had good reason for her peculiar behavior, Paula saw with sudden clarity. Extending forward from the sand as if groping for the ball, complete with three gaudy rings sparkling in the sunlight, was a woman's hand.

CHAPTER TWO

Afterwards, Paula was never certain which was the more traumatic event of the day. The golf round was never finished; the police came, driving their patrol cars and vans right to the fourth green. The pristine fairways of the Kamiak Hills Country Club would never be the same. Bodies, after all, had to be removed, even if groundskeepers gnashed their teeth. Paula thought that the physical scars of the day would be there to remind people long after the murder was solved. She never doubted that it would be.

"Is it okay if we forgo having lunch today?" she asked Ellen as they headed away from the fourth green. "I don't know about you, but I seem to have lost my appetite."

Ellen nodded. "I feel the same. Looking at that hand . . ."

"Uh—yes." Would anyone who was there this awful morning ever forget the sight? Glancing at her neighbor, she saw that Ellen was definitely still green around the gills, an apt expression. Neither spoke again until Ellen parked behind the Pappas house.

"Oh, shoot. I have to return the clubs," Paula said.

"I'll do it," Ellen volunteered. "It'd be easier than you getting your cart out and transferring them."

"Well . . . Thanks so much."

Paula waved goodbye, then hurried into the house. She was just brewing strong coffee when the phone rang. Startled, she almost dropped the coffee can. Recovering, she set it on the counter and reached for the phone, absently swiping at a few spilled grounds.

"Pappas residence," she answered. So far, all the calls had been for the absent owners.

"Mother?" a quavering voice inquired.

"No, I'm sorry—at least . . ." There was something about the voice that nagged at Paula's subconscious. "Whom did you wish to speak to?" She clutched the front of her blouse, scrunching the cotton material into a wrinkled lump.

"You, I think," the voice answered. "Mother, this is Jennifer."

Paula groped for a kitchen chair, then sank into it. Shock made her mind refuse to function. "Jennifer? My daughter?"

A giggle on the other end sounded like the girl she remembered. "The one and only, at least I think so. You and Dad didn't have any more after I left, did you?"

"No, of course not. Jennifer—I'm overwhelmed. Where are you?" Paula glanced around quickly, as if her absent daughter could be approaching somehow instead of talking on the phone. "Are you here?"

"Where's here?" Jennifer inquired. "What are you doing away from home?"

A flash of irritation made Paula's voice sound curt. "What are *you* doing? Where have you been for the last sixteen years and four months?"

"So you've been counting?" Jennifer's voice sounded as if she was laughing. "You did think about me once in a while?"

"Of course I did! Didn't you think I would? Why didn't you let us know where you were? Your father . . ." Paula realized suddenly that Jennifer wouldn't know. "Your father's dead," she said numbly. "He—had a heart attack."

"I heard," Jennifer answered. "That's why I'm calling. I did write, Mom. Why didn't you answer?"

"I never got any letters."

Paula felt anger boiling over the silent humming of the line before Jennifer answered. "So he confiscated my letters." Her voice was bitter. "That sounds like Father."

"He wouldn't have."

"Oh, yes, he would," Jennifer informed her. "He always went through my things."

"Well," Paula said, sighing, "that's over and done with. We can talk about it when I see you. When are you coming?" Her responses came from deep within her without true thought.

"Well," the voice hesitated, "actually, I'm not. It's Laurie . . ."

"Who is Laurie?" Paula somehow knew before Jennifer answered, and she felt herself gasp for breath.

"Why, my daughter, of course. Your granddaughter. I wrote. Didn't Dad see fit to tell you? But of course not. Always the bastard. I was as good as dead, as far as he was concerned."

"Maybe he didn't read the letters before he destroyed them." The minute she said it, Paula knew it wasn't true. It was so like Fred, the way he controlled everything, always insisted on knowing what was going on. Fred had undoubtedly read the letters, known about the child, Paula's granddaughter, and hadn't seen fit to tell her. At that moment, Paula's heart hardened against the departed Fred. She would never again mourn him.

"If you can believe that, you'll believe anything," Jennifer said dryly. "But that's not the point now. It's Laurie."

"What about Laurie? Tell me about her. How old is she? What does she look like?"

"Oh, she looks like you and me, Mom. Strong genes I guess. She's got a mop of brown curls, and she's small for her age . . ." For an instant, Paula pictured Jennifer at about three, but that vision popped away like a broken light bulb when Jennifer continued, "She's thirteen."

In its place, Paula suddenly had a view of her daughter at thirteen, wild dark hair, a scrawny build, and defiant gray eyes.

"Well," Paula said, "when can I see you both? You still haven't told me where you are."

"Oh, New York," Jennifer said casually. "That answering service of yours didn't want to give me your number, but I persuaded them when I told them I was your daughter and it was an emergency."

"Emergency?" Paula's heart tightened. "What's the matter? You said Laurie . . ."

"Calm down, Mother," Jennifer said. "It's not that kind of emergency. And you will see Laurie. I'm sending her for a visit."

"A visit?" Paula's voice squeaked. "I—I mean, I want to see you, both of you, I'll send the money, but—I'm house sitting . . ."

"What difference does that make?" Jennifer's voice was curious.

"I don't know what the Pappases would think. They surely would not have wanted a house sitter with a teenage—how long will she be staying?"

"I had in mind the summer."

"But the carpets are *white*." To her horror, Paula realized how inhospitable that sounded. Nevertheless, she doubted if a teenager with drippy sandwiches and dirty feet had ever trod the floors of the Pappas residence.

"You always did worry too much about what the house looked like," Jennifer snapped. "A clean house isn't the most important thing in life, you know."

"Of course I know. That wasn't me; it was your father," Paula told her.

"Well, you should have learned to stand up to him."

"You tried that—and you ended up running away. I didn't have that option." She took a deep breath. "Of course. Send Laurie. What's up, after all these years?"

"I have a chance to go to Europe is all," Jennifer said. "With a friend."

Paula knew without asking that the "friend" was male. Who was Laurie's father? Had Jennifer married? She was bursting with questions, but this didn't seem the time. She'd cope, somehow. "All right. Send Laurie," she said. "We'll manage. Will you come visit as soon as you get back from Europe?"

"Of course, Mom."

The words were pleasing, but there was something evasive about the tone that made Paula uncomfortable. Jennifer had spent her entire stint as a teenager, until she ran away at seventeen, arguing with Fred while Paula ineffectually tried to make peace. However, there were two sides, even if Fred had been hard-headed. Jennifer had been impulsive and selfish. Paula had tried to tell herself that those were normal traits for teenagers. And they were. Jennifer, however, was now—Paula knew exactly, without figuring—thirty-three, almost thirty-four. Impulsiveness and selfishness were traits that were supposed to disappear by that age, particularly when a person had acquired a child.

"When will she be coming?" Paula asked. "Next week?"

"Well, no, actually. Today?" Jennifer answered with a slight question in her voice. "We made reservations as soon as I heard, before I realized you weren't home. It's been hard raising a child alone, Mom," she said, her voice pleading. "It's time I got on with my life."

Paula realized suddenly that she herself had never gotten on with her own life. She'd always been someone's daughter, wife or mother. Now, it appeared, she was to be someone's grandmother. Well, that was what she was used to. She only hoped that Laurie was more amenable than her mother had been at thirteen. She knew immediately that this was a vain hope. Jennifer would not be so anxious to be heading for Europe, to be "getting on with her own life," if Laurie were the sweet child that an eight-year-old, for instance, tended to be.

"Let me give you my address here," Paula said. "You will want to stay in contact with Laurie while you're traveling?"

"Of course, Mom. Let me get a pen." Paula heard a rustling in the background. Would her daughter even have thought of getting that address, or for that matter, of the possibility of sending cards to her own child? Her heart sank a little. Jennifer, it would appear, was still the flighty, thoughtless person she'd been when she disappeared.

"Okay. What is it?"

"Thirteen-ninety-two Sienna," she said, adding the town and zip code. "It will be exciting for your . . . for Laurie to get cards from so far away," she said. "You will remember . . ." She bit her tongue. That wasn't going to do any good, might actually have an adverse affect.

"Of course, Mom." Her tone was aggrieved.

Paula didn't blame her. She probably remembered similar conversations as well as Paula herself did. Whether she also recalled how ineffective the results had been, who was to know? "What time's the flight getting in?" she asked, sighing.

The plane, it developed, was to land at midnight. Keeping her thoughts to herself about the inconvenience of the hour as she wrote down the pertinent information regarding the flight, Paula somewhat wistfully said goodbye to her daughter. *My daughter,* she said silently several times. It produced a warm spot somewhere in the region of her heart. *My granddaughter,* she tried experimentally. That worked even better.

Paula arrived at SeaTac Airport at 11:30, after checking in at a nearby motel where she and Fred had stayed often before an early flight. By the time Laurie arrived, it would be much too late to make the drive north to Kamiak Hills, especially after such a stressful day. Even getting out of the house had not been easy. At the last minute, Carioca had decided to take a stroll and came back only when she was good and ready. If only the two spoiled pets had been indoor cats, she thought with a touch of rancor.

Just before she left, Ellen had phoned. "I heard it on the news. The body's been identified as Martha Abingsford."

"Oh?" Paula answered calmly. She'd never even heard of the woman.

"You wouldn't have met her yet, I know. She's not well-liked . . . But murdered? Why on earth would . . . ?"

Ellen clearly wanted to talk about the woman, and normally Paula would have been happy to oblige, but this time she put her off. "I'm sorry to interrupt," she said. "But can we talk tomorrow? I'm just leaving for the airport to pick up my grand-daughter."

"Your granddaughter? My goodness!"

If Ellen's response to the news of Laurie's arrival had sounded dubious, she didn't blame her. Paula was dubious, too, about introducing Laurie into the Pappas house. Otherwise, she was more excited than she had been about anything for years.

The flight was late, which seemed to be normal these days, but finally the jet arrived and sleepy-eyed passengers began to stream past security by the hundreds. Paula stood on tiptoe, trying to see over the family waiting in front of her. Each time a small, dark girl came through the doorway, Paula's heart jumped, but each time, the girl was either not alone, was claimed by someone or confidently strode off toward baggage. Paula watched, her hand clutching her throat, as one slim, brown-haired figure walked toward her. Only as her hand started to reach forward and her lips began to form a welcome did she re-alize that the young person was male. It was hard to tell sometimes, especially in one of slight build.

Finally, a tousle-haired girl dressed in spotted jeans so tight they looked uncomfortable, an oversized blue sweater and what appeared to Paula's astonishment to be pink high-topped tennis shoes, hesitated as she came into the terminal. "Laurie?" Paula inquired cautiously, waving her hand. The girl pushed her way through the crowd and approached. "Paula?" she asked.

Taken aback momentarily, Paula answered, "Yes. Your grandmother, Paula." They stared at each other for a second, then Paula reached forward and hugged the girl. Her body was stiff. *Don't move too fast,* Paula warned herself. After all, Laurie had never seen her before. Paula, however, could see her daughter at that age in almost every feature. Only the eyes that would be a bright blue when they weren't dulled with sleepiness were really different. "Come along," she said. "Let's get your baggage. We're going to stay in a motel across the way. It's too far to drive tonight."

"Good," Laurie answered, then was silent.

Paula made several attempts at conversation but elicited little more than grunts from Laurie after that one word. *She's sleepy,* Paula told herself. *Pray to God she's not just sullen.* They followed the crowd toward baggage.

By the time they reached Kamiak Hills late the next morning, Paula had concluded that sullen Laurie was not. During the last hour of the drive, Paula would almost have settled for an attack of the sulks. She wasn't accustomed to constant chatter, especially first thing in the morning. Good Lord, was she facing a summer of this, of conversation that required an answer from the time Laurie first set foot out of bed? Even Fred had grunted noncommittally until he'd had a cup of coffee, and by that time he was settled behind the *Wall Street Journal.*

Laurie, however, had things to say from the time her blue eyes, bright now instead of sleepy, had flown open. "When's breakfast? I hope the hotel has a restaurant. I'm hungry."

Perhaps, Paula thought hopefully, once they were settled, her granddaughter would sleep late as all teenagers were reputed to do when they had an opportunity. Uneasily, she had a faint memory of Jennifer arising with the dawn.

The buildings of Seattle didn't impress Laurie much, even the domed football stadium, Quest Field, or the Space Needle, but the scenery did. "Wow," she had said when they came out of the motel and saw Mount Rainier's truncated cone gleaming in the morning sun. "Has anyone ever climbed to the top of that?" When informed that, yes, indeed, they had, that reservations had to be made to make the two-day climb, she looked thoughtful. When they crossed the high bridge over Seattle's shipping canal, Laurie peered over at the parade of small boats and the University beyond, making comments all the while. "Does everyone here own a boat?" she inquired.

"Practically," Paula answered, smiling. She and Fred had never had one, but many of their friends did. As they drove north through the more rural areas, Laurie was fascinated. "Are those things actually cows?" she asked as they passed a field. "I've never seen one before!"

Paula glanced sideways at her in amazement. While Laurie appeared intelligent and curious, obviously there were gaps in her knowledge.

An advantage of her granddaughter's garrulousness, Paula found, was that she did not need to ask many questions. Jennifer had been married, it seemed, but, "Daddy did coke," Laurie informed her, and, "Mom got sick of it and . . ." She snapped her fingers dismissively.

Street-wise if not farm-wise, Paula thought. "Do you ever see your father?" she decided to ask.

"See him? I don't even remember him."

"Then how . . . ?"

"Do I know? Mom told me. When I started asking why I didn't have a father. Of course Mom has had lots of friends since then," Laurie said, sounding proud. "Gary—he's the one Mom's going to Europe with—he always asks me to call him

Dad, but I don't."

Paula raised an eyebrow inquiringly.

"I don't like Gary much. I don't think he's good for Mom."

Paula would have liked to ask why but decided not to press. The way Laurie talked, she was likely to tell Paula without prompting. Sure enough, after a short pause, Laurie continued, "Mom needs someone to do the managing. Gary's no good at it."

That sounded ominous, but Paula tried to shut out the picture of her daughter flitting around Europe with a man when, according to Laurie, neither of them "managed." Would she hear from Jennifer when things broke down? Very likely, now that they were back in touch, Paula decided with a queer feeling. And who managed normally? Paula glanced speculatively at Laurie.

Laurie was impressed when Paula pulled into the driveway of the Pappas house. "This is where you're staying?" she inquired with raised eyebrows. "You must have rich friends."

"They're not friends of mine," Paula answered, without explaining that she lived in a house that would, no doubt, appear equally impressive to Laurie. "I just agreed to housesit."

For a moment, she considered suggesting Laurie remove her shoes when they walked in the front door. Then she decided to wait. She could establish rules later. Anyway, those peculiar things Laurie had on her feet couldn't have gotten too dirty on the airplane.

"Let's pick a room for you," she suggested. "I rather think the peach one on the left would suit you the most, but as far as I'm concerned, you can choose. This is mine," she said, holding open the door of the room with the green-and-yellow spread.

For once Laurie was speechless, as she peeked into the four remaining bedrooms. Finally she nodded, standing in the doorway of the one with the peach chiffon spread. "This is okay," she said. "I'll get my suitcase."

While Laurie got settled, Paula fixed lunch, heating some of the cabbage-patch soup she had made earlier. It would be easier cooking for two again, she realized. So many of her favorite recipes made too much for her to bother fixing them just for herself.

They ate the soup while Laurie continued to talk. Paula was aware that the lengthy story involved somebody named Kiki, but otherwise she tuned out her granddaughter as she began to seriously worry. She honestly couldn't remember what Jennifer had done to amuse herself at thirteen other than to storm into her room after one or another of the endless arguments with her father. What was she going to do with Laurie for the summer?

CHAPTER THREE

Laurie watched her grandmother as she dished up orange sherbet in classy glass bowls. Paula looked just like Mom probably would when she got old, with the same brown curly hair as Mom's, except shorter and mixed with gray, and the same gray eyes. A strange feeling swirled in Laurie's stomach. Mom had talked about her mother a lot, but to Laurie, a grandmother was like somebody in a book, not real. Now this grandmother, who was smiling happily to herself as she spooned sherbet, *was* real. At the front of the house, a doorbell chimed. "Oh," Paula said, handing the spoon to Laurie, "finish for me, would you? Please?"

Laurie stood up. "Sure." Paula's face had lost its cheerful expression. She knew who was at the door and was annoyed, Laurie figured. Couldn't be any big deal, though. Paula had only been here at—what was the name of this place? Oh, yeah. At Kamiak Hills—for a few days. She couldn't know that many people.

"Mer-ow." Laurie looked down, startled. A cream and brown cat stretched and rubbed against her ankles. Another, almost like it but smaller, watched nearby, ears quirked curiously.

"Oh-h," Laurie said, reaching for the cat at her feet. Paula hadn't told her there were any pets here. The cat purred loudly and climbed onto Laurie's shoulders as she stooped to pick up the other. "Oh, wow!"

Paula came back into the kitchen, followed by a blond

younger woman who'd eaten too much for too many years. "Why didn't you tell me, Paula?" Laurie asked. "What're their names?" The first cat rubbed against her ear, and Laurie could feel the purr clear to the tips of her toes.

"That's Mum-mum around your neck," Paula said, "and the other's Carioca."

"Well, my goodness," the woman said, her expression astonished. "Those two cats won't go near my kids."

"I've always gotten along with animals," Laurie said. "I'm Laurie. Who are you?"

Paula winced, and Laurie wondered why. The blonde said, "I'm your next door neighbor, Ellen Cogsdill."

"Mrs. Cogsdill," Paula said. "Let me introduce my granddaughter, Laurie . . ." She stopped, suddenly, looking embarrassed.

"Hi, Ellen," Laurie said.

"Nice to meet you, Laurie. You'll have to come over and get to know Josh. He's about your age, I think. How old are you?"

"Thirteen."

"Well, Josh is twelve, but . . ."

Laurie wrinkled her lip. "Twelve-year-old boys are children." She removed Mum-mum from her shoulders and sat down. The orange sherbet was melting. She stuck her spoon in and took a bite, then glanced up at her grandmother. Her mouth had opened, but she shut it quickly when her eyes met Laurie's.

Ellen smiled. She was almost pretty when her face lit up like that. "This particular twelve-year-old's best friends are twin boys who are fourteen," she said.

"Um." Laurie took another bite. "I'll meet him, I guess." Fourteen-year-olds might be interesting, at least. Human.

"Well, come over whenever you feel like it," Ellen suggested.

"Won't you join us for dessert?" Paula asked, gesturing towards her own rapidly slumping sherbet.

"Oh. No, thank you. I'm sorry. Please finish. I shouldn't have just dropped in. I wanted to talk about the murder. I can't get it out of my mind, and since you were there, Paula . . ."

Laurie choked.

Paula quickly filled a glass with water and handed it to her. "Take a drink, dear."

Laurie swallowed fast, then asked as soon as she could speak, her voice croaking, "Murder? Where? When? You were there, Paula? Wow!"

Now Paula did look unhappy. So that's why she hadn't wanted to answer the door. She knew it was this Ellen and that she'd want to talk about a murder. Why should Paula mind? Laurie would have found out about it sooner or later.

"I was just a bystander," Paula said. "Laurie, you can run along since you've finished eating."

Laurie hadn't finished, and she had no intention of "running along," but she quickly scraped the dish. "Oh, wow," she repeated. "A murder here. A guy got stabbed downstairs last year, but that wasn't anything. Just a drug deal that went sour. I want to hear about this one." A shiver of excitement traveled up her backbone, and she hugged herself.

Ellen glanced at Paula, her eyebrows raised.

"Murders happen anywhere," Paula murmured. "It's unfortunate, of course. But this one doesn't have anything to do with us," she finished firmly.

"Yeah, but it's still exciting. I think I might like to be a detective when I get through school," Laurie said. "Tell me about it, please."

Paula winced again but poured two cups of coffee. Laurie shot a pleading glance at Ellen, who appeared happy at the chance to share what she knew. This summer might not be as boring as she'd figured it would be, Laurie thought.

Ellen sat down but ignored the coffee in front of her as she began what turned into a monologue. Paula quietly sipped hers, and Laurie perched on her chair, avidly listening. "And," Ellen finished the story with a shudder, "they've definitely identified her as a woman I know—knew—named Martha Abingsford. I was sure those rings looked familiar, but my thoughts weren't too clear at the time. It was . . . it was so horrible."

"Do drink some of your coffee at least," Paula urged. "You'll feel better."

"You're right. I would. But do you suppose we could take it outside? Mark and Susan are playing checkers on our deck, or they were when I left. Josh is supposed to be keeping an eye on things, but he gets engrossed sometimes. I can half watch the place. At least, if Josh blows something up . . ."

The summer definitely wasn't going to be boring.

"Blows—something up?" Paula, obviously appalled, repeated Ellen's words as her own hand holding the mug stopped in midair.

"His chemistry set, you know."

"Oh. Of course." Paula suddenly looked weary, but she stood, opened the sliding door and stepped aside. She hadn't been around kids much lately, she'd admitted, and it showed. Laurie almost laughed but managed to squelch it. Ellen strode out the door, and Laurie jumped up and followed quickly before her grandmother could get any more ideas about getting rid of her. The cats trailed along.

Ellen stretched on tiptoe at the far end of the deck. "All okay," she announced, then turned and settled on a red-and-white striped chaise. Laurie picked a chair at a table under an umbrella. Mum-mum, who was the friendlier of the two cats, jumped into her lap, and Carioca rubbed against her leg. Having the cats around was going to be fun.

It was nice out here on the deck. Wow, all that space behind the house! It looked like a park, but as she watched, a woman got out of a little cart thingie, pulled a club from her bag on the back end, and swung at a golf ball. The ball dribbled about fifty feet. Laurie laughed, and then she sniffed. Definitely smelled better than New York. Cooler, too. Their apartment had been awfully hot before she left, even though it was only June. Paula sat down on another red-and-white chaise and tucked her green dress carefully around her. She still had good legs, Laurie noted, especially for an old lady.

Ellen sighed and ran a hand through her hair. "I just can't get it out of my mind. I thought it might help to talk about it."

Laurie pulled her chair closer as Paula sighed. *She* didn't want to talk about it, but Ellen wasn't noticing, which was great. "It must have been much worse for you than for me," Paula said, "since you knew her, and of course, you were the one to . . ." She bit her lip and stopped speaking.

Ellen's face paled suddenly. Laurie held her breath, hoping Ellen wasn't going to faint or something awful that would shut her up.

"Tell me about Martha Abingsford," Paula said quickly, obviously changing the subject. "Will she be missed?"

Ellen straightened, and her cheeks regained some of their color. "Well," she said, "I hadn't thought about it. I suppose so. Isn't everyone, in one way or another? But she was—come to think of it, I don't know of anyone who was a close friend, and she was widowed years ago, I guess. At least I never knew a Mr. Abingsford. She was always just . . . there, always talking. She reminded me of that animal, you know, a shrew."

"A shrew?" Laurie asked. "How come? I didn't think shrews were noisy."

"Oh, I didn't mean that. I guess . . . well, she was tiny and dark-haired, and she had a pointed nose and receding chin."

"And . . . ?" Paula prompted.

"And, the way she moved. Always in motion to begin with

31

and darting hither and yon. She drove you nuts to play golf with. She'd talk when you were putting or driving, and if she wasn't chattering, she'd be wiggling somewhere just on the edge of your peripheral vision. And . . . well, to be honest," Ellen said, looking guilty, "that pointed nose was always in other people's business."

"Gosh," Laurie said, "she doesn't sound like anybody'd like her very much."

"Well, I'm quite sure people didn't. I remember someone once saying, 'I could kill her.' "

"You do?" Paula asked. "Shouldn't you tell the police?"

"Oh, it wasn't that sort of remark." Ellen shrugged casually. "I think she'd shouted at someone on the next fairway just as one of her partners swung. Anyway, I can't remember who said it. I'm sure I would if it had been a serious thing."

Paula agreed. "As irritating as that kind of behavior is, people aren't usually sincere when they say something like that."

"What did you mean about her sticking her nose in people's business?" Laurie asked. "That sounds worse than shouting on a golf course."

"Well," Ellen said, grinning, "that might be because you're not a golfer. Anyway, she was nosy. There was no doubt of that. And, of course, there was that other thing." She set her coffee mug down and stood, peering toward her own gray-shingled house, just visible through the trees. "Damn, I don't see the kids anywhere."

Laurie felt herself squeak as Paula frowned. How could Ellen quit right in the middle of what she was saying? Especially something important like this?

"Ellen," Paula said firmly, to Laurie's relief, "what other thing are you talking about?"

"Huh?" Ellen turned. She was obviously thinking about her kids instead of Martha Abingsford. "Oh. I forgot you wouldn't have heard about it." She glanced anxiously toward her own house, then continued, "It's just that someone has been sending notes—nasty, malicious little things. Not always about anything important, but usually devastatingly accurate. Like, 'Your husband wasn't really working at the office. He was playing poker and drinking with the boys.' Marcia Stoneham got that one."

"What's that got to do with the murder?" Laurie asked.

"Oh," Ellen said in a maddeningly slow manner, "just that people figured that it was Martha sending them, that's all." She stepped off the low deck. "Thanks for the coffee. I think I'd better go. I'll call later, and we can set up that lunch."

She isn't going to get away from me that easy, Laurie thought. "Mrs. Cogsdill," Laurie said, hurrying after her, "I think I'd like to meet Josh now. Is it okay if I go with you?"

"Certainly, Laurie."

Laurie glanced over her shoulder, grinning. Paula didn't look happy at her leaving. She was showing signs of being bossier than Laurie was used to. She was accomplishing two things. She'd show Paula right now that she made her own decisions, and, if she was lucky, she'd find out more about the murder.

She caught up with Ellen. "Did this Martha person ever write you a letter?" she asked.

CHAPTER FOUR

Paula sighed and looked at the cup sitting beside her. She didn't want coffee. It was much too warm a day for it; what she really wanted was something tall and cool. She picked up the mug and went into the kitchen. She'd make a pitcher of lemonade, then return to the deck for some serious thinking. It was overdue.

She mixed up the lemonade, poured some over ice in a glass, then, on impulse, opened the cupboard where she had stashed the vodka she'd brought with her in case she wanted to serve a drink to anyone. She poured a generous dollop into the glass.

Returning to the deck, she again settled on the chaise and then took a swig of the cool drink. That was better. She leaned back and shut her eyes. Uncharacteristic for her, having alcohol at this time of day, but somehow necessary, she felt.

Laurie. She sighed. Already she sensed a bond, possibly one-way so far, but she also was worried. She didn't understand teenagers, perhaps never had. This one clearly had been allowed to go her own way without direction, although maybe she wasn't being fair to Jennifer. There was no way to tell. Conceivably the problems she was seeing with the girl's manners were related to the differing demands of the society she'd come from and those of the one she'd suddenly been thrust into. A house in Kamiak Hills was a far cry from a New York apartment with its drug dealers and murderers. Although, she realized, disconcerted, not the latter. Murder had found its way here, too.

She would need to establish some rules, regardless. Rules that would protect the white carpet, anyway. Paula smiled ruefully to herself. Maybe such things *were* too important to her, as Jennifer had often said. Nevertheless, she felt an obligation to return the Pappas home in the condition she found it.

Also, she suspected, she needed to establish right now that Laurie must ask permission before departing as she had to the Cogsdill house. This time her going had been inconsequential, but the fact that it had not occurred to Laurie to ask Paula first indicated that she was not accustomed to doing so

And then there were Laurie's clothes. Paula wondered what else was in the small amount of baggage they had retrieved at the airport. Was there anything suitable to wear should they go into the city or to someone's home, if the occasion arose? She wouldn't look, of course, but she should consult with Laurie as soon as possible and make a shopping expedition if necessary.

She still hadn't a clue as to what Laurie would want to do with her time. It was a blessing that she was willing to meet the young man next door, with or without his teenager friends. Or, was it? After all, Paula didn't really know Ellen and hadn't met the children. A boy whose mother feared he might blow up the family home might not be a suitable companion. Anyway, had Laurie been interested in him or had she wanted to pump his mother about the murder?

The murder. Paula sipped her drink as she reflected on how that word kept intruding, as if all paths led there. She tried to remember the other residents of Kamiak Hills whom she had met so far. All except Ellen had been encountered on the fourth green of the golf course. She discounted the police. The plainclothes officer in charge had introduced himself, but Paula had paid no attention. Shocked as she had been, she found that all of the other police blended into one uniformed man. And a woman, she amended. One of them had been female.

But before that. Before the police arrived. A cart carrying a couple had hesitated on the fairway behind them like a skittish bug, then had scurried forward when it became obvious there was a problem. The driver was a man, a doctor providentially, who commented that he was a friend of the Pappases and had intended to stop by the house to introduce himself. What was his name? Oh, yes. Dr. Cordiner. David Cordiner, if Paula's memory served her right. Ellen and the two Griffins had precipitately turned over the management of the situation to him. Until then, Ben Griffin had shown every sign of being a manager, but by the time Dr. Cordiner drove up, the skin on Ben's bald head had been pale and dappled with even more perspiration than the temperature of the day warranted. He had been very willing to abscond from decision making. Dr. Cordiner called 911 on his cell phone; then, with an unreadable glance at Ben, he suggested that the Griffins meet the police at the clubhouse. Ben and Babs had climbed into their cart with obvious relief and departed.

Paula pictured the scene. Dr. Cordiner, his graying hair carefully styled, appeared to be in his early sixties and holding. Hours at the gym led to the trim physique, Paula felt sure, although regular golf could account for the tan. His gently lined face, even though not handsome in a conventional sense, was the sort that implied a world of experience and generally was attractive to women. He definitely did not match the cart he was driving, which was painted robin's-egg blue and decorated with waving fringe. The doctor had ordered, "Trish, take your cart and go on. I'll be here for a while."

Trish had not been happy, and her tone was petulant as she argued, "David, must you? I mean, why is it necessary for you to stay? You have nothing to do with . . ."

"Of course I'll stay. Run along."

Paula had stared at the woman, her curiosity aroused by her

lack of compassion. Trish was a bit much. She was dressed in a cute little golfing outfit that was color coordinated with the cart. It sported a skirt that stopped too soon for Paula's taste, and her socks featured tassels. A straw hat with a jaunty ribbon in a deeper tone of blue-green perched on her head. She was, Paula, guessed, older than she appeared at first glance, at least late forties, and perhaps more. The blond hair which appeared below the hat was in perfect array. Paula had reached up automatically to smooth her own dark curls, which she was quite sure were pooched out by the golfing visor.

Her eyes had flicked toward Dr. Cordiner in assessment. He didn't strike her as the sort to be attached to Trish, whoever she was. Although it might be difficult to tell. He was smooth looking and perhaps flattered by the attention of a younger woman. He wasn't, however, paying any attention now to Trish, who drove away without further comment. He was obviously used to issuing commands and having them obeyed.

"I'd suggest you two leave, also, except that you found the body . . ." He looked questioningly at Ellen who shuddered. "I'm sure the police can talk to you later if you'd rather."

"No." Ellen made an obvious effort to pull herself together. "I'd rather get it over with."

Dr. Cordiner nodded his approval, then said, "Oh, hell. Here come more golfers." He raised his arm to wave the cart forward as Paula abstractedly watched. "There's been an accident," the doctor called as the cart approached. "Perhaps you could notify the clubhouse to stop play."

"What kind of accident?" A middle-aged woman with improbably dark hair climbed out of the passenger side and walked toward them. Her path took her past the edge of the bunker and she glanced down to where Ellen's club still lay, pointing as if a marker. "Oh! I see," she said, bending forward curiously.

"I'd get away if I were you," Dr. Cordiner suggested calmly.

"Oh, nothing like that bothers me. You know I'm a nurse. That's Martha Abingsford, of course. I'd recognize those rings anywhere." She bent down again. "I always did wonder if they were real or paste."

A man had followed her slowly out of the cart. "Alice," he reproved mildly as the doctor's lips tightened, reflecting the disgust Paula also felt.

"Well, I don't care, Edward," the woman said, straightening. "I can't tell. There's too much sand. You know as well as I do that Martha Abingsford was a thoroughly annoying woman. She probably talked one time too many when someone was putting. I've wanted to do it myself."

"Alice!" Edward admonished, shocked.

"Even for you that comment was remarkably distasteful." Dr. Cordiner's voice remained calm, but a tiny tic near his mouth showed his tension. "Why don't you make yourself useful? Go back and stop the other golfers. The police should be here soon, and I'm sure play will be suspended."

"I didn't say anything everyone else won't be thinking, David Cordiner," Alice said with a sniff. "But you're right about stopping the golfers, I suppose, although everyone'll be unhappy. They're playing matches now, for the club championships, and I don't know what this will do to the tournament."

"Come along, Alice, and we'll do what David suggested." The gray-haired man took her by the arm.

"Oh, very well. I'll expect you to keep me informed of what happens, though, David," she announced. "Or you, Ellen." Her glance was dismissive. For the first time she seemed to notice Paula. "Or you. Who are you, anyway?"

Paula had been rendered speechless by the woman, and she was glad when the doctor stepped forward menacingly. "Are you going to get in that cart, or am I going to have to put you there?" he demanded.

"I'm going, of course." She slid into the seat. "But don't think you can threaten me!" She pointed at the doctor as the man Paula assumed was the woman's husband drove the cart quickly away. No one but a husband would put up with her.

"I wonder," Ellen said with a weak grin, "why someone didn't murder her instead."

Dr. Cordiner's mouth twisted wryly. "Give them time."

The three of them silently watched the cart as it intercepted a group on the fourth tee. Paula had tried, unsuccessfully, to quiet her mind as well. How long was it going to take the police to get there? She'd found herself nervously clenching and unclenching her fingers and taking deep breaths that came out sounding like sighs. Nothing helped. She was acutely conscious of what lay behind them, as if the body was sending out little waves through the air as it struggled to get out of the sand.

Paula tried to concentrate on a small bird that flew down and pecked at something on the green, but that only made her apprehensive. What if the bird should decide to descend into the hazard? She watched, her teeth grinding, but the bird moved on to a small fir tree where it trilled a cheery song that was distinctly out of place. David Cordiner glanced at her once, and a flicker of a smile indicated that he understood what she thinking.

The police arrived in due course, and very likely the wait had been a tenth of what it seemed. Ellen and Paula did not dally when told that they could leave. Dr. Cordiner was still talking to a uniformed officer as the two women climbed into the cart. "A wonderful man, that Dr. Cordiner," Ellen commented as they drove away.

"Oh?" was all Paula said.

"Yes. A great doctor, but a good man, too. He devotes time every year to a clinic in Latin America somewhere, and he's always the physician for local sports teams. Everyone loves him."

An alarm bell rang in Paula's brain. In her experience, no one was quite that good. "How nice," was all she said.

Fists clenched so tightly they hurt brought Paula back to the present, and she looked down at her hands in surprise. She hadn't intended to relive the entire scene. Stupid, she thought. She'd learned long ago to put unpleasant experiences behind her. Doing so was the way to maintain control and serenity. She'd needed to, in order to live with Fred.

She picked up her glass and looked at it in surprise. Somehow she had drunk its entire contents. Had the alcohol done any good? It wouldn't seem so, as tense as she felt. Stretching, she tried consciously to ease tight muscles.

"Hi, Paula," Laurie's voice called.

Paula turned and looked toward the Cogsdill house. Laurie had just come across the grass between the two places. Behind her, scurrying to keep up, was a boy. He was much shorter than Laurie, which, assuming he was the twelve-year-old Josh, meant that he was quite short for his age indeed. His brown hair was spiky, and as Paula watched, his glasses slipped down on his nose. Absently, he pushed them back into place without missing a step.

Laurie moved up the steps onto the deck, then flopped down on a chaise. The boy hovered just at the top of the stairs. "You must be Josh," Paula said. "Won't you sit down?" One more lesson in deportment went on the list for Laurie that Paula was compiling. "I'm Mrs. Madigan." She introduced herself in a manner which she hoped would forestall first-name intimacy if Josh was so inclined.

"How do you do, Mrs. Madigan," he answered with a friendly grin. "My mother's mentioned you."

No doubt she had, what with the events of the past day. At least Josh had good manners. Perhaps they would rub off on

Laurie instead of Paula having to nag. Feeling cheered, Paula smiled in return.

"What's for dinner?" Laurie inquired, her expression hopeful.

"Dinner? Oh, my." They'd just finished lunch! Paula hadn't thought far enough ahead to plan the next meal. Her own appetite was small at best since Fred's demise, and she would often eat on impulse when she found herself hungry, her choice of food dictated as much by what was available as by desire. A teenager's eating, though, would need to be planned for. She had forgotten.

"I'd thought," she improvised hastily, "that we'd go out to eat. To celebrate your arrival."

Laurie's expression indicated that she saw through Paula but was willing to go along with her. "Great," she said. "Where?"

"Um, I'm not familiar with what's available yet," Paula admitted. "Do you have a suggestion, Josh?"

"Sure. How about the Cedar Harbor Inn? It's up north. Right on the water. We saw a killer whale there once. Food's good, too. That's where we go when it's Mom's birthday or something."

"Sounds perfect." Paula was relieved. "How do we find it?"

After Josh gave directions, Paula glanced at her watch. There would be time to make a trip to the store to avert another meal crisis. "I need to grocery shop," she said, standing. "I'll be back . . ."

"I'll go with you." Laurie bounced to her feet. "Goodbye, Josh," she said firmly.

Startled, Paula glanced at the boy, fearing his feelings would be hurt. "Laurie . . ." she began, but Josh grinned cheerfully and departed, waving over one shoulder. "Don't you think that was a little—abrupt?" she asked her granddaughter.

"Abrupt? Oh, you mean rude? Nah, I didn't ask him over in

the first place. Anyway, I don't want to encourage him. He's a nerd."

Paula rolled her eyes but clamped her lips shut. She was being cowardly, no doubt of that, but she definitely had lost any knack she might have had for dealing with teenagers. It was going to take time to get her confidence back, if she'd ever had any.

The faint rumble of an expensive car woke Paula the next morning. Sleepily, she looked at the marble clock on the bed stand. Eight o'clock exactly. The motor suddenly ceased, and she realized that the reason she had responded to the sound was that the car had stopped in the Pappas driveway. Quickly, she threw back the covers, leaped out of bed and grabbed the robe she had laid on a chair the night before.

Who could be calling at this hour? Sliding her arms into the sleeves of the silky robe—a silly thing, really, that Fred had given her—she hastened toward the front door.

When she heard a key being inserted into the double-bolted lock, her heart thumped. The door swung open as Paula cinched the waist of the robe around her with the sash. A tall woman stepped over the threshold.

"Oh," Paula said, suddenly realizing who this was.

"Good morning," the woman said cheerfully. "You must be Mrs. Madigan. I'm Cynthia Lamphear." With a raised eyebrow and a questioning tone, she continued, "Lynn Pappas must have told you I'd be here. It's Friday."

"Oh," Paula repeated. "Yes. I'm sorry. I did forget. I should have been ready."

"No need," Cynthia said with an airy wave as she slid out of a soft sweater that appeared to be cashmere. "Lynn didn't usually get up before I came. She knew I didn't need her."

Paula responded weakly, "Fine. I'll be out in a minute."

The woman picked up a basket beside her that Paula hadn't really noticed. A short-handled squeegee rose above assorted bottles of cleaning liquid. Cynthia smiled faintly, then strode down the hall. "I always start in the kitchen," she said over her shoulder.

Paula watched her go, then turned and brushed aside the curtain covering the window next to the front door. A sleek, silver-colored car stood in the driveway. Something fancy. Not a car she recognized. This was clearly not an ordinary cleaning woman. Why hadn't Mrs. Pappas warned her? Not that it really made any difference, Paula thought as she hurried toward her bedroom. She was always polite. She prided herself on not hurting people's feelings. Still, there was a subtle difference between a woman who arrived in cashmere and in an expensive car to do up the house and those counterparts Paula had always employed.

Glad that she had showered the night before, Paula dressed hurriedly in slacks and a blue cotton shirt. For an instant, her hand hesitated over her coral silk blouse, but then she jerked it back. She wouldn't normally wear it in the morning at home, so why should she now, just because the cleaning lady had arrived in cashmere?

Coffee was doing its thing in the maker on the counter, Paula saw gratefully as she walked into the kitchen. "It'll be ready in a minute," Cynthia said, scrubbing vigorously at something in the sink. "I've got the stove apart. Thought I'd have it done before you'd need it."

"I won't need it," Paula informed her. The coffeemaker gave a last burp, and the red light came on. She reached for a mug, then took down two. "Coffee?" she asked.

"Thank you. Yes." The woman continued to scrub.

Paula filled the cups, set one on the counter near Cynthia, then sat down with the other and really looked at her for the first time. All she had been aware of in the hall was that Cynthia was tall. Statuesque would have been a better description, she decided. Even leaning over the sink, there was something dignified about the well-proportioned figure. Her chestnut-colored hair, fastened in a bun on top of her head, added to the impression.

"Have you worked long for Mrs. Pappas?" Paula inquired, curious about the woman.

"Only a year," Cynthia answered, screwing the knobs back on the stove. "But we've been friends ever since we moved to Kamiak Hills four years ago."

"Oh. I see," Paula said.

"Good morning." Laurie, rubbing one eye and trailed by both cats, ambled into the kitchen. "I thought I heard voices. Hi. I'm Laurie." She opened the refrigerator.

Cynthia turned away from the stove, her green eyes taking in the girl. "I'm Cynthia," she said. "I'm here to clean." She didn't ask a question, but one was implied by her tone.

Laurie picked up on it. "Well, I'm here to spend the summer with my grandmother." Both cats began to yowl as only Siamese are equipped to do, and they didn't subside until Laurie poured milk into the individual bowls Mum-mum and Carioca insisted on. As they contentedly began to lap and purr, Laurie lifted out a container of orange juice and closed the door.

"Oh? Lynn didn't tell me."

"She didn't know," Paula admitted. "Neither did I." She deliberately made her tone flat. It really was none of the cleaning woman's business.

Her ploy didn't work. "Where are you from?" Cynthia asked.

"New York. My mother has gone to Europe."

Would Laurie have enough sense to stop right there? Probably not, Paula feared, considering the personal information Laurie had volunteered to Ellen yesterday.

Paula was right. She cringed inwardly as Laurie spoke. "Wow, it must be neat to have someone else clean for you. Mrs. Padersky across the hall worked for people in some of the ritzy condos. She thought they were all slobs." Laurie poured juice into a glass, then took a drink, leaving an orange mustache.

Cynthia's eyes gleamed with humor. "Some of them are. Is your mother in Europe on business?"

This had gone far enough, Paula thought. "A vacation," she murmured quickly, shooting a glance at Laurie before she had time to answer. Mercifully, it worked. Laurie didn't proffer any of the personal details that Paula feared she would.

Instead, she asked personal details of Cynthia. "How did you—I mean, you don't look like any of the cleaning ladies I know. I guess you can earn lots of money, though. Mrs. Padersky always said . . ."

Cynthia grimaced. "Not lots," she answered. "But more than you'd think. I've a daughter about your age. Fourteen?"

Laurie nodded, looking pleased, but when she saw Paula's face, she answered, "Well, almost."

"My daughter's name is Serita, and she's in Colorado training for her figure skating."

"Wow, like the ones on T.V.?" Laurie's expression was awed.

Cynthia nodded. "That's what we hope, anyway." She paused, and then a pleased grin crossed her face. "Albert—that's my husband—and I are going to visit her soon and see how much she's progressed," she said. "We're going the first weekend of August."

"Oh," Paula said. "You'll miss one of your times here?"

"No, no. It's all set up. We're flying out Friday night, and we'll get back late Monday. I've already made arrangements with my Monday ladies. Won't interfere here at all."

Paula wondered if she, herself, now was the "Friday lady." Also, for the second time, she reflected on the fact that Laurie's impulsive talking provided answers to questions that she herself would have been reluctant to ask. Nevertheless, probing wasn't polite. Laurie needed to learn that. Besides, it was obvious that Cynthia, who had stopped all pretense of cleaning, could not talk and work at the same time. "I think you should get on with your breakfast, Laurie," she suggested in what she hoped was a gentle tone, "and leave Cynthia to her work."

"Okay," Laurie said, "but I'd like to hear more about your daughter. Serita? That's a neat name."

"She's a neat girl," Cynthia said. However, she must have noticed Paula's hint because she began to wipe a cupboard off vigorously. "I'll show you a picture some time," she said.

Laurie stood, rustled in the cupboard that contained breakfast cereal, and filled a bowl. "You must know everyone around here, don't you?"

"Most everyone, yes." Cynthia continued with her work, bending over and removing fingerprints from the door that Laurie had just finished opening.

"You must have known what's-her-name, Martha Abingsford, huh?"

"Laurie . . ." Paula began, shuddering.

"Wow, it's really exciting." Laurie opened the refrigerator again and the cats reiterated their noises of hunger.

"Feed them, please," Paula suggested. With luck, doing so might divert Laurie's train of thought, and at worst, it would save Paula from getting up from the table. Suddenly she felt very weary.

"Yes, I knew her, of course," Cynthia answered Laurie's question. "Everyone here did. She got around."

"Have you any idea why anybody'd want to kill her? Josh and I are going to do some investigating . . ."

"Laurie!" Paula was disconcerted. "That's a terrible idea."

"We're just going to ask questions, that's all." Laurie's voice bordered on whiny.

"At the very least, that would antagonize everyone in the community. This is murder, Laurie. You seem to think it's some sort of game! There's a killer out there somewhere. Keep that in mind, and leave investigating to the police. Martha Abingsford's death doesn't have anything to do with us," she finished firmly.

"I agree with your grandmother, girl," Cynthia Lamphear said. "Stay out of it. You could get hurt that way." Turning to Paula, she went on, "I'll be working in the living room next if you need me, Mrs. Madigan."

Chapter Five

"It was a mistake coming here." Paula glanced nervously over her shoulder at the other inhabitants of the dining room of the Kamiak Hills Country Club. The tables were interspersed among healthy, large plants, giving an illusion of intimacy. It hadn't taken long for Paula to come to her conclusion. From the minute they had walked through the French doors that led to the restaurant, they had been the focus of attention. Fred would have reveled in the situation.

Most of the diners, admittedly, were polite enough to feign deep interest in their food as they glanced surreptitiously over their forks and cups. Paula felt like hiding, but she wasn't too sure about her companion, who gave every appearance of thriving in the glow cast by her one-time performance as the finder of the body. Paula assumed, anyway, that the ghastly event was not to be repeated.

Glancing up, Ellen suddenly seemed to realize what Paula had said. "Because they're looking at us? Oh, they'll get over it." Absently, she said, "I think I'll have the eggplant, fontina and pesto pizza. The salmon's very good, if you like it. Actually, most anything on the menu is. Where is that waitress? Oh." The girl, dressed in a sleek but short black shift, materialized at her elbow. "What are you going to have, Paula? My treat, remember."

Paula smiled her acknowledgment, then ordered. "The chardonnay chicken salad sandwich, I believe. With iced tea." With luck, the lunch that Ellen's mother was feeding the children would be large enough that dinner tonight wouldn't be a concern. Perhaps Laurie would be willing to settle for popcorn, as Paula often did after eating out at noon.

"The pizza, please." Ellen discussed the options of dressings and drinks with the girl, who wrote down the orders and departed.

Thinking of the children had reminded Paula. "Nice of you to include Laurie for lunch, by the way. Frankly, I was relieved that she was willing. She does like to feel that she's much older than Josh."

Ellen giggled. "I know. She told me. She informed me that she was only there because she thought it would be good for you to get out of the house and that she didn't have anything else to do, anyway."

Paula wasn't surprised at Laurie's comments. As they had walked toward the Cogsdill house, Laurie said, "I don't need a babysitter just because Ellen asked you to go to lunch."

"No, I'm sure you don't."

"I'm going because there's nothing else to do."

"Yes." Paula sighed. Entertaining Laurie was going to be a first-class challenge. "I know."

Now, Paula rolled her eyes and began to apologize. "Her manners . . ."

Ellen placed a hand on Paula's. "Don't worry. She's refreshing. There's no prevaricating with Laurie: I can see that already. She gives the appearance of being a very self-sufficient girl, coming all the way across the country on her own. My children wouldn't do that."

"I think she is." Paula was quite aware that Ellen anticipated continuing the conversation on the subject of the unexpected appearance of Laurie. She had no intention of doing so. There were things about Laurie she did want to discuss, though. "Did you know that she and Josh have big plans to be detectives?"

"Oh, no." Ellen grimaced. "I should have guessed. It sounds like Josh. It won't amount to anything, though. What can they possibly do? They're just playing."

"Laurie seemed to have in mind asking questions. She's— very outspoken, in case you haven't noticed. I don't think it's a good idea."

With a wry twist to her mouth, Ellen answered, "I'll speak to Josh." There was something about her tone that made Paula suspect that "speaking to Josh" might be a recurring event in the Cogsdill household and, very likely, was not particularly effective.

Glancing across the room, Paula realized that the woman who had been with Dr. Cordiner on the golf course the day of the murder was lunching with a man much younger than the doctor. The man was speaking, dangerously waving a hand that contained a wine glass, but Trish's gaze roved around the room. It passed over Ellen and Paula as if she had never seen them before. "That woman, the one who was on the golf course . . ." Paula began, and Ellen glanced over her shoulder.

"Oh, her. Not one of my favorite people." She turned back to the table. "I do hope they're not too slow today. It's busier than usual."

"Is she Mrs. Cordiner?" Paula asked with unaccustomed outspokenness.

"Mrs. Cordiner?" Ellen laughed. "You mean David's wife? Thank goodness, no. He has much too much sense for that. Trish Miller's just the most rapacious single woman around. Widow, not a divorcee, for what difference that makes. I don't know who that is she's eating with, but if he's married, his wife had better keep an eye on him. We all watch our husbands in her presence. I was surprised to see David playing golf with her. She probably snared him at the clubhouse. If you need a doctor while you're here, by the way, he's the man."

"I'll remember that." Paula reached for one of the crusty whole-wheat rolls and buttered it.

"Such a sad story." Ellen clearly was prone to tantalizing, unfinished remarks. She added cream to her coffee and stirred, then took a sip.

Paula would have liked to ignore the statement just to see if Ellen would follow up on it, but she found that she couldn't. "How so?" she asked, then bit her lip in frustration.

"Oh, his wife. She died a few months ago, some sort of weird illness. We didn't see much of her that last year. David acted so brave, but you could tell he was deeply worried about her."

"That *is* sad." Paula could empathize with the trauma of being widowed. She hoped, for the doctor's sake, that he'd not had reason to become disillusioned about *his* marriage.

"Oh, look! Here come Alice and Edward Ramsford, and they've actually been playing golf! How could they, after seeing that . . . that . . ." Ellen's face began to crumple, and she reached for her purse and extracted a floral handkerchief. Her hands were shaking, Paula was sorry to note. In spite of Ellen's façade of being calm and happy, she still had not recovered from the experience on the fourth green.

"Don't, Ellen," Paula soothed. "Crying won't help."

"I know." Ellen's voice was tremulous as she surreptitiously wiped her eyes. "But I don't know if I can ever play golf again," she continued, "and especially on this course. Don says I'm being silly, that that's why we bought a house right on the fairway. He's—going to very angry if I won't play in that best ball twosome competition that's coming up." She sniffled into her handkerchief.

"That *would* be a problem. I know exactly how you feel, though. I guess, well . . ." Paula found herself confiding in a manner most unusual for her. "Well, my husband died on the eleventh green at home, a heart attack, you know, and I've always been quite sure I'd never play on that course again."

"Oh-h." Ellen's eyes widened, and now tears threatened to overflow. "How sad. How hard for you this must have been."

Paula concentrated on making her voice matter-of-fact. "I'm sure it was for everyone, and a death always will be. But, you know, the place it occurs—it really isn't that important. I'm not sure that I couldn't, after all, play on my home course again."

What she didn't say was that her new-found resentment of Fred most probably contributed to her feeling. What Ellen didn't know wouldn't hurt. "But now, let's talk about something else. Let's . . ." Her mind fluttered onto different subjects before settling on one that she felt would be truly diverting to a woman who did appear to enjoy gossip. "This Alice." While the penetrating tone of Alice's voice could be heard above the rumble of conversation of the other diners, the words were indistinguishable. It should be safe to discuss the woman. "Tell me about her. Is she always as obnoxious as she was the other day?"

Paula's diversion worked. After one last swipe at her eyes with the handkerchief, Ellen put it away in her purse and managed a smile. "As far as I'm concerned, yes. Not everyone feels that way, though. She's supposed to be tremendously capable. She was even president of the women's club a year or so ago."

"She said she was a nurse?"

"Not a practicing one. I think she did some private duty until recently, but now she specializes in trying to run everything."

One good thing about the arrival of the Ramsfords was that the attention of the other diners was diverted to them. They had, after all, also been on the spot, and Alice clearly did not have any compunction about telling the story. While her docile husband studied the menu, she talked. She talked to people at the surrounding tables, and she talked to a couple who were just leaving and passed nearby. A word or two, "hand," and "rings," drifted across the room.

An athletic-looking woman dressed in a purple velour running suit threaded the tables and headed in their direction. "Hi, Ellen," she said as she approached.

"Hi, Sally. Where's Bob today?" Ellen inquired.

"He had to go to San Francisco on business." The woman turned toward Paula. "You must be Mrs. Madigan. I'm Sally Gunderson, by the way. We're friends of the Pappases."

"How do you do," Paula murmured conventionally, but the woman had already swung back toward Ellen and attacked the subject that Paula feared. "How horrible for you to find the body. I can't imagine . . ."

Ellen's nose began to turn red, and Paula decided to intercede. "It *was* horrible, and we'd decided to avoid the subject."

"Oh. I *am* sorry. Well, please give me a call if I can be of any help. I told Lynn to leave my number."

Paula did remember seeing her name on one of the lists Mrs. Pappas had left. Now, realizing that the woman's eyes expressed genuine sympathy and chagrin, she smiled and said, "I'll do that." She smiled even more when the woman rapidly departed. Ellen didn't need to discuss the murder, even though she had initially appeared to be blasé.

"You were right. We should have gone somewhere else." Ellen pushed her plate away. "I'm not hungry suddenly."

Paula hastily took two more bites, then set the remnants of her sandwich on her plate. "I've had enough, also. Shall we go?" She'd mostly had enough of the oddballs who lived at Kamiak Hills, even though she would have enjoyed a piece of the pie Ellen had told her was featured at the country club.

Josh and Laurie were gone, Ellen's mother told the two women when they arrived back at the Cogsdill house. "They said they were going to go detecting." Mrs. Anderson, a grey-haired older version of her daughter, chuckled. "Such bright children. I do think it's wise to encourage their imaginations, don't you?" Without waiting for an answer, she picked up her purse from the hall table. "I must go, Ellen, I completely forgot that I promised Helen to take her shopping this afternoon. My neighbor," she said in an aside to Paula. "She's recovering from a broken hip. Susan's in her room, and Mark left on his bike with a friend."

A necessity to breathe finally caused her to pause. Paula watched in fascination as Mrs. Anderson, who had obviously run out of air, visibly inhaled. Fuel, Paula decided, to feed vocal cords.

"Laurie's such a sweet girl," Mrs. Anderson, refreshed, rambled on. "Josh is completely smitten. I do think . . ."

"Yes, Mom." Ellen leaned forward and kissed the older woman on the cheek. "You'd better be running along. You've told me how slow Helen can be."

A glance at her watch confirmed that her daughter was correct. "Oh, my yes. It was delightful meeting you, Mrs. Madigan, and your lovely granddaughter. Call me, Ellen." Her departure seemed to leave the air swirling in disarray.

Ellen smiled in apology as Paula quickly composed her own features which, she realized, had included an open mouth. Ellen's tendency for rapid, disjointed conversations had clearly been inherited; fortunately, on a lesser scale.

"I will speak to Josh about this detective business," Ellen promised. "Mom is so sure he's perfect she never thinks of consequences. She was the one to buy him the *large, advanced student chemistry set* for Christmas."

Paula chuckled. She could picture the scene, the parental consternation perhaps hidden in deference to the holiday but unnoticed, anyway, by the indefatigable Mrs. Anderson.

"Come in and have coffee," Ellen invited warmly. "I'm afraid

I rushed us."

Paula shook her head. "Thanks loads. But I do need to be getting on. If Laurie comes here, please send her home. I'd like to take her shopping. She arrived woefully unprepared in the clothes line." Paula remembered her own shock the previous evening when she had suggested a dress might be suitable for the dinner at the Cedar Harbor Inn. A dress to Laurie, it had developed, meant another spotted garment which barely covered her round rump.

"Good luck." Ellen laughed. "If she's anything like my friends' daughters . . ."

"Oh?" Paula inquired inquisitively, figuring that the old adage *forewarned is forearmed* might be appropriate. "I haven't shopped with a teenager for—many years."

"Well, it's just that their taste is so atrocious. You have noticed what they're wearing these days?"

Paula shook her head. "I really haven't paid attention. Although, now that you mention it . . ." She recalled some very odd appearing youngsters she'd noticed while shopping at the mall recently.

Ellen nodded at the expression on Paula's face. "Exactly. And the prices! Some of their clothes couldn't be made out of more than a quarter of a yard of fabric, so it isn't the cost of goods that determines the price. You'll see. Thank God Susan isn't old enough yet. Maybe they'll be wearing something decent by the time she's a teenager."

Paula glanced at Ellen speculatively. She was probably in her late thirties, at least. Paula remembered the era when Ellen would have been a teenager quite well. "And when you were that age you wore . . . ?" she couldn't resist asking.

Ellen's laughter bubbled explosively. "I'd forgotten. I had a . . . Oh, well, I have a few years before I have to worry about it."

Laurie was not at the Pappas house when Paula arrived. That didn't surprise her, since Josh hadn't showed up at the Cogsdills' either by the time she left. By mid-afternoon, Paula was annoyed, and by dinnertime, she was seething. Although, to be honest, she couldn't decide whether the turmoil that was stirring up her insides was anger or worry. The two children had left, presumably, to do some "detecting," and that, Paula was convinced, was foolhardy.

At five she called Ellen. "Oh, they'll show up," Ellen assured her. "Their tummies won't let them miss a meal." Ellen didn't seem the least alarmed, and Paula did not remind her what Josh and Laurie were up to. There was no point in frightening Ellen. It wouldn't do any good, at least now. She only hoped it wouldn't become necessary later. Paula ground her teeth as she prepared the chicken and artichoke-heart casserole they would eat for dinner.

As usual when Paula was cooking, Carioca and Mum-mum sat on one end of the counter and watched. She had tried to persuade them that cats didn't belong on counters at all but failed. She wondered how Lynn Pappas had ever convinced the two that they could come so far and no farther, but there obviously was an invisible line they wouldn't step over. A mousetrap, maybe? She chuckled, picturing the result if she set one on their favorite spot, but then reluctantly decided she couldn't. She had, after all, promised to care for the animals in the manner they were accustomed to, and Paula feared that she would somehow see Lynn's accusing face should she succumb to temptation.

The cats sensed Laurie's approach before Paula heard anything. They leaped down together and headed for the front door, yowling the entire way. Paula heard the door shut and Laurie's voice as she headed toward the kitchen, flattering the cats as she went.

Paula took a deep breath and told herself that she had managed composure. "Where have you been?" she demanded simultaneously with Laurie's cheery, "What's for dinner?"

"Chicken casserole. Now answer me."

"Paula! You sound mad! I was only out and around with Josh. You knew that. At least if Mrs. Anderson . . ."

"That isn't what I meant. Where did you go?"

"Well, we went over and met his friends, the Severan twins. Honestly. I guess neither of them ever goes anywhere without a soccer ball under one arm. They looked like the dumb things had grown there or something. Besides, I don't think they know how to talk and they . . ." Laurie rattled on, her gaze somehow never quite managing to meet Paula's.

"Laurie," Paula interrupted, waving the paring knife she was slicing tomatoes with, "I think there's something you're avoiding. Did you or did you not go 'detecting' with Josh?"

"Well, uh, sort of. I mean, we didn't *do* anything. We just sort of asked some questions and listened to people. You'd be surprised what people say to each other in the grocery store when they don't realize someone's listening." Laurie's expression suddenly became vivacious. "I heard one woman say how she'd hated sex ever since menopause . . ."

Paula gasped. "Eavesdropping, you mean! Laurie, I specifically told you to forget this snooping business, and you promised . . ."

"No, I didn't, Paula. I never make a promise that I don't intend to keep." Her head rose proudly.

"Laurie! What do I have to *do*?" Paula's voice was definitely rising. Paula hadn't shouted in years, if ever. Was this what teenagers did to one? But what did one do to a teenager? She couldn't exactly lock her granddaughter up. "Doesn't your mother ever expect you to obey?"

Laurie shrugged. "Mom's . . . well, she's sort of spacey

sometimes. Besides, she treats me like an adult. She trusts me," she said accusingly, her eyes narrowing and her lower lip thrusting outward. "I'm the one who keeps things going. Which reminds me. Don't you keep a list of things you need at the grocery? It really helps. I couldn't find any peanut butter, and we need . . ."

"Stop changing the subject!" Paula took a deep breath, all the while realizing that she had not kept a grocery list since Fred died. He had insisted on organization. She'd rather enjoyed shopping according to impulse in these last months. *Be reasonable,* she told herself. *You won't get anywhere with anger.*

"Laurie, I think you just don't realize what you're doing. You're not going to find out people's serious secrets eavesdropping in the grocery store. Do you really think someone's going to confide over the broccoli that they murdered Martha Abingsford?"

"No, but Martha Abingsford didn't get murdered because she wiggled when someone putted or whatever, no matter what you golfers think. When a person gets murdered, there's something going on. With the one in our apartment house, it was drug dealing."

"Martha Abingsford wouldn't have . . ."

"Probably not." Laurie shrugged. "But I'll bet she was up to something. Everybody's hiding something, don't you know that?"

Not for the first time, Paula wondered about the environment that Laurie was being raised in, and she felt sorrow. No thirteen-year-old should sound so cynical. "I don't believe . . ."

"You'd better believe, Grandmother Paula. How have you gotten along for so many years?"

Fred, Paula thought, not answering.

"Just for starters, your buddy, Ellen. She's got a secret she hides from everyone."

"Don't be silly!"

"Yes, she does."

"Oh, but—how did you find out, then?" Paula couldn't resist asking.

"Well, first I asked Ellen if she'd gotten one of those letters, and . . ."

"You didn't!"

"And then Josh told me. He doesn't think it's any big deal. He's got this stepbrother, see, that Ellen doesn't tell anyone about. He's at the pen. Armed robbery. He was a user." She added matter-of-factly, "Probably still is. And Ellen doesn't want anyone here at Kamiak Hills to know. It happened before they moved here. Her husband's lots older, and Gary's his. She figures everybody'd cut them dead if it got out.

"So. When do we eat?"

CHAPTER SIX

Paula did not sleep at all well that night. What was she going to do about Laurie? She felt woefully inadequate. More so, certainly, than at any time since the tumultuous days before Jennifer's departure from home. Was she as naïve as Laurie intimated? Had Fred shielded her from most of life's unpleasantness?

Probably, she admitted to herself ruefully. And she had accepted it without complaint, without even questioning. Had she ever had to face life with all its foibles on her own? Perhaps not. Her parents had been well-to-do. Paula, their only child, had arrived late in their reproductive years and had been loved and cosseted. It was only with reluctance that they had allowed her to live on-campus when it came time to attend a university. They chose the college she would attend, a conservatively run religious school that had an impeccable reputation for scholarship. Not the sort, however, that encouraged students to think for themselves.

Untangling herself from a nightie that had somehow wound itself in a coil around her like a morning glory around a lily, she thought about her early years. She'd met Fred Madigan when he'd come to the campus to visit his sister. Their parents had held similar viewpoints on women's roles. Liberal state institutions, with their intellectual challenges and social diversions, were not for their daughters.

Fred had liked her dependency, she realized now. Why, oh

why, had it never occurred to her that being on a protected pedestal was not the way to experience life? Nor was it—she pulled herself back to the issue at hand—preparation for dealing with a thirteen-year-old who thought she knew everything. What on earth was she going to do?

She finally fell asleep much too long after midnight and consequently slept late. Cats yowling awoke her. Pulling on her robe and feeling bleary-eyed, she made her way toward the kitchen. Laurie was eating breakfast and so, purring contentedly, were the cats.

"I started a grocery list," Laurie told Paula. "Peanut butter, and we'd better get more milk next time. Maybe one of those jugs like we use at home."

"No place to recycle them here," Paula grumpily answered, filling the coffeemaker.

"Well, two half-gallons, then. And if you'd decide what we're going to have for dinner . . ."

"After I've had breakfast," Paula snapped.

Laurie looked huffy. "Well, I was only trying to help."

"I know." Paula forced a smile. "Just let me have some coffee first."

"You're just like Mom," Laurie commented. "I guess I must have gotten some of my genes from my father. He might have been an okay person if he hadn't gotten involved with coke."

"People usually do—get their genes from both parents, I mean," Paula answered, watching the coffeemaker begin to do its thing.

"Well, if we're going clothes-shopping, we can stop at the grocery store on the way home."

"All right," Paula acquiesced. Was this why Jennifer needed a vacation away from her daughter? Plans before breakfast?

Somehow Paula survived the shopping expedition. She was exhausted, though, by the time they came home, the car loaded with bundles from department stores and boutiques, not to mention the three large sacks of groceries in the trunk. She had won a few points but lost the rest. She remembered how important it was to a teenager to look like everyone else, but nevertheless insisted on two outfits that would be suitable for occasions with adults.

She was slicing carrot cake for dessert when the phone rang. She put down the knife and reached for it. "Pappas residence," Paula said automatically, then hastily added, "Paula Madigan speaking." They were, after all, beginning to get calls of their own.

"Good evening," a pleasant male voice said. "This is David Cordiner. I tried to call earlier, but there was no answer. I was wondering if I might drop by this evening."

"Uh—why, certainly," Paula answered. She was tired from the shopping expedition but couldn't think of a gracious way to say no. Anyway, she was curious as to what the doctor wanted.

"Shall we say half an hour?"

"That would be fine—or sooner. We were just going to have dessert. Perhaps you'd join us? Carrot cake," she added on impulse.

He chuckled appreciatively. "My favorite. I'm on the way."

Paula hung up, then began to dish up one piece. "Dr. Cordiner's stopping by. I'll wait and have cake with him." She handed a plate to her granddaughter.

"Oh, I'll wait, too." Graciousness oozed from every word.

Paula glanced at her suspiciously. No doubt she remembered David Cordiner's role at the murder scene.

"Well, you did ask him to have dessert with 'us.' " Laurie's mouth quirked. "Don't worry. I won't ask questions about the murder. I just want to meet him. Anyway," she said plaintively, "I don't have anything to do. Josh went to soccer practice. He plays the stupid game, too."

"All right." Paula gave in, then headed toward her bedroom. "I'm going to take off these heels before he gets here," she said, looking over her shoulder and frowning. "Promise? No questions?"

Laurie sighed dramatically. She was good at that. "I already said so."

Laurie heard the shower running, and then closet doors opening and shutting. Paula must have decided to do more than change her shoes. The doorbell rang and she raced to answer it. The doc was early, but hey, that'd give her a chance to talk to him before Paula got there. "Hi," she said, opening the door. "I'm Laurie Shuler. My grandmother will be here in a minute."

"Nice to meet you. I'm David Cordiner," the man said, smiling.

"Come on in." Laurie studied the doctor as he stepped over the threshold. Gray hair cut by a salon, a "trust me" grin, little crinkles at the corner of his eyes. Looked like he should be in a commercial. Like, one where an actor in a white coat was trying to persuade people on the other side of the TV that the goop in the bottle would grow hair on a basketball.

The roses he carried were beautiful, not like any Laurie had ever seen. Lush, all different colors, and she could smell them as he stepped past her. The last ones Gary had brought Mom had been red, all exactly alike, no smell. Mom might have gotten over her mad sooner if Gary had brought flowers like these.

"I thought your grandmother might like these," the doctor said, "but I hope you'll enjoy them, too. Good year for roses. It's been the dry weather. Not even any mildew."

"Good evening, doctor. Won't you come in?"

Laurie turned to see her grandmother. Yeah, she'd showered, done her make-up again and changed to pants and a coral-colored blouse. This guy must be important to her.

"What lovely roses," Paula said. "Laurie, would you like to put these in water? I noticed a cut-glass vase in the cupboard above the stove that would be perfect."

"Sure." Laurie took the flowers. She detoured through the dining room, leaving the door slightly ajar. She wouldn't miss anything that way. She found the vase and filled it with water, straining her ears.

There was one of those awful silences in the living room. Even grownups had them once in a while. Then they both spoke at once. "I promised Lynn . . ." the doctor said at the same time that Paula said, "So good of you . . ." Then they both laughed and began to talk. Not that they said anything worth listening to. Boring. How to grow roses and what a great golf course Kamiak Hills was and Paula really ought to try it again. With him, maybe? Laurie decided she might as well go back.

She carried the vase with the flowers in it and set it on the coffee table. "I fixed the cake, Paula," she said, "while you were changing. It's all on a tray. Shall I get it?"

Looking surprised, Paula answered, "How nice. Please."

Laurie had found the good china, and the tray looked special, if she did say so herself. "There're roses on the plates," she pointed out as she set the tray down next to the real ones.

"So there are. Thank you, Laurie." Paula busied herself with pouring coffee. "Sugar or cream?"

Dr. Cordiner shook his head. "Plain black, please."

Another one of those silences. Laurie opened her mouth, then shut it. Shit. She'd promised Paula not to ask about the murder. What else was there to say? "Do you have a house here on the golf course, too?" she asked.

"Yes, I do."

"Oh. Are you married?" she asked, with a sideways glance at her grandmother. Paula pursed her lips and didn't look like she appreciated it. Somebody had to ask these things. Mom forgot sometimes.

"Widowed last year," the doctor answered.

"Do you have any kids?" Laurie asked.

"Yes," the doc said. "One. He's in medical school in the east, the same one I went to."

"Oh, did you live back east, too? I'm from New York. When did you come out here?"

"Well, I've been here, in Washington, that is, for twenty years, but we moved to Kamiak Hills when it was developed. Let's see, my son was in high school . . ."

"Oh," Laurie said. "Do you . . ."

Paula frowned.

What was her problem? Laurie wasn't talking about the murder, was she?

"Do you like it here in Washington?" the doctor asked, forking a bit of cake. "Must be different from what you're used to."

"Oh, it is," Laurie agreed. "I live in an apartment, just my mom and me. Well, Gary lives there now, too. It's interesting, though. Something always going on." Maybe if she just mentioned the stabbing it would bring up the subject. "There was a drug dealer, and . . ."

"Laurie," Paula interrupted, "are you almost finished with your cake? Isn't it about time for Josh to get home from soccer practice?" Her eyebrows rose hopefully.

Laurie glanced at her watch and then down at her plate. "Yeah, almost," she conceded. She'd only taken a few bites. Paula wanted to get rid of her. Did she have a thing for this doctor? Laurie narrowed her eyes and studied the two of them. They both sat on the black leather couch, but there was a cushion between them. Paula's face was flushed, but he looked perfectly ordinary, maybe better looking than most old guys, but not flirting with Paula or anything like that.

Maybe she should go and give her grandmother a chance, if that was what she wanted, Laurie decided impulsively. She took two quick bites.

"Laurie's mother is traveling in Europe," Paula explained.

Laurie'd bet that the doctor wouldn't picture the way Mom and Gary were traveling: hitchhiking with backpacks.

Laurie scraped up the last of her cake. It was good. Almost as good as Mom's. "Okay, I'm done," she announced, standing.

"Now you and Josh won't . . ." Paula stopped mid-sentence, but Laurie knew exactly what she'd been going to say.

"Nah, we won't do anything you wouldn't want us to do," she promised. "Not tonight, anyway. Goodbye, Doc. Nice to have met you," she added as an afterthought as she pushed through the swinging door to the kitchen, carrying her own plate.

Paula sighed, a heartfelt, deep exhaling of air. It seemed she was doing a lot of that lately.

"Problems?" David asked, his expression one of wry sympathy.

"Well, yes. Laurie . . . I'm not experienced at coping with teenagers. She seems to think she's going to solve the murder by snooping around with the boy next door."

David laughed. "I'm not surprised, having met her. Not shy, is she?"

"Not at all!" To her surprise, Paula found herself explaining about Josh and Laurie's activities at length. David Cordiner was the sort who managed to elicit pertinent information without appearing to pry. Finally, Paula gestured apologetically. "I didn't mean to burden you."

He shook his head dismissively. "I promised Lynn and Hal I'd stop by and see if there was anything I could do. I didn't really expect that there would be, but I've been told I'm a good listener, and that's what a person needs sometimes. Anyway, I wanted to get to know you better. And I guess I have." His smile was warm. "A beginning, anyway."

What exactly did he mean by that? Paula wondered, self-consciously refilling coffee cups.

"And, I think I could make a few suggestions regarding Laurie."

"Oh? Please do," she said in a rush.

"Nice girl. You'll adjust."

Paula nodded.

"I think what you might try, is keeping her busy. She has a bright, inquiring mind . . ." She nodded again, vigorously, and he continued speaking. "There're a lot of classes available around here for kids in the summer. Golf, soccer, or maybe she'd like swimming. There's a good recreational team, and the kids have a lot of fun. And, with two practices a day, they don't have much time or energy left over to get into trouble. If she doesn't like sports, she might be interested in art. Or a foreign language. Then, of course, since she's never been here, there's sightseeing. The waterfront in Seattle, with the Aquarium and Ye Olde Curiosity Shop. That alone is good for at least an afternoon."

"Doctor," Paula said enthusiastically, "I think you've just saved my life. I can't understand why I didn't think of these things myself, but I've been in a rut. I haven't been to Ye Olde Curiosity Shop myself for years. I seem to remember a mummy . . ."

David nodded. "That always fascinates kids. I haven't been there for years, either. Perhaps we can make it a date?"

"Absolutely."

By the time he left, after a second piece of cake and uncounted cups of coffee, Paula felt as if they were old friends. No wonder everyone raved about him so much. He'd certainly given her a prescription that just might be the wonder drug she needed in dealing with Laurie.

It seemed that most of her problems were solved, Paula thought by the next Wednesday. Laurie loved the swimming pool, and swam well enough that the coach suggested she join his "B" team. She signed up, surprisingly, for a knitting class. "It looks like fun," she said, "and I can make myself vests, and scarves, and gosh, maybe some presents for people."

Paula thought some of the projects she had in mind would take much longer than Laurie anticipated, but she happily bought her some lovely, surprisingly expensive yarn, the needles, and a book of patterns. Soon, her first project, a multi-colored scarf, began to take shape.

David stopped by twice, bringing fresh lettuce from his garden once and staying for dinner the next time. Paula's life was becoming more enjoyable than it had been for years. Spending time with Laurie was a lot more fun than being an adjunct to Fred on various committees. For that matter, to be honest, David was better company than Fred had ever been, at least in recent years since his tendency toward pomposity had gotten out of hand.

As he'd suggested, Laurie skipped practice on one of David's days off, and they went to the Seattle waterfront. Besides the fascinating curiosity shop, they toured the sculpture park with its huge works of art and then took the cable car to Pioneer Square.

"There's a great Italian restaurant here," David said. "Appeal to you two?"

"I *love* spaghetti," Laurie said.

"Sounds good to me," Paula seconded.

When he dropped them home later, Paula said, "Thanks so much, David. The waterfront has changed so much since I've been there. It's been a lovely day."

"Yeah, Doc," Laurie said. "I didn't think it would be, but it's been fun."

Paula and David exchanged amused glances.

But then came the day that she got the letter. The plain white envelope with the address printed in blue would not have been particularly noticeable, except that it was the first addressed to her here at the Pappas house, not forwarded. Nevertheless, it was only afterward that she studied it with care. It had been mailed locally and had no return address.

The message inside was crudely printed. It said,

STAY AWAY FROM DAVID CORDINER UNTIL YOU FIND OUT WHAT HAPPENED TO HIS WIFE. YOU DON'T WANT TO BE NEXT.

Life had been too pleasant, Paula realized. Her first reaction, that David Cordiner was too good to be true, had perhaps been right. Although, in all fairness, she should give him a chance to explain.

But, perhaps of greater interest to the police at least, the anonymous letter writer was still at work. Martha Abingsford had been unfairly maligned when people thought her to be the malicious author.

Was there a possibility that she had been murdered in error?

CHAPTER SEVEN

What was she to do? Mesmerized, Paula stared at the paper with the stark message. Clearly, she needed to phone the police. It was crucial to their investigation that they know about this.

But what about David Cordiner? She took a couple of deep breaths as she thought. Her original reaction to the doctor, on the golf course, had been positive. He'd handled a difficult situation admirably, dealing with two obnoxious women while he saw that play was stopped and the police notified. It was only later, as praise was heaped on praise, that she had begun to have doubts. She'd never encountered anyone who was truly as perfect as David was portrayed.

In the normal course of things, she'd have found out his flaws, no doubt, if they continued their burgeoning relationship. Perhaps he liked to eat garlic, never being aware of its effects. No, not that, she decided. A doctor would surely know that garlic eaters so often, to be blunt, stank. But he might . . .

Stop dithering, she told herself. She would give him a chance to explain. That was only fair, but contacting the police took precedence. What was the name of that officer who'd been in charge? Oh, Lord. She was getting old. She hadn't the faintest idea.

She was still holding the letter. Carefully, she laid it on the kitchen table. Fortunately Laurie was over at Josh's house, and the cats hadn't yet returned from their nighttime foray in search of game. She'd seen enough movies and read enough books to know that she should avoid handling the letter. Too bad that her fingerprints were already festooned across the top and bottom.

She extracted the phone book from the upper drawer in the kitchen cabinet and, with a little searching, found the number to call. "Hello," she answered to the query on the other end, "I need to talk to whomever is in charge of the investigation of the murder the other day on the golf course. I have information that I think is pertinent."

"That would be Detective Jack Compagnio," she was told. "Hold on."

She pulled up a chair, sat and waited. Interminably, it seemed. But no. Glancing at her watch, she saw that it was just another of those stressful intervals that only seemed to last forever.

"Good morning," a deep bass voice finally spoke. "This is Detective Compagnio. I understand you have information for me."

"Yes, Detective," she said. "This is Paula Madigan. I was one of the group of golfers . . ."

"Yes, Mrs. Madigan," he interrupted. "I remember you. The newcomer to Kamiak Hills."

"Oh. Well, I seem to be the recipient of one of those anonymous letters that people have been receiving. I thought that it might indicate that Martha . . ."

"Hmm, yes," he interrupted again. "That Martha Abingsford was not the author of the other missives." He was silent for a moment. She could almost feel his thought processes emanating across the line. "I assume that you have handled the letter?"

"Yes," she answered. "But as soon as I realized what it said I set it down, and . . ."

"And what did it say?"

There was one of the all-too-common faults that David might have had. Constantly interrupting. But perhaps the detective

71

was to be forgiven. The news about another letter must have been a shock.

Paula quoted the letter exactly. " 'Stay away from David Cordiner until you find out what happened to his wife. You don't want to be next.' "

"You have been seeing the doctor then, I gather?"

A little irritated, as if it was any of his concern, she snapped, "If you consider my going into the city with him accompanied by my granddaughter 'seeing' him, yes."

A touch of humor lightened his voice. "Just trying to get the picture. Have you spoken to Dr. Cordiner since you opened the letter?"

"No. I intend to," she said firmly. "It's only fair to hear his side of the issue."

"I agree. But may I ask you to refrain until we have the letter in our hands?"

"Yes, certainly."

"Good. I'll be over to the Pappas house as soon as I can get there. I have a meeting in ten minutes, but I'll come immediately after."

"I'll be here," she promised.

Restlessly, she began her morning chores. She finished cleaning up the kitchen, wiping off the stove and counters but avoiding the table. Then she went to her bedroom, made the bed, and started a load of wash.

Every time she passed through the kitchen, the letter drew her attention like a magnet. Finally, she placed an upside-down mixing bowl over it. It wouldn't do to have the cats return and step on it, or, worse yet, to have Laurie grab it to read.

"I'm going home," Laurie said. "That's a stupid game. I'd rather work on the scarf I'm knitting."

Josh looked at her over the top of his glasses. "You're just a bad sport because you keep losing. We can do something else, though."

"I don't think so. See you later, after swimming practice."

Josh shrugged. "Do what you want. I don't care." He turned back to the computer. Laurie stuck out her tongue and slammed the door on her way out.

As she walked into the kitchen, she could hear voices in the living room. One of them was unfamiliar, deep and growly. It sure wasn't the doc.

She crept into the dining room and gently turned the handle so that a tiny crack appeared and the voices became clearer.

"I assume your fingerprints are not on record," the voice said.

Fingerprints? Laurie pressed her ear to the crack.

"No, I've never had them taken."

"At your convenience then, please stop by the department. You do realize that we'll need to have them as we try to identify the letter writer?"

"Of course," she said. "I *have* read a few mysteries."

"Probably isn't necessary," he said. "The writer of the other letters also read or watched TV. There were no discernible prints on any of them."

He hesitated, then went on. "I probably shouldn't say this, but the letter writer could be almost any adult—or even a teenager—in this community. Except you and your granddaughter. From what you've just told me, you have no prior connections with anyone here. So, if anything comes to your attention, anything at all that seems suspicious, please contact me."

"I would, of course," Paula said. "But I'm unlikely to. It's good to know that you realize we're not involved."

"I didn't say that. Murder in a community potentially involves everyone."

Paula shook her head. "Not us."

"Let's hope not."

"Am I free to phone David Cordiner now?" she asked.

Huh? Laurie thought. Had Paula received an anonymous letter about the doctor? Wow.

"Any time. And now . . ." It sounded like the man, apparently a policeman, was laughing as he spoke, ". . . you might see who's eavesdropping behind that door over there."

Oh, shit, Laurie thought. Thinking quickly, she opened the door wide and walked into the living room. "Hi, Paula," she said. "I just got home. All Josh wanted to do was play some computer war game. What's up?" She opened her eyes wide, something she'd practiced in front of the mirror. It made her look innocent, she figured.

Grandma Paula was not fooled, it appeared, from the look on her face. "Laurie!" she scolded. "Did your mother approve of your eavesdropping?"

"Of course not," Laurie said, "I'd never . . ."

"We'll talk about it later," Paula said.

The man had risen when she walked in. He held out his hand. "I'm Detective Compagnio," he said, "from the local police department."

He had a face she'd have liked if he hadn't caught her doing something she shouldn't. It wouldn't be good to have this guy after you if you had committed a crime, she decided. She studied him carefully. Dark eyes, ones her mother would have called soulful, tightly curled gray hair, lines on his face. Not grumpy ones, she decided. There might be some laugh lines among them.

She held out her own hand. "Hello. I'm Laurie Shuler. I'm spending the summer with my grandmother."

"Glad to meet you," the policeman said. "Hope you're having a good summer."

"Yes," she answered. "Yes, I am!" She was surprised at her own answer. She hadn't really thought about it, just taking things as they came. But their apartment in New York was probably roasting hot now, and she had a lot of cool new clothes. The swim team was fun. She was actually going to be in a race soon, the coach promised.

"Good." Turning toward Paula, he said, "Thanks for calling me so quickly. I think it would be just as well not to tell anyone about the letter. You haven't, have you?"

"No, of course not," Paula said. She was the one who sounded grumpy.

On the way out, the man patted Laurie on the shoulder. "Hope I'll see you again."

"Uh . . . sure." Why had he said that, she wondered.

As soon as he was out the door, she asked, "What was that all about?"

"You heard the detective," Paula said. "He doesn't want me to talk about it."

"But I already know you got one of those letters. You have to tell me."

"I don't think so," Paula answered. "Yes, you know I received an anonymous letter. But I'm not going to tell you any more than that."

"And I know it was about the doc," Laurie said slyly.

Paula threw her head back and blew out air. A lot of it. "Laurie . . . No amount of wheedling is going to get me to tell you what the letter was about. I hope you'll let it go right there. David Cordiner is a very nice man. No one should believe an anonymous message anyway, and it would be extremely unfair for him if this gets out. So far, only I, Detective Compagnio, and now you, know I received it. Can I have your promise to keep it that way?"

Laurie thought for a minute. Paula and the doc might have a

thing going, and that could be good for her grandmother. He seemed like an okay guy, and he was probably rich. "Okay," she agreed. "Only, one more person is going to know."

"Who?" Paula said sharply.

"Why, the doc, of course. You told the policeman you were going to call him."

Paula put her hand to her forehead. "Yes. You're right. I'm not looking forward to it. And, no, you are not going to listen to the conversation."

"Grandmother, I would never have thought of such a thing!" Laurie blinked her eyes and grinned. The summer was also turning out to be more interesting than New York would have been.

Paula had a headache. Whether it was in reaction to the letter or to Laurie, she wasn't sure. What a pain in the neck that girl could be. Or, in this case, pain in the head.

She would have to wait until evening to call David. He worked long hours, and this was one of the days that he made rounds at the local hospital after he left the clinic. She'd rather speak to him in person, making it absolutely impossible for Laurie to overhear the conversation. Perhaps she could meet him somewhere to talk.

Laurie squealed, out in the kitchen. "Mum-mum, no!" she yelled.

Curious, Paula hurried to the kitchen. Mum-mum was placidly sitting in front of the cat door that led outside, washing her face with her paw.

Laurie, however, was not placid as she grabbed a broom from the closet. Seeing Paula, she said, "That stupid cat! She brought in a mouse! And it's alive!"

"Ooh!" Paula's first thought was to sit down and raise her feet. She liked most animals, but in their proper places. A mouse in her kitchen was not in that category. Instead, she opened the back door. "Where is it?" she asked.

"Over there!" Laurie pointed at the quivering rodent who lurked in a far corner.

"Okay," Paula said, grabbing Mum-mum. "I'll come from this direction, and you use the broom, and let's hope we can shoo it out the door."

It took several attempts. Finally, the mouse scurried outside. Paula shut the door and set the cat down.

Mum-mum was not happy. The cat had shown her dislike for Paula earlier, and now, Paula was sure, she had cemented their, she was sorry to say, mutual antipathy. Oh well, they only had to put up with each other for a little over two months. And then she could return to—to where? Not to the house she had shared with Fred, that was for sure. It was time to put it up for sale and to look for another residence. That would take some think-ing. Where did she want to live? Kamiak Hills? Well, maybe. And maybe not. The way things were going, unpleasant memories might prevent her from being happy here, also.

That evening, feeling like a sneak, Paula dialed David's number from the pay phone at the clubhouse. She'd told Laurie that she was going over to check on possibly joining the Women's Club. That might be a good idea, anyway, she concluded. She could meet other women of the area and find out whether Kamiak Hills was totally populated with oddballs, or if it had a cadre of normal women. Regardless, she was ready to start playing golf again.

David sounded weary when he answered the phone. In the background, she could hear classical music playing, either his stereo or TV. The poor man was probably trying to unwind from a grueling day, and she was the bearer of bad news.

She wouldn't hit him with it tonight, she concluded. Anyway, it would be better to talk to him in person. One could gain so much from seeing the expressions on the listener's face, she told herself. But no. That really wasn't the cause of her reluctance. It just didn't feel right, as nice as he'd been, to potentially break off whatever their relationship was without doing it in person.

"David," she said, "I've just had some disturbing information. Would you—is it possible to get together sometime soon so we can talk about it? Without Laurie's presence?"

"Of course, Paula. Did you have a place in mind?"

"Anywhere private." She could, of course, suggest he come while Laurie was at swim practice, but it seemed best to be in a neutral location. Not the Pappas house and not his. She had yet to be to his house, anyway. Sort of a mutual decision to keep tongues from wagging.

"There's a nice, short hike that circles Lake Padden, near Bellingham," he suggested. "Can you get away from Laurie on Saturday morning?"

"I will, somehow."

"How about I pick you up about ten? I'll bring a lunch."

"How thoughtful," she said. "Yes, that would be good." David had not sounded surprised, she concluded as she hung up.

But how was she going to get rid of Laurie? Well, perhaps the best thing was just to be blunt. Laurie shouldn't expect to be included every time she and David chose to do something together.

So, Friday evening, she brought up the subject. "I'm going to be leaving tomorrow morning before you get home from swim practice," she said. "I assume you can amuse yourself until I get back. David and I are going on a hike he recommends, and he's bringing lunch."

Laurie and she eyed each other, Paula holding her breath.

Rather to her surprise, Laurie quickly agreed. "Sure." With a smirk, she added, "If you two want to be alone, that's good by me."

"It isn't . . ." Paula started to say, but then firmly shut her mouth. Let Laurie think what she wanted. What *was* important was bringing into the open the information in the anonymous letter.

So, at ten o'clock, Paula was ready when David swung into the driveway of the Pappas house. Without waiting for him to come in, she ran out and hopped into the front seat of his BMW.

"It's a beautiful day, isn't it?" David said. "I think you'll enjoy this hike. It's easy, but on Saturday it'll likely be crowded. We can find a spot to ourselves, though, I'm sure."

He didn't press her. They chatted about Laurie, about the pressure of David's work, about Paula's life before coming to Kamiak Hills. "Somehow the woman you're describing doesn't sound like the Paula I'm coming to know," he said, an eyebrow raised.

"I'm not the same person," she admitted. "Someday I'll explain."

He turned the car onto a short drive through woods, and they came out at a parking lot half filled with other cars. Beyond, the intense blue lake had attracted loads of other people. Dads pushed strollers, kids tossed balls on the grass, sweating joggers swerved through the congestion.

"How about over there?" he suggested, pointing to an unoccupied bench on a slight rise. "From your tone when you called, I gather this is something you'd rather get over with?"

She chuckled wryly. "You could say that."

They walked to the bench in silence and sat down. He placed his arm casually across the slotted back of the park bench.

"David," she began, her voice croaking. "David, this is very awkward for me. I've enjoyed your help and support so much, but . . ."

He raised one eyebrow.

"Oh, heck. I received an anonymous letter two days ago," she blurted.

"And? I gather it was about me?"

"Yes," she admitted. "I had to take it to the police because everyone has assumed that Martha Abingsford was the writer of those letters so many people, evidently, have been receiving. But my first reaction was to talk to you. It said . . ." She paused, finally deciding that a direct approach would be best. "It said that I shouldn't see you until I found out about your wife's death." The words rushed out of her mouth.

He removed his arm and leaned forward, placing his elbows on his knees and his chin in his hands. "I'm not surprised," he said. "I'm well aware of the rumors that swirl maliciously through a community like Kamiak Hills. Any community, no doubt."

He took a deep breath, obviously gathering his thoughts. "My wife had osteoporosis of the spine. It's a very painful and disabling disease. You may be aware of it . . ."

Paula nodded. "Yes. A friend of mine in Bellevue had it. She had those debilitating small fractures of her spine and was in great pain. She'd shrunk a number of inches before . . . Oh, David, I'm so sorry."

"Yes, well, you understand then what my wife went through as she deteriorated. Medications helped for a while, but then . . . When Anne died, there were those who thought I'd assisted her in suicide. I loved my wife very much, Paula. I'd have done anything in the world to help, but there was no help, beyond what was being done."

"Oh, David," Paula said, putting a hand on his forearm. "I'm so sorry to have brought up such painful memories. I feel . . . rotten. And I think it was absolutely inexcusable for anyone to write that letter. I hope whoever it is will be caught."

"I do, too. Particularly since the letter writer may very well be the murderer," he reminded her. "Do you want to go home?"

"Of course not. Not unless you want to. I just felt that I had to bring this out in the open."

"I'm glad you did. We've cleared the air, I hope?"

"Absolutely. Now, do you want to show me the rest of the lake?"

He stood, took both of her hands, and pulled her to her feet. "Let's go."

It was only later, at about the halfway point, when sweat was dripping down her face as the day grew warmer and her thighs were registering the fact she hadn't been getting enough exercise in recent days, when she realized he'd never actually said whether he'd helped his wife die. Had he given her just the little extra painkiller that was the difference between life and death? Did it matter?

No, probably not. Not to her. If she'd been in the same situation, with a loved one dying slowly and excruciatingly in front of her, what decision might she have made?

She'd never know, unless she was someday faced with such a dilemma. God help her, she hoped that she never would be.

CHAPTER EIGHT

On Tuesday morning, Paula dropped Laurie at the pool, where other young people were arriving for swim practice. They looked like good kids, Paula noted; clean-cut, fit and tanned. They were extraordinarily fortunate, she thought. Typical mid- to upper class and involved in an activity that, with luck, would keep them out of trouble.

"So long, Grandmama," Laurie said, with a casual wave as she sidled up to a lanky youth at least a couple of years older than she. Paula smiled. She was getting used to being called various names, and she liked it. Seemed like Laurie was getting comfortable in their relationship. They both were.

It had taken a certain firmness earlier, however, to convince Laurie that she was not going to drive the cart today. After all, it was the first time they'd taken it out from its cubbyhole under the deck. "Go faster," Laurie had pleaded, her eyes gleaming in excitement. "Let me drive. You're too pokey."

"They aren't meant to go faster," Paula had explained. "If they did, they'd damage the course. I'm not complaining; I remember when I pulled my clubs behind me in a funny little contraption."

"But . . ."

"Later," she'd promised. "I'll take you for a test drive. But now you'd better get in there. It looks like practice has already started." Heads bobbed in the aqua-blue water of the pool, which could be seen through a chain link fence to the east of the clubhouse. Coach Soriano, or "Coach Sorry," as the kids called him, not to his face, she hoped, was pacing alongside and gesturing.

"Oh. Yeah," Laurie said. "See you at lunch."

Paula hadn't known if she'd need her own cart or would be joining another woman for Ladies' Day. The space in front of the clubhouse swarmed with carts, and women juggled huge bags as they switched to join their playing partners for the day. How many clubs these women carried, Paula realized, as she again went in to pick up her rental set. She couldn't imagine ever needing quite such a variety. One of these days, she'd return home to pick up her own clubs, along with a few other items she'd overlooked. She also would make arrangements to list her house for sale.

She was playing with Sally Gunderson, she was pleased to note on the chart. Sally had seemed like an especially nice woman when they'd chatted in the Clubhouse dining room, even if she had inadvertently brought up a tender subject.

As Paula carried her clubs out the door, she saw Sally wave to her from her cart. No fringes, no gaudy colors, Paula was happy to note. Somehow the plainness matched the Sally she'd chatted with so briefly.

"Hi, Paula," Sally said. "Ride with me." She hopped out of her cart to assist with installing the clubs on the back. "So glad you've joined us. When I saw you'd signed up, I asked if we could be partners. I'd like to get to know you better."

"I, too," Paula answered. The morning was cooler than some of the days they'd been having and was perfect for a round of golf. "You may not enjoy playing with me, though. I'm rusty, and I never was the greatest, as you may have guessed from my handicap."

"You think I'm a champion?" Sally grinned.

The women used staggered starts, so they had to drive to the fifth tee to be ready to begin at nine o'clock. That boded well for the day, Paula thought. She'd get to play all of the other eight holes before tackling the dreaded fourth.

They were soon joined by another cart. One of the women was Babs Griffin, whom Paula had played with on the awful day of the murder. Paula was a mite relieved. Babs had appeared to be innocuous, except for her unkind jabs at her husband. The other woman, a mild-mannered blonde named Pat, was obviously a good friend of Babs. It looked like they would be a congenial group to spend the morning with.

When a siren indicated the start of play, they began. Again, Babs hit a short shot straight down the middle. Her partner's appeared to be similar but longer, until it took a wild slice. "Oh, damn," Pat said. "I took a lesson this week, and what good did it do me?" Everyone laughed, although sympathetically. It could happen to any of them, they knew.

Paula's play, as she had expected, was erratic. It didn't matter, though. She was enjoying herself. It was great to be outdoors on such a nice day, and in the company of a group who were, as she'd hoped, good companions. By the time they reached the eighth tee, where there was a delay because of slow play ahead of them, she felt they were becoming friends.

So far, they had studiously avoided the subject of the murder. Perhaps Sally had warned the others that Paula didn't want to talk about it. They did gossip, though, as they waited. If one could truly call it gossip when they were really chatting about their activities and mutual friends.

After discussing the serious illness of one of their friends, one Bill Jackson, the topic switched to include David Cordiner. "Reminds me of when Anne Cordiner was so ill," Pat said, "except this time it's the husband who's so sick, and his wife, Gerri, who's so supportive. What a thing for partners to go through," she added. "I sure hope it doesn't happen to me or

Wes. How can people be so brave?"

"You do what you have to, I imagine," Paula contributed, hoping they'd change the subject. It was not to be.

"Even if it's assisted suicide?" Pat asked. "Like people are saying happened to Anne? They're still talking."

Still talking? Why? Who was doing the talking? Paula took one of the deep breaths she so often used for courage. It wasn't fair, truly wasn't, to spread stories about such a nice man. Making her voice as calm as she could, she nerved herself and asked, "Who would be so despicable as to spread a story like that?"

"Well, you're right. One should always consider the source. It was Alice Ramsford I last heard saying it, but she hasn't been the only one. There was no question Anne didn't take her illness without a whimper. We all felt sorry for David, being so patient and understanding as Anne deteriorated, both physically and emotionally," Babs said.

"Humph." Sally picked up her club preparatory to teeing off. "How do any of us know how we'd react to an illness like Anne's? Who wouldn't be angry? I don't understand why anyone pays attention to Alice. We all know how malicious she can be."

Paula was surprised to hear Sally express such a sentiment. So far, she'd continued to be gracious and had not made any negative comments about anyone. Paula suspected that Alice had few, if any, friends.

When they got to the fourth tee, Paula felt her nerves tighten. Sure enough, she managed to top her second shot, send the third well over the green, and back to the shoulder on the other side with her next. At least she'd avoided the sand hazards, she thought, as she turned her body in such a way that she didn't need to look at the grim reminder of the murder.

Sally came up alongside her and whispered, "Just take it easy. This first time'll be tough, but then you'll have it behind you."

Paula nodded. "Thanks." And then to her surprise, she

chipped the next shot so well that it bounced once, then rolled slowly into the hole. A bogey, but she'd take it, all things considered. Everybody laughed and cheered. Even Babs. Paula realized that she, too, had been affected by the sense of place and had been completely silent. She'd played her ball even more conservatively than usual, so there hadn't been the least chance of going near the hated hazard.

Paula was glad to finish the round. However, she felt stressed enough that she thought she'd take a short nap after lunch. Sally was right, though, she was sure. Next time would be easier, and maybe, eventually, she could tuck thoughts of that grim day in a far corner of her brain.

Her grandmother decided to come to watch the afternoon practice of the swim team, much to Laurie's surprise. Even more of a surprise, Paula suggested they ride to the clubhouse in the cart, and she let her drive.

"Wow," Laurie said. "This is so cool!" She tried a couple of experimental turns. "Whoops! Oh, well."

They were on one of the numerous cart paths that laced the community, and she'd veered off the asphalt and wandered onto the grass.

Paula smiled. "Take it easy, Laurie. Remember, this isn't our cart. You wouldn't want to put a dent in it."

"I won't," Laurie promised. "Thanks. Thanks a lot for letting me drive."

She had sort of figured that her grandmother would make excuses and never let her behind the wheel. Grandma was sure turning out to be cool. She stayed at the pool the whole time they practiced, talking to some of the mothers, and hadn't looked bored at all.

Coach Sorry stopped her before she went into the dressing room. "Laurie," he said, "your freestyle's really coming along nicely. You should be ready to enter that meet that's coming up in a couple of weeks at the city pool."

"No kidding?"

"No kidding." He smiled, looking really pleased. "And maybe we'll enter you in the breaststroke also. Won't hurt, and you'll get experience."

"Hey, far out!" She knew her backstroke was only fair, and as far as the butterfly, she'd never swam it before, and she had an awful time making her arms and legs work the way they were supposed to. He wouldn't be putting her into any races in that event, but that was okay. She wanted to have a chance, maybe, of winning, in any races she did enter.

Alan looked like he was waiting for her when she came out of the dressing room, and that was cool. They walked out together, and she saw Paula raise an eyebrow. But then she smiled. Paula let her drive, too, even though she was still wet. Alan looked impressed when she got in behind the wheel, she thought, as she watched him out of the corner of her eye. And when they got to the house, Gramma let her park the cart in its little place under the deck and plug it in.

"You don't want to forget that," Paula said. "Otherwise the battery will run down."

She was starved. Paula had made potato salad earlier, and they barbequed hamburgers out on the deck. Rich people sure had it made. Mom was never going to make it, and that made Laurie sad, but maybe she, herself, could. She wasn't sure what she wanted to do when she got out of school, but Grandma had already been talking as if she assumed Laurie would naturally go on to college. That might be cool. Mom never said things like that. All the older kids on the team were already buzzing about where they wanted to go, the U-dub, Wazzoo, and a bunch of places she'd never heard of. Places like Whitman and Pomona.

Afterwards, they'd had ice cream sundaes for dessert, and

Paula let her put any topping on it that she wanted.

She went to bed early. Swimming twice a day made her sleepy. Grandma was still reading when she went to her bedroom, but when she woke up later, the house was still and it had grown dark outside. Why had she woken up?

She was almost asleep again when she heard a noise. That's what had woken her, she was sure. Something rattled, somewhere down below. She sat up and listened. Then she heard a clank.

Somebody was poking around close by, under the deck, she figured out. Why? And who? She'd better get her grandmother.

She tiptoed quickly into her grandmother's bedroom and shook her shoulder. Paula snorted, then reared up, her eyes wild, like a cat cornered by a dog.

"Sh!" Laurie whispered urgently. "There's somebody outside. I think they're fooling around with the cart."

She was glad when Paula caught on quickly and acted. She swung her legs to the floor, and the two of them hurried toward the kitchen, where they could hear better.

The door below squeaked. "I think someone's trying to steal it!" Grandma whispered. "Why ever . . ."

"I'll go see!" Laura said.

"Not on your life. I'll call . . ."

Laurie ignored her, opened the kitchen door, and ran outside.

"Laurie!" Paula didn't even try to be quiet, which was dumb. Laurie figured that if she got out there in a hurry, she might see what was going on and who was doing it. Grandma was blowing it.

When she reached the railing, she could see that she'd been right. The cart was racing away, as quickly as it was able, but she couldn't even tell whether it was a man or woman driving. Defeated, she went back into the kitchen.

"What a foolish stunt!" Paula scolded. "I told you to stay

put! You don't know if someone was dangerous, even had a gun or something."

"Get real," Laurie said. "It was probably kids."

"I'm going to call the police!"

"Ah, they'll probably bring it back. It's . . ." She glanced at the clock. ". . . It's two in the morning. Police don't like being called in the middle of the night for some little thing like this," she said. "I remember the time . . ."

The look Paula shot her shut her up. Maybe it was just as well not to squeal. Maybe police in New York were different from the ones here, but she'd bet not.

Grandma ran her hands through her hair, making it stand up like a witch. "It probably is too late now," she said. "All right, we'll wait until morning. Let's get back to bed. We'll want to sleep late."

"Oh! Grandma. I'm glad you said that! I forgot. They've got something going on at the pool when we're usually there, so the coach scheduled an early practice. We have to be in the pool at six o'clock! It's not fair!"

"Well, those things happen, Laurie. We'll just have to . . ."

"You don't have to get up, Grandma. I can grab a bowl of cereal. I'll have to get out of bed . . ." She glanced at the clock. ". . . Oh, ugh, three hours from now. Do we have an alarm clock?"

"There's one in my room. We'll just move it. That's good of you. I feel guilty . . ."

Laurie looked at her grandmother's woeful face. "Don't," she said, and on impulse, she hugged her, then drew back, sort of embarrassed. Paula seemed to like it, though. At least she smiled.

Paula didn't hear the news until Laurie returned from practice the next morning. Her granddaughter burst in the door, her face excited and chagrined. "Grandma," she almost shouted,

"Somebody found another body on the golf course. It was a woman! It was in a water hole! And there was this golf cart left there, too. The police are trying to find out who it belongs to!"

"Ohmygawd! Did you tell anybody, the coach or someone, about what happened here last night?"

"Well, yeah, sure. Why not?"

Why not indeed? Before she could decide what to do, the phone rang.

CHAPTER NINE

"Mrs. Madigan." The voice was deep male, and Paula recognized it instantly.

"Yes. Detective Compagnio? I was just reaching for the phone to call you."

"You've heard, then?"

"Indeed. My granddaughter brought home the news from swim practice. Everyone was talking about it."

"Am I correct that your cart was stolen last night?"

"Yes. I'm afraid so. I'm sorry I didn't call the police, but Laurie persuaded me they wouldn't appreciate it at that hour."

"Which was when?" he asked.

"Just about two."

"Well, needless to say . . ." He stopped speaking.

Paula was quite sure he'd almost said what a big mistake she'd made. Perhaps they would have caught the murderer disposing of the body. If only she'd listened to her own impulse. Weakly, she repeated, "I'm sorry."

"Officers will be descending on you as soon as I radio them. And I'll be over as quickly as I can get there."

"All right. Certainly." Her voice wavered like some old lady's. She was not looking forward to Detective Compagnio's arrival. He had every right to be angry. Errors in judgment like hers could have a serious impact on an investigation, she imagined. Only . . . surely she wasn't the first innocent who'd made a mistake.

It wasn't long before she heard a knock sound on the rear door, the one leading to the kitchen from the deck. Laurie answered, saying, "Hi."

"Hi," a woman's voice responded. "We'll be working below." The same officer who'd helped with the investigation on the fourth green? Paula wondered. Did they employ her to be a liaison with women and children? "The detective will be here shortly to talk to you."

"Sure," Laurie said. "We've been expecting you." Her voice was formal, as grown-up sounding as she could make it.

Laurie, Paula feared, was going to enjoy the proceedings. She, too, knew few of the people who lived here, so would undoubtedly feel exhilaration rather than sorrow. She was, after all, a child, although surely she didn't think of herself as one. Paula hurried into the kitchen. Laurie'd left the door open and was now leaning over the railing of the deck watching the action below.

Two officers were studying the ground behind the house, and from the sounds, others were inside the cart room.

"Do you know who the woman you found was?" Laurie called.

The woman officer looked up, a trifle irritated. "You ought to know we can't answer questions."

"Oh. Sure. Yeah, I understand." That didn't stop Laurie from watching intently, her hands grasping the railing as she stretched over it.

"Maybe I'll be a policewoman," she muttered to herself, then jumped when she realized Paula had moved up beside her.

"What brought that thought on?" Paula asked.

"Oh, I've been wondering lately what I'll do when I get out of school. Do policewomen get rich?"

"Police didn't use to," Paula answered with a smile. "Honest ones, anyway." She knew full well that dishonest cops weren't as rare as they should be, but mentioning that didn't seem like a good idea. Although likely Laurie knew, having apparently lived in a disadvantaged section of New York. "I understand there are several women who now are chiefs in major cities, though, and likely they do quite well. Not what I'd call rich, probably."

"Oh. Well, I'll probably look for something else then."

Paula, chagrined, opened her mouth to give a little speech about what was truly important in life, but shut it again when the front doorbell rang. She hurried through the house to answer it.

"Good morning, Mrs. Madigan. May I come in?" The detective was dressed more formally today, with a blue blazer and subdued paisley tie. Probably in deference to the "meeting" he'd just attended, she surmised.

"Of course. Please do." She led him into the living room. "Coffee?" she asked.

Chuckling and patting his stomach, he said, "No, thanks. Our meetings run on coffee—and doughnuts." He waited while she seated herself in an armchair and then settled on the couch. Opening a notebook, he pulled a pen from his breast pocket. "Tell me about last night," he requested.

"Well, Laurie woke me, saying she'd heard sounds from below . . ." She proceeded to relate the events as he took notes.

"My officers tell me that apparently the door to the room where the cart is kept was unlocked."

"Unlocked? Oh-h." She put a hand to her forehead. "*Mea culpa.* How could I? Laurie and I were . . . and I was thinking about dinner preparations, and . . . Oh my goodness. It *is* my fault."

"Murdering someone was not." His expression was grim. "If the perpetrator hadn't found your cart available, I'd be willing to bet that others around here have lax security also. You'd be surprised how many people don't even lock up their houses.

They think just because this is an affluent community, that there'll be little crime. And there is, relatively. But it's not absent."

He shut the notebook with a snap. "You do recall your remark about murder not affecting you?"

"Oh, do I! I was so smug. You must have wanted to smack me across the face!"

Suddenly he grinned. "No, but 'I told you so,' does cross my mind now. Among other things."

What other things? she wondered. What an expressive face the man had. A somewhat craggy countenance was transformed into an incredibly attractive one by the smile. Whatever had come over her? It wasn't like her to ogle men like a teenager, and now she'd been analyzing the sex appeal of two men. Was it because she no longer had any feeling for Fred? Perhaps she'd never had as much as she thought. Fred, after all, had convinced her that she was cold and unfeeling in bed.

She realized suddenly that she'd been off in another world, and the detective was looking at her strangely. "Oh," she said, apologetically. "Sorry. I was just remembering . . . I suppose the body was found by early golfers, just like the other day?" Let him think that she was remembering the scene of the first murder.

"Yes. It was."

Would the victim turn out to be anyone she knew? she wondered. Not likely, considering how many people lived here and how few she'd met. Although, come to think of it, "a woman" could very well have been one of those who milled around at the country club before the golf session on Tuesday.

The detective pushed himself to his feet from the rather soft sofa. "Need to get back to business," he said.

"I apologize. I have been wool-gathering, have I not? Detective Compagnio . . ."

"Why don't you call me Jack?" he suggested. "Much less cumbersome. And I have a feeling we'll be talking again."

"Jack," she said, smiling.

He shook her hand and departed.

Maybe she shouldn't be in too big a hurry to sell her house. At least, until she considered other areas as possibilities to live in. Kamiak Hills was looking less desirable all the while.

Paula found it difficult to concentrate on the stuffed pile of paperwork she'd been neglecting—bills and correspondence. Her mind kept returning to that day when she'd been part of the group discovering Martha Abingsford's body. What sorrow this day would bring to someone. But someone else, no doubt, was feeling satisfaction because he or she had solved what was perceived as a problem. Sighing, Paula bundled up the papers and returned them to her file.

When the phone rang, it was a relief, at least until she heard Ellen's frantic voice. "Oh my God, Paula," Ellen cried. "I've just heard about Babs. Oh my God, what is Kamiak Hills coming to! I said to Stan just this morning, maybe we should move, and he was mad at me for saying it, but . . ."

"Ellen!" Paula snapped. "Stop it! I don't know what you're talking about!" And then her words sunk in. "Babs? Do you mean she was the latest . . . ?"

"Yes!" Ellen interrupted. "Babs Griffin! I thought you knew by now. Laurie went dashing off when we heard. She and Josh. It was Babs whose body was in the water hole. Oh, poor, poor Ben!"

Paula remembered the taciturn banker whom she'd played with that awful day. And now he, too, was left to grieve. Babs could have been an annoying woman for him to live with, she surmised, with a tendency to put him down, but on the golf course Ben had shaken off her remarks as if he was totally used to them, and probably didn't really hear.

"Where did Laurie and Josh go?" she asked.

"I don't know. I assumed they were going to your house."

"What do you want to bet," Paula said, "that they went off 'detecting' again?"

"Oh, I hope not. I spoke to Josh about this little fantasy, and I thought he understood that the police were the only ones equipped to investigate."

"You did point out the danger to amateurs who poke their noses into the wrong places?"

"Oh, well, yes, I did. But no one would take seriously what a couple of kids were up to, surely."

Paula sighed. She'd been right. Ellen had not done her part to stifle her son. And, thus, Laurie. There was no point in saying anything more, except, "I hope you're right, I truly do."

The only one who was in the kitchen when Laurie burst through the door after swimming practice was Cynthia, who was again cleaning the stove. "Where's Paula?" Laurie asked.

Cynthia shrugged. "I don't follow her around," she said. "But she's here somewhere, I imagine because I didn't hear her car leave."

Huh! As if that meant anything. Grandma had been getting to know more people and lots of times walked to their houses. "Why not?" she'd asked when Laurie wondered why she didn't at least take the golf cart, now that they'd gotten it back from the police.

"The exercise is good for me," she'd said.

Laurie thought it more likely that she had not wanted to sit down in a cart that had last contained a body. A bloody body, from what she'd heard. The woman's head had been bashed in. She shivered. She hadn't been in a hurry to ask to drive it again, either. But she would, one of these days.

She'd look through the house, anyway, to see if Paula was here. She really, really wanted to tell her the latest gossip she and Josh had heard. The sound of a toilet flushing sent her into Paula's bedroom in time to see her grandmother exiting the bathroom, still tugging up her pants.

"Oh!" Grandma said. Her cheeks turned pink. She was actually kind of bashful. "You startled me."

"Sorry," Laurie said, although she didn't see why she should be. "I heard some more gossip," she burst out.

"Laurie! I specifically asked you not to do any more snooping."

"I wasn't snooping!" Laurie replied indignantly. "We weren't!"

"Oh, so Josh is still at it, too?" Grandma sat down at the dressing table and began to brush her hair. Hard.

"Why don't you listen to me ever? We were not investigating! All we did was listen to the kids at the swimming pool. They know everything that's going on. I made a list . . ."

Paula frowned at her in the mirror.

"Oh-kay!" Laurie said. "Then you're not interested in the fact that Mrs. Gunderson's husband is having an affair with . . ." She turned to leave.

Paula sighed. "With whom?"

"Trish Miller, that's who," Laurie said triumphantly. "If you want to know the rest we heard, I'll tell you later. Right now, I have to go. Josh is waiting for me."

Before she turned away, she triumphantly watched Grandma's face reflected in the mirror. Her mouth opened and shut and then opened again. Laurie scurried away before words could come out. *Let her fume,* she thought. That'd teach her.

When she returned from the later swimming practice, Grandma was dishing up some casserole. Laurie glanced at it suspiciously. "What's in it?" she asked.

"I'll tell you after you eat some," Paula said, laughing.

Laurie wrinkled her nose. Well, it smelled decent. Good actually, and she was starved. She always was these days. She took a bite, then another. Yeah, it was good. She said so. "It's okay," she said. "But what's in it?" she poked at a suspicious lump.

"Oh, liver, and . . ."

"Yuck!" Laurie pushed the plate away.

Grandma laughed. "Only teasing. It has cheese, and onions, and eggplant . . ."

Laurie made a face, but took another bite.

"I've been thinking," Paula said. "About the gossip you and Josh have been picking up. I really hate to see people passing on things like you told me about Sally. She's a nice lady, and it must be bad enough that her husband's cheating, but to have the whole community find out just isn't fair."

Laurie shrugged. "It happens."

"Well, what I mean is I really don't think someone's affair would cause murder. Unfortunately people cheating is all too common these days for . . ."

"Don't you watch the news? Mom used to, every day, and I heard things. People do murder each other all the time and lots of times somebody's been in the wrong bed. And," Laurie added, "what about blackmail? I heard that somebody's blackmailing people around here. Don't you think that would make someone mad enough to shoot? Grandma, I think you have lived a very sheltered life. You'd better wise up."

Laurie had managed to zero in on her character defect in a short time, Paula thought. Why had it taken her so long to figure out what a detriment it had been to blindly follow the paths that others had picked for her? Sheltered life. Yes, indeed. She'd missed so much. Bad things as well as good, of course, but now she suspected that the bad things shaped one's attitudes, and thus one's life, as much as the good.

Well, this was all changing and so was she. She'd have to remember to thank Kay Morris for steering her in a new direction.

She'd been reading before plunging into self-reflection, and now, glancing out the window, she realized it had gotten dark. She glanced at her watch. Laurie should be home by now. She and Josh had gone to a soccer match at the local high school field. Surely it would be over by this time unless they played under lights.

But sometimes the kids stopped for pizza after a match, and that was no doubt what they had done. Perhaps she should get Laurie a cell phone after all. She'd been whining that she was the only kid her age who didn't have one. Since she was Paula's responsibility for such a short period, it hadn't seemed logical to set her up with one now. She'd need to have a local circuit when she returned to New York.

But probably Josh had a phone, if it was true that "everyone" did, and Ellen would call her if they were delayed. But would she? Obviously Ellen was not a worrier like she herself was, and very likely would not expect Josh to check in about little things like delays.

Stop dithering, she told herself. *Why not just pick up the phone and check with Ellen?*

Before she could, however, it rang. She recognized the agitated voice as Ellen's immediately. "Oh, Paula," she cried, "the kids have been in an accident. I just got called. They're at the hospital. Oh, Stan isn't home . . ."

Paula interrupted. "I know Sally would baby sit for an emergency. Call her, and I'll get my car out in the meantime and pick you up. But quickly, tell me what kind of an accident? They were walking, what could . . ."

"They were hit by a car!" Ellen said. "Knocked into a ditch.

And the driver didn't even stop! That's all I know."

"Oh, my God!" Paula said, beginning to shake. "I'll be there in about two minutes."

CHAPTER TEN

The Laurie lying under the white coverings looked more like a child than the teenager Paula had come to know and love. Her heart lurched when she saw the still body, the face almost as colorless as the bedding, and the drip doing its thing into her left arm.

The doctor had warned Paula that Laurie was unconscious. "However," he'd said, "the scan showed no serious head injury. We'll know more after she wakes up, of course, and we expect that she will before long. No broken bones, no apparent internal injuries. She'll be a very sore young lady for a while, though."

Paula took Laurie's flaccid right hand, and, with tears in her own eyes, studied her granddaughter. A large, angry bruise was forming on her forehead. She was going to sport two black eyes, judging from the discoloration already there. She was likely, Paula suspected, to be even more unhappy about how she looked than how she felt when she woke up.

"Laurie," Paula said softly, as she gently rubbed the hand.. "I'm so sorry. The doctor says you'll be okay, and Josh, too. Only, no more soccer for Josh this season. His leg is broken. I wish your mother was here, and I'll bet you do, too, but I'm here, I'll do everything I can, and . . ."

She broke off to blow her nose and wipe her eyes. Talking to an unconscious person seemed so useless, but she'd read time and again that those people indicated afterwards that they had heard.

101

"Who did this to you? Was it an accident? I hope you'll be able to tell us."

Did Laurie's hand tremble under hers? Yes! She definitely was moving it slightly. And then she mumbled and groaned. Paula rang for the nurse. Was she helping by asking these questions, or was she somehow disturbing Laurie in an unhealthy manner? She needed to know.

The nurse wore a scrub with brightly colored cavorting cats on it. What a nice change from the traditional sterile white, Paula thought irrelevantly. "You rang?" the nurse asked.

"Yes! Laurie moved her hand. And she mumbled."

"Oh, that's a good sign. Let me check her vitals."

Paula held her breath, while the nurse used her stethoscope, measured oxygen content, and checked the monitors.

"Looking good," she finally said, smiling at Paula. "The fact that she's responding is great."

"I've been talking to her, and . . ."

"Keep it up," the nurse suggested. Looking sympathetic, she patted Paula on the shoulder. "She's going to be okay." She glanced at her watch. "It's after one. You're looking pretty tired yourself. Wouldn't it be a good idea to go home and rest and come back in the morning? We'll take care of her, I promise. And of course we'll call should there be any adverse event. But the doctors aren't expecting any."

"All right. Good idea." Paula rubbed her own forehead. She *was* exhausted. "Give me just a little more time, okay?"

After the nurse nodded and left, Paula talked to Laurie gently for a few more minutes. If Laurie was somehow assimilating this, she wanted to leave her with pleasant memories, not those of the accident. "The weatherman is predicting a spell of good weather. When you're home, I thought we might take a trip up to Mount Rainier. You'll love it. It's one of the ten biggest mountains in the world, you know, and the flowers should be at their best. Ellen'll take care of the cats so we can go, I'm sure."

She turned her head when the door opened. Surprised, she saw Jack Compagnio walk in quietly. "How is she?" he asked.

"Doing well, it appears. Even her color is looking better. What are you doing here?"

He raised his eyebrows. "Investigating a murder," he said. "What else?"

Paula's heart jumped. "Murder? Is Josh . . ."

"No, no. Sorry to have scared you. But we're assuming this thing with the kids wasn't an accident. They've been asking too many questions, we're told, and they may have asked the wrong person."

"Oh! Oh, my!"

"I've talked to Josh," Jack said. "Unfortunately, he never saw the car that hit them. I'm hoping Laurie will have better recall."

"Well, she'll have to regain consciousness first," Paula said sharply.

"I know that. Just thought I'd check on you. The nurse tells me that very likely I'll be able to talk to her in the morning. We like to have a family member present. Thought I could arrange to meet you here. I'm assuming you'll be spending the morning with your granddaughter?" His smile was compassionate.

"Of course."

"If nothing interferes, I'll be here in late morning. Give the medical people time for anything they have to do. At best, they don't expect her to be released for a couple of days, I'm told. Now. Can I give you a ride home?"

Paula stood, easing her stiff back, and picked up her purse. "That's very kind of you. However, I drove, and Ellen came with me. Let me check with her and see what her plans are. I haven't seen her since . . . since we separated to see the kids, after the doctor talked to us."

Laurie kissed her granddaughter, and whispered, "See you in

the morning. Sleep tight." The latter was a wish that her family had always said to each other upon bedtime. Silly, she thought now, since it referred to medieval beds with ropes. At least there'd be no bedbugs here, like the rest of the wish.

As they walked out of the room, the detective took her arm. She *was* shaky, she realized, and he'd noticed. He also knew where Josh's room was, which helped, since the two women had split up when they were told they were free to see the kids.

"Come in," Ellen responded to their knock. "Oh, Paula," she said. "I so wish I'd paid attention when you urged me to help stop Josh and Laurie from . . . from . . ." She burst into tears.

Paula hugged her. "We're lucky. They're going to be okay."

"I know." Ellen reached for the tissue box on the bedside stand, and blew her nose noisily.

Josh was asleep, Paula saw. "How is he doing?" she asked.

"Oh, I feel so blessed. Just think, Paula, they could both be . . . be . . ."

Paula patted her on the shoulder, saying only, "I know." Ellen was not one, she decided, to call for support in an emergency.

"I'm sorry," Ellen said, reaching for another tissue. "I'm such a dolt in times of trouble. If only Stan had been home. But Josh is doing okay. We talked. He says he never saw what hit them, just felt it, and felt the pain, and panicked when Laurie couldn't answer him. I'm afraid he's just like me when it comes to . . ." She blew her nose yet again. There was a lot of nose-blowing around here, Paula thought. The hospital must go through cases of tissue.

Jack Compagnio intervened. "I understand," he said to Paula, "that they checked thoroughly. The doctors are satisfied that his only injury was to his leg."

"His leg," Ellen said. "Oh, the first thing he said was, 'I can't play soccer, Mom. I'll have to quit the team.' I didn't think I should point out how much worse it could have been, that

Laurie, with her head injury . . ." She blinked. "How is she?"

"Still unconscious but showing signs that she might be coming out of it. They suggested I go home and rest so I could be ready in the morning when she's talking."

"Talking. Oh, I do hope she knows more than Josh does. They have to catch whoever did this. It's despicable that people . . . It was dark, they could have lain in that ditch all night . . ."

"How *were* they found?" Paula asked. It hadn't crossed her mind to wonder, she'd been so involved in the medical aspects.

"An SUV wasn't far behind the accident," Jack Compagnio said. "The driver, a local woman, realized the car in front of her had hit something; she saw the kids fly into the ditch, although she assumed it was an animal. Fortunately, she stopped to see and had a cell phone. The aide car was there in just minutes. The woman," he added, "was so shook up they had to treat her, too."

"Didn't she . . . wasn't she able to describe the car?"

He shook his head. "Too dark. And she was so rattled. Always a chance she'll remember something later, but we're not counting on it."

"Well, we must thank her," Paula said, "when this is over. Don't you think, Ellen, that it might be a good idea for you, too, to go home and rest? When's Stan getting home?"

"He's flying in tomorrow morning. He cancelled a meeting, and he plans to come straight to the hospital."

"Well, then," Paula said, "shouldn't we both go? Jack here offered to drive us, but we won't have to bother him if you come now."

"That would be good. I guess." Ellen rustled around gathering her jacket and purse. She looked like she wanted to hug Josh but decided against it.

"I'll see you both in the morning," the detective said, after he escorted them to Paula's car.

Laurie opened her eyes. Ooh, she hurt all over.. Her body, her arms, but mostly, her head. She couldn't see anything, but then, gradually, she realized she was in a strange bed in a strange room, and it was dark because it was still night. But where was she? What an awful feeling. What was she doing here, and why was she hurting so much?

A nurse slid into her vision and whispered softly, "You're awake?"

"Sort of," mumbled Laurie. "Where am I?"

"You're in the municipal hospital."

"Hospital? Why? What happened?"

"You were in an accident, dear," the nurse said. "Here, let me take your temperature." She shoved a thermometer into Laurie's mouth.

Laurie groaned, but the thermometer was removed quickly. She tried to think as the nurse bustled around her.

She and Josh had gone to a party at the Nelson house after the soccer game; she remembered that much. Most of the team was there. They'd eaten pizza and popcorn. Eeuh. The thought made something vile rise in her throat. She swallowed quickly.

And after that . . . ?

She couldn't remember. "What kind of an accident?" she asked.

"A car hit you," the nurse replied. "You and your friend were knocked into a ditch."

"Josh! How's Josh?"

"He's going to be okay, dear. He has a broken leg, though."

"A broken leg? He won't be able to play soccer! That sucks."

"It could be much worse," the nurse said, which didn't make Laurie feel any better.

"I feel awful."

"I'll give you a little pain medication now that you're awake," she said. "The doctor authorized it."

Laurie tried to move her arm, but the nurse put a hand on it. "You have a drip in that arm," she said. "Be a little careful." She inserted a needle into the tube. "Now go back to sleep," she suggested. "You should feel better when you wake up."

The next time she opened her eyes, it was daylight. And Grandmother was here, sitting beside the bed, reading. She glanced up and laid her book down. "You're awake," she said.

Dumb thing to say. She wouldn't be opening her eyes and looking around if she wasn't. Ooh, she still hurt. But maybe not quite so bad, she decided, as she moved her legs.

"Yeah," Laurie said. "I'm awake. Sort of. What happened?"

Grandma sighed. She looked tired, like maybe she was the one who should be lying here. "You and Josh were walking home from your party, and somebody hit you both. But we won't talk about that now. Are you hungry?"

Laurie thought about it. Even that took effort. "No," she said. "I feel sort of urpy."

"Why don't you go back to sleep, then," Paula suggested.

That sounded good. Laurie shut her eyes. Strange, flashing lights appeared before her eyelids. Somehow, when she woke up the next time, she realized she had been asleep again. Experimentally, she moved her legs, then her arms.

"You're awake again," Paula said. "Good morning."

"What's good about it?" Laurie said, opening her eyes.

"Well, you're alive, and you're going to get better, and someday this will all be a bad dream."

"I did—I was having bad dreams," Laurie said. "Flashing lights . . ."

"Detective Compagnio will be here in a little while, and he's going to want to hear everything you remember. But, now, are you hungry?"

"Hungry? Yes," Laurie realized with relief. She felt much better than before. "When's breakfast?"

Paula laughed. "Hold on. I'll see what I can rustle up. I need to stretch my legs, anyway." She went out the door.

Laurie looked around her. One reason her arm hurt, she realized, was that she had that dumb tube stuck in it. And, wow, she had to pee. She struggled to a sitting position.

The door opened, and a nurse walked in. "And how are we this morning?" she asked. At least Laurie guessed she was a nurse. She had on a bright yellow figured top, and she had curly dark hair.

"Oh, man," Laurie said. "If I don't get in that bathroom real quick, you're going to have a wet bed."

"Here. Swing your legs over to your left side, and you can take your dolly along with you. I'll help. And when you finish, your breakfast will be here."

Laurie hoped she didn't mean she was going to follow her into the pot, but she didn't, just helped maneuver the thing through the door.

When she came out, feeling a lot better, food was sitting on a bedside tray, and Grandma was back in her chair. The nurse helped her into bed and then pushed buttons so she was sitting up.

"I'll wash your hands and face quickly," the nurse said, "and then you can eat. Although this is almost lunch, not breakfast. Soft food, though. You have to let your digestive system rest a little."

Soft food meant some sort of soup, some Jell-O, and a dish of applesauce. Laurie thought she'd starve on a diet like that, but she was surprised how full she felt as she finished. Grandma watched her eat, her face still tired looking, but her eyes bright.

Just as she finished, the detective arrived. He'd brought her flowers and, of all things, a little brown stuffed dog with a red ribbon around its neck. She was too old for stuffed toys; didn't he know that? But somehow, as the nurse cleared away the table, she enjoyed the feel of the little dog nestled in the bend of her elbow.

"Do you take gifts to all your victims?" Grandma asked him.

"Only the special ones," he answered with a grin.

Again, Laurie thought what a nice guy he seemed to be, not like most of the policemen she'd had anything to do with.

"Are you ready to talk to me? About what you remember?" he asked, as he sat down in a chair the nurse brought in.

"Yeah," she said. "Only . . ." She thought for a minute. "We went to the Nelson's after the match, for pizza. Mrs. Nelson— her kid's on the soccer team—she offered to give us a ride home. But we only had a few blocks to go, and we thought . . ."

She sighed. "I wish I remembered more."

"Take your time. It's likely to come back slowly. You don't have to hurry."

Grandma didn't say anything but watched with anxious eyes.

"Well, we'd only gone a little ways. I remember that, and I remember . . ." She shut her eyes. "I remember the sound of a car motor, just starting up." Her eyes snapped open. "Do you suppose the jerk was waiting for us?"

"I think that might be a reasonable assumption," the detective said.

"I remember flashing lights . . . Only I don't know if they were car lights or in my head. I've been seeing flashing lights like stars every time I shut my eyes."

"Just relax a little, put your head back, and let your thoughts flow." His voice, even if it was deep and rough, was relaxing.

"It was dark, but not completely. There was a streetlight . . ." Laurie didn't open her eyes, just let thoughts in her mind tumble on, "and I turned around when I heard the car coming.

I tried to warn Josh, but he was singing. If what he does can be called singing. And the next thing I knew . . ."

They were all silent, Grandma and the detective waiting for her to speak. If only she could remember. She put her hand to her forehead. "I think," she said. "I can't be sure because it was so dark, but I think the car was gray, or maybe silver. But then—I don't remember anything more. Will that help?"

"A little. I hope so. Was it big or little, a Cadillac or a Honda size?"

"Big. Definitely. It sure looked big to me, but, yeah, it was."

"Good. You were able to tell us much more than Josh did."

Laurie ran her fingers through her hair. Ouch! That hurt. "I think . . . I don't know, but I'm pretty sure there was something else about that car . . . I'm not sure what. If only I could remember."

"It may come back," the detective said as he shut his notebook. "I hope so. And you'll let us know if it does, of course," he said. "It wouldn't be unusual to have this sort of memory surface later.

"Just"—he smiled that great smile again—"stay off dark streets, why don't you? And I understand your grandmother had suggested you stop asking questions. She warned you," he said, "that it wasn't smart. Leave those things for the police, please. That's what we're here for. But if you remember anything, anything at all more, let us know right away, won't you?"

"I will." She was getting tired. But there was something—she knew there was—that was different about that car. If only she could remember.

CHAPTER ELEVEN

"I'm going to have lunch in the cafeteria here before I leave. It's really quite good. And healthy." Jack Compagnio patted his stomach. "Want to join me?"

"Why, yes," Paula said. "That sounds good." She really hadn't eaten much breakfast, a banana and coffee was all. She'd been in a hurry to get to the hospital. Now, what with seeing Laurie so much better, she found she was quite hungry.

"You'll excuse me?" she asked Laurie.

"Of course, Paula," Laurie said. "Scram. I'm going to take another nap." Then, looking hopeful, she said, "You are coming back?"

"Of course." Paula leaned forward and kissed her lightly. "Be a good girl."

"I will, Grandma. I won't do anything you wouldn't do." She laughed.

Jack, as Paula was beginning to think of him, shook Laurie's hand. "Thanks for your help," he said. "Stay out of trouble."

Laurie giggled. "What do you two think I'm going to do? Just wait until I get home, okay?"

"That's what I'm afraid of," Paula muttered as they exited.

"She's quite a girl. You must be proud of her."

"I am." Jennifer had done a good job; that was obvious, in spite of a difficult situation. Maybe, just maybe, it wasn't too late for her daughter to salvage a decent life, and maybe, with luck, they could again have a relationship, Paula thought.

"What's with this first name stuff she uses sometimes?" he asked. "Do you prefer it?"

Paula chuckled. "Actually, no. I was rather floored when she hit me with it originally. Being 'Grandmother' or 'Gramma' is actually an improvement. She didn't call me that until she became, I think, more comfortable in the relationship."

"Oh, you hadn't spent much time together in the past, I take it?"

"No." Paula hoped her tone would forestall any more questions along those lines, and it seemed to work.

They were a little ahead of the noon rush, and so were able to quickly pick out their food at the appetizing buffet. They carried their trays to a table near the window, which looked out on a small garden. It was a peaceful scene, with garden art set among blooming flowers of soft pastel colors. Probably planned to give respite to harried medical personnel and anxious visitors, she figured.

Jack had been right about the food, even though the plateful he held wasn't going to reduce his waistline, she noted. She'd chosen mostly from the salad bar, her favorite food, but included a couple of the more substantial choices along with the fruit and a tossed salad. The chicken cashew had been especially appealing. They'd both succumbed to the tempting lemon meringue pie.

"I'll get the drinks," Jack said. "What'll you have?"

"Coffee, I think. I'll need it to stay awake this afternoon. Black, please."

They ate in silence for a few moments, each deep in thought. Finally, Paula slowed and spoke. "I'm angry. Deeply angry. I never thought I'd feel that I, personally, could go after someone physically. What kind of a person would do this?" she asked. "Attack two good kids and not care whether they lived or died?"

Jack grimaced. "A desperate person. Someone who considers

more killing is necessary to avoid being caught. I hate this kind of murder. It's miles removed from the gang-related, drug-induced, what have you, that's so common these days. I think when we find that person, he or she will be someone who appears to fit right into the Kamiak Hills community. If circumstances had been different, they'd never have resorted to murder. What we have to do is figure out what those circumstances were."

"You're thinking a woman could have done this?" Paula was surprised.

"Either sex, of course. But some of the aspects of the case—the anonymous letters, for instance—are perhaps more typical of the female gender."

"Umm," Paula said, wondering if the detective was being sexist. "And," she asked, "are you implying that many of us are capable of murder?"

"Yes. Yes, I am."

He looked sad, Paula thought. What a depressing job he had.

"They say anyone would be, given sufficient motivation." Jack took a swig of coffee. "Were you able to notify her mother?"

"No, there's no way to reach her. They're . . . rambling, I guess is the best way to put it, I'm afraid Jennifer isn't the most responsible person in the world."

"I see," Jack said.

Paula was quite sure he didn't really see. There was no way he could picture Jennifer and Laurie's life among drug dealers in a scummy apartment. An environment where, yes, murder was not unexpected. And she wasn't going to tell him. He seemed to respect Laurie. Let him think she was a perfectly normal kid. Paula was determined, she knew suddenly, to make sure that life continued that way for Laurie. How she was going to accomplish this, she didn't know yet.

"Do you really think Laurie's meager description of the accident will help?" she asked.

He shrugged. "Not much. Have you ever noticed how many gray or silver cars there are around? Even big ones. But I wanted her to feel she was helping. With luck, she'll remember the elusive thing that's tantalizing her."

He seemed to be thinking as he stared out into the garden. Paula remained quiet.

Turning back to her, he asked, "What do you think of the Seahawks' chances this year?"

Paula set down her fork. "Detective Compagnio, are you changing the subject on purpose?"

He shrugged. "You might say that."

Paula was irked. "Well, before we discuss the Seahawks, I want to know what we're going to do about the situation."

Jack took a bite of pie. "*We* aren't going to do anything about it," he said. "*I* am, with the help of my associates. Umm, delicious."

Paula lost her appetite. "You are infuriating! Of course I'm going to do something about it."

"You heard what I said to Laurie. Our department will take over. That's what we're here for. It's police business. We're trained for this. Civilians are not."

"Don't patronize me. You're the one who pointed out, just a few days ago, that murder is everyone's business. The golf cart was taken right from underneath the house Laurie and I were sleeping in. That was a murderer, Jack, prowling around just a few feet away. If that and the fact my granddaughter was attacked don't make it my business, what could? I'm getting to know the people in the community, and you don't and never will. I can bring a personal touch, I can look at cars, I can listen . . ."

"Paula!" He almost shouted, and a silver-haired woman nearby glanced up, startled. He lowered his voice, "Paula, you're a very nice woman. I'd like to see more of you. Alive, not on a slab waiting for an autopsy like the others. Don't buck me on this."

Was he trying to shock her into compliance? If so, he had underestimated her determination.

"I don't think you understand me," she said in a steely voice. "Laurie has become the most important person in the world to me. I'd do anything for her. I don't care if I put myself in danger. I'm getting old. I lost my daughter sixteen years ago, and I'm not going to lose Laurie!"

She hadn't meant to spill her personal life, but it had happened, and it didn't matter. "I saw a killdeer on a golf course once. She thought we were too close to her nest, and she pretended to have a broken wing as she tried to lead us in the other direction. That's me. If I have to put my life on the line, I'll do it."

Jack took another bite of pie.

That was the last straw. "Here," she said, shoving her untouched pie toward him, "put this on your waistline, too."

She shoved back her chair. And then . . . and then she realized he was laughing at her. She fled from the room.

Paula helped a shaky Laurie into the house with one hand under her elbow.

"Do you feel like you need to climb into bed?" she asked.

Laurie shook her head. Too hard, evidently. "Ouch, that hurt! No, I do not want to go to bed. What do you think, Grandma? I've been there for two days. Put me in the front of the TV, I guess. Although I looked at enough of that in the hospital, too. What stupid shows they have during the day!"

Silently agreeing, Paula asked, "Do you feel like reading?"

"Maybe. What have you got that's interesting?"

"I'll probably have to go to the library for you. I'm reading an expose on Washington, D.C. politics, but I don't think it would appeal to you."

"You are *so* right, Grandma. Take me with you to the library. I can do better than that."

Paula hesitated before answering. The doctor's directions had specifically stated that Laurie was to restrict her activities. Would a trip to the library be stretching things too much? "Umm, tomorrow, maybe," she finally said.

"Sure. Oh, gosh, I forgot! I look so awful. I can't go looking like this!" She gestured at her swollen nose and two garish-colored eyes. "TV, I guess it is." Still clutching the stuffed dog that Jack had given her, she plumped on the sofa and reached for the remote.

The phone rang, and Paula hastened to answer it. "Hi, Paula," Ellen's voice said. "I saw your car come in. Did you bring Laurie home like you hoped?"

"Yes. I'm so glad to have her here. How's Josh doing?"

"Bored to tears. He wants to talk to Laurie."

"Sure. Just a second." She handed the phone to Laurie, who raised her eyebrows.

"Hey, man," she said. "How're ya doing?"

A rumble was all Paula could hear from the other end.

"I look awful, like one of those creatures in a haunted house . . . Hey, that sounds good. Let me check with Paula." Holding the phone to her chest, she said, "Josh wants me to come over. Says he doesn't care what I look like, at least I can move around. He's stuck. Would that be okay?"

"Is it okay with his mother?"

Laurie nodded. "He says his mother's tired of him bugging her."

"Then, fine. When do they want you?"

"Now. She says to come for lunch."

"Well, okay." Obviously, Josh wasn't up to much activity

either. Surely a visit with him wouldn't be too stressful. She'd been looking forward on one level to having Laurie enliven the now empty seeming house, but on another, she'd worried about what she'd do with her during convalescence.

So a few minutes later, she accompanied Laurie across the grass to the neighboring house, one hand under her elbow in support. Josh, on crutches, was waiting eagerly. "Wow," he said, "you look like hell."

"Josh!" Ellen admonished, shocked.

"That's mean! Do you want me to go home, lame-boy?" Laurie glared at him.

"Nah. Of course not. I don't care what you look like. I can still beat you at games."

"Just try." She stuck out her tongue, but then laughed.

Ellen had been waiting eagerly, too, it turned out. "Stay for lunch, why don't you? I've already set a place. And then I have a big favor to ask. My larder is empty, and I have a long-standing dentist appointment at three. Could I possibly ask you, please, to keep an eye on the kids for a couple of hours? It's a big favor, I know, but sometimes it's harder to get a sitter during the summer when the kids are all into activities, and . . ."

Ellen was capable of continuing for some time with explanations. "Of course," Paula interrupted. "I have nothing else to do. Then maybe when you get back, I can run to the library to find some appropriate reading to entertain Laurie. I find, and I guess you're like me, I don't want to leave her alone."

Ellen nodded vigorously. "We'll never feel the same, will we? Become overprotective, I guess. But what else can we do? At least until this murder is solved."

"I'm not very experienced with kids the ages of yours, though," Paula said apologetically.

"Don't worry. They completely entertain themselves." A hubbub from the direction of the rec room indicated that they were, indeed, entertaining themselves adequately. Whether the rec room would ever be the same, she'd let be Ellen's worry.

Ellen had prepared a plate of chicken salad sandwiches and another of peanut butter and jelly, the staple of preadolescents, she did remember. And adolescents, it turned out. That plate was quickly emptied, and Ellen made more. "Being in an accident sure didn't hurt the kids' appetites, did it?" she asked, laughing as they quickly grabbed at the refilled plate.

"Thanks so much for staying," Ellen said, an hour later as she prepared to leave. "I think . . . I think I'd rather have Mark and Sue stick around home. You understand. If any of their friends come over, that'd be okay, at least if it is with you . . . ?"

"I'll cope," Paula said. "Run along."

She sat down on a porch swing after refilling her glass of iced tea, leaving the deck door open except for the screen. The kids were loud enough that she could keep track of them. Josh and Laurie kept insulting each other, through the dings and dongs of the computer, but then they'd laugh, so they seemed to be doing okay. The noise in the rec room quieted, though, so she went in to check. Mark and Susan were playing some kind of board game and didn't even notice her, so she backed out silently.

On her way through the kitchen, she refilled the glass yet again. She'd be running to the bathroom, but it sure tasted good on this day that was turning out to be quite warm. The weather hadn't deterred the golfers, though. With much the same view as the one from the Pappas house, she was able to watch the passing parade of golfers. Most appeared to be enjoying themselves. An occasional oath drifted toward her. That was golf, she thought. Mostly enjoyable, sometimes oh-so frustrating. Like her own life, maybe?

Sitting down again, she found her thoughts turning to, what else, the accident. And what Jack had said. And what she could do about it. He was right, of course, that she had no trained abilities for police investigation. She hadn't held a real job, her only experience being her volunteer work. She'd never been one for self-analysis, but now, as she recollected her life with Fred, she cringed. What had she ever done besides subjecting herself to Fred's every whim?

Well, she'd been efficient and had actually worked rather hard on various sub-committees she'd been attached to. She'd always been diplomatic, prided herself on not ruffling feathers, even when she had to bite her tongue to keep her thoughts to herself. A future politician, after all, could not be encumbered by a wife who did otherwise. As a result, she'd always been a good listener. People confided in her.

Could she use this listening ability to advantage now? Laurie and Josh had heard secrets by eavesdropping. Would it be possible for her to learn even more by encouraging people, lonely people perhaps, who were anxious to have a listener?

Who, though? Kamiak Hills was large enough that it was unlikely the murderer was among her acquaintances. Except, as she'd pointed out to the detective, for the golf cart. Someone knew exactly where to find it. Someone who most likely was familiar with the Pappas house.

The most logical route of investigation might be to find out more about the anonymous notes. Perhaps she should concentrate on ascertaining who wrote them. Maybe this person was the murderer, maybe not. After all, from what she'd heard, the notes were petty. Somehow she didn't picture people who got their thrills from such activities as being the violent sort. Unless, as Jack had pointed out, events forced them into it.

She was going to have to come out of her shell and socialize. Paula knew she had the skills to do so. But where should she start?

First, though, she needed to have a heart-to-heart talk with

Laurie. She waited until after dinner. They'd moved into the living room, where Laurie was studying the books Paula had brought from the library.

"These look good," she said, making a stack, "but this one—ugh!" She laid it to one side. After she read the flyleaf of the next one, she turned to page one and started reading.

"Before you get too engrossed," Paula said, "you and I need to have a talk."

"Oh?" The glance Laurie shot over the still open book was suspicious, wary. "What about?"

"I've been thinking," Paula said. "I talked to the detective quite a while at the hospital."

"Yeah, big surprise," Laurie said. "He's got the hots . . ."

"Laurie! Don't be silly! And, that's . . . that's gross! Of course he doesn't. We've barely met."

Laurie's smile was smug.

Paula knew she was blushing. How could Laurie think such a thing? Especially as her granddaughter had made it clear that she thought everyone in their sixties was old.

"Anyway," she continued, "we spent the entire time arguing. That stupid man thinks . . . Well, Detective Compagnio was not what I wanted to discuss. Except for the fact that he's bullheaded and doesn't have any respect for what you and I could accomplish."

"You and I . . ." Laurie said warily. "What do you mean?"

"I mean, he ordered me, and you by extension, not to do anything further concerning finding out who hit you. Yes, I know, I told you not to do any snooping, and I was right, wasn't I?"

Laurie shrugged.

"It's just that, well, I'm angry. I care more about finding out who did this to you and Josh than who the murderer is, although, of course, likely it's the same person. Not necessarily, though. You may have heard another secret someone doesn't want disclosed. I'm planning to become better acquainted with people who live here, and I'll listen. That's what I'm okaying for you. Listening. No prying questions. That's undoubtedly what got you and Josh in trouble."

"We didn't 'ask questions,' Grandma. You specifically told us not to." Her expression oozed innocence.

"You have to admit that somehow you made someone very angry."

"Well, yeah. I guess."

"Okay. What I have in mind is that we'll share notes on anything we find out, anything at all, that could be important."

"We're going to be detectives, Grandma? Cool!"

"Please use your head, Laurie. You have a good one. Restrain Josh if you need to."

Laurie laughed. "He won't be going anywhere for a while."

"No, he won't. I'm hoping, of course, that the police do their job and our little efforts won't be needed. But if either of us hears anything pertinent, let's share it."

"Oh-kay!" Laurie held her hand up for a high-five, and Paula returned it. What Paula didn't say was that she also thought being "open" would be a way for her to keep track of the activities of these two adventuresome kids.

She stood, and as she walked past the back of the couch, impulsively she hugged her granddaughter, and whispered, "I love you, Laurie." And then she hurriedly left the room

It was the first time she'd told her granddaughter how much she cared, and she didn't want to embarrass her. She realized it was also the first time in ages she'd said it to anyone. Had she ever said it to Fred? Perhaps not.

Had she ever loved him? If so, when had that love faded away?

CHAPTER TWELVE

What Paula hadn't admitted to Laurie was that she herself fully intended to ask questions. She was, after all, an adult who presumably had better judgment that any thirteen-year-old girl. She also, as she'd realized when she'd analyzed her abilities, was more close-mouthed and tactful than many. Moreover, as she'd told Jack, she didn't care what happened to her. She'd do what she had to.

And where better than to start with the Pappas's cleaning lady, Cynthia Lamphear? Not only had she lived here many years, but she had access to a number of households. People tended to confide in their help. That, or forget that they were there entirely, like a piece of furniture, when they talked on the phone or entertained.

She set her alarm so that she wouldn't sleep late, as she'd tended to so often lately, after restless nights. She wanted to be ready, not groggy, when Cynthia arrived, so that her mind would function at its best.

So, showered and dressed, she was just finishing breakfast when Cynthia walked into the kitchen. "Good morning," she said.

"Oh. I expected you'd still be in bed," Cynthia said, "with all that's been going on. I was so sorry to hear about that girl of yours. How is she? Is she still in the hospital?"

"Oh, no. She came home on Monday. She's doing fine. Still sore, but she's spending a good part of her time over at Josh's house. He isn't as mobile as she is, of course. I picked up a number of books at the library for her, and I'm pretty sure she read late. At least, there's no sign of her yet this morning.

"Won't you sit down and have some coffee with me before you begin working?" Paula suggested. "The house doesn't need much but touching up this week, what with Laurie and me both having been gone much of the time. You must put in long days, with all the people I understand you clean for."

Cynthia hesitated, then reached for the coffee. "Thank you. I could use another cup. I'll just sit for a moment."

Good, Paula thought. Now if she could just steer the conversation in the right direction . . . "You always do such a fine job. Tell me, how many households do you clean for?"

"Well, let's see. There's the Morrisons on Monday morning, and the Ramsfords in the afternoon." She held out a finger for each one. "The Gundersons on Tuesday, and the Millers in the afternoon." She named two or three others that were unfamiliar to Paula, who tried to commit them to her memory bank.

"And the Griffins . . . That one won't be much longer, I hear. I understand he's putting his house up for sale. So sad. And the . . ."

To Paula's disappointment, she quit naming the households, but counted silently on her fingers between sips of coffee. "That's eight," she said. "I keep one morning and one afternoon free for my own appointments, doctors and such, you know. A mammogram this week." She wrinkled her nose.

"You've come to know so many people," Paula said. "Tell me, just out of curiosity, since I don't know as many as you do, who do you think did write those anonymous letters?"

Cynthia looked startled. "Why, Martha Abingsford, of course," she said. "Everyone had figured that out. She was so nosy. And really, I hate to speak ill of the dead, a generally unpleasant woman."

"So I've heard, but . . ." Paula realized that word must not have gotten out about the letter she'd received, and actually, there was no reason it should have. She hadn't told anyone, Laurie had promised not to, and certainly neither David nor Jack would have. Would Jack be angry if she mentioned it? Mentally shrugging, she decided, sure. He would. But so what? He was already put out with her for her perceived interference.

She realized Cynthia was looking at her strangely, waiting for her to finish her sentence. No wonder. She sighed, and shook her head. "Sorry. I was thinking. No, Martha didn't write the letters, it turns out. Not all of them, anyway. There's been at least one more since Martha's death."

"What?" Cynthia set her mug down so quickly, coffee sloshed on the place mat. She got up and grabbed a cleaning cloth. "I hadn't heard that. Who got it?" She scrubbed, more vigorously than Paula thought necessary.

"I don't . . ." Paula began.

Cynthia eyed her suspiciously. "You? You got one?"

"I promised not to identify . . ."

"It had to be you," Cynthia said. "What did . . ."

Paula shook her head. "I'm not going to say any more." She stood up, taking her empty bowl to the sink to rinse. Peripherally, she noted Cynthia gulping the rest of her coffee before setting her cup on the counter..

"I'd better get back to work," Cynthia said, her face expressionless.

Paula chided herself. Instead of finding out anything, she'd divulged information. So much for her ability as a questioner. Her skills were rusty. She'd need to buff them up before her next attempt at, as Laurie put it, "detecting."

Cats' meowing anticipated Laurie's arrival, as so often happened. "Good morning. I'm hungry," she said as she came into the room.

"Good Lord, child," Cynthia said, dropping the cloth she was now wiping a cabinet with. "Your face . . ."

Laurie sighed. "I know. It's even worse today. Some of these spots are turning yellow." She touched her face. "And green. I can't be seen in public! I'm never going to look the same."

Drama queen, Paula thought, as her granddaughter continued to whine. Then she chided herself. Laurie had good reason to feel sorry for herself. But some stoicism would be welcome about now.

Cynthia's expression was almost enough to laugh at, Paula decided. The dropped jaw, which she quickly snapped shut, and the wide-open eyes, reflected horror.

"Nobody asked you to look," Laurie snapped, setting down Mum-mum, and turning away.

"Oh. I apologize. It's just that . . ."

"I know. I look like a freak. I am doomed to stay in this house forever."

"Of course you're not," Paula soothed. "You didn't break anything. There's no permanent damage. In fact, Coach Soriano called and suggested you come back to swim practice. I thanked him, but told him I didn't think you were quite ready. But perhaps by Monday . . ."

"I am not going back to swimming practice. Not today. Maybe not ever. I'll be so far out of shape . . ."

My, that girl could be dramatic. Maybe she should have joined a little theater group this summer. They might even be putting on a horror show. Paula quickly stifled a giggle. "You could do some exercises to stay in shape. There's even a treadmill out in the garage, I noticed."

Laurie was not in the mood for rational suggestions, it was obvious, as she threw open a cupboard door, slammed a bowl on the counter, and reached in another cupboard for cornflakes.

Paula usually limited herself to one cup of coffee in the morning, but she refilled her mug. "I'll be out on the deck," she told Laurie. "If you want to find me." She shut the door behind her.

Grandma just didn't understand! She'd probably never even had a pimple on her chin. And her hair was always perfect. Well, except when she got agitated and stirred it up. Cynthia was looking over her shoulder at her, and she looked lots more sympathetic than Grandma.

"My daughter's had lots of bruises during her years of skating. And even pulled muscles. She did get better, you know, and the bruises went away. But, I'm proud of her. She just kept skating." Cynthia frowned. "I did have to persuade her, at first, but she got over that. Her goals are too important to let injuries interfere."

Goals were important? To what's-her-name, or to Cynthia? Laurie wondered.

"Yeah, but I'm never going to be an Olympic swimmer. Some of the kids on the team think they're going to be, but I figure I'm starting too late, and from what I hear, the ones that make it don't do anything else but swim laps. Eight hours a day! Can you imagine looking at the bottom of a pool for eight hours a day?"

"Well, no, I can't. At least a skater has variety. But don't be hard on your grandmother. This all has been difficult for her, too. After all, receiving an anonymous letter . . ."

"She told you?" Laurie was astounded, but when she saw the smug look on Cynthia's face, she thought, *Oh, shit. I've blown it!* "I mean, she told you she'd heard about another letter?" *Nice try,* she told herself. Except it clearly didn't work.

"Strange, isn't it? The two of you haven't been here at Kamiak Hills that long."

"It wasn't Grandma."

Cynthia smiled. "Well, I'm done here. I'll do the bathrooms

next, if your grandmother needs me."

Laurie felt like a worm. What a detective she'd turned out to be. Instead of finding out anything, and this would have been a great chance, she'd spilled the beans, as her mother always said. Should she tell Grandma?

Sighing, she decided she had to. She quickly scraped the bottom of her cereal bowl, then opened the refrigerator and poured herself a glass of orange juice.

"Grandma," she said as she carried her glass out the door, shutting it firmly behind her even though a quick glance confirmed that the cleaning lady was no longer in the kitchen, "I did something stupid."

Paula looked surprised. "How could you? You haven't been anywhere. But don't look so scared. I won't bite your head off."

"Well, I wouldn't blame you. I was an idiot. I told—well, actually, I didn't tell—I just didn't say she was wrong . . ."

Grandma set her cup down. "It can't be that bad, Laurie. Just tell me. Oh. The only person you've been talking to was Cynthia. Is it about her?"

Laurie nodded. "She . . . said something about you receiving an anonymous letter, and I . . . I should have acted like I didn't know anything about it, but I just . . ." She took a deep breath. "I let her know that I knew you had." She couldn't look at Paula; she just couldn't, so she hung her head.

Grandma's voice was quiet when she answered, and she didn't sound mad. "She's obviously a clever woman," she said. "Don't blame yourself. Tell me exactly what was said."

So Laurie did.

"And you say she looked smug?"

"Yeah, like Mum-mum when she's managed to eat Carioca's share, too. Why should she be glad?"

"That's a very good question, Laurie. Indeed. Why should she?"

"Well, she could just be glad to see someone else have problems."

"Maybe. But we'd better watch ourselves around her. That was very clever of her, to get that out of you." Paula patted Laurie's arm. "Don't feel bad. Actually, you did find out more than you realize. Now we know how very interested in those letters Cynthia is. We have to wonder why. And we've learned to be very careful what we say around her. She may just be nosy. That wouldn't surprise me.

"I just remembered something," Grandma added. "Cynthia drives a big, silver-colored car. Haven't you seen her pull into the driveway in that humongous vehicle? I've often wondered why she wants anything that big and pretentious. Why don't you wander out in front and see if there's anything about it that looks familiar?"

"I'll do it! Right now!"

"It's hard to imagine her as a murderer, but we should keep our minds open. Don't look too obvious. I know! Pretend you're going to the mailbox. It's about time for the delivery anyway, and that would make sense."

"Okay. Hold everything. I'll be right back."

Laurie could hear the vacuum running in Grandma's bedroom as she tiptoed down the front hall. Parked in the driveway was a pickup, a green one.

Wow! Why had she changed cars? Laurie had never paid attention to what Cynthia drove before, but Grandma had said it was an expensive car, like rich people drove.

She grabbed the mail out of the box and hurried back through the house to the deck. She'd let Grandma handle this, she decided.

"Grandma," she said, as she thrust back the sliding door to the deck, "what would you say if I told you Cynthia's driving a different car?"

"I'd say," Paula said as she stood, "that you've found out something important. Now, what are we going to do about it?"

Laurie liked the way Grandma planned to include her in the action, whatever it was going to be.

Grandma leafed through the envelopes, then exclaimed suddenly, "Laurie! You didn't look at the mail. You actually—I mean, you have a postcard from your mother! It appears"—she turned the card over and looked at the picture—"that they must be in Italy. How exciting!"

"Gimme!" Laurie snatched the card. She'd never believed her mother would send one, and it was obvious that Grandma hadn't expected her to, either. The picture was of the Coliseum. Even she recognized that. Turning it over, she read silently, then aloud so Grandma could hear it also, *"We're in Rome. How weird to actually see the place where the gladiators fought. The Vatican was stupendous. Heading north tomorrow as it's awfully hot here. Love, Mom."*

Mom hadn't said anything about missing her, or wishing she was with them, but at least she had remembered to send a card. Laurie decided she'd save it forever.

CHAPTER THIRTEEN

Thank God Jennifer had sent a card, Paula thought. Maybe she *had* remembered how fragile the feelings of a young teenager could be. If she could see Laurie's face now, she'd certainly be more thoughtful in the future.

But now, getting back to the discovery that Cynthia was presently driving a different car, what should she do? Surely, this pleasant woman who'd lived in the neighborhood for years and was friends with so many could not be a murderer. What possible reason could she have?

She had access to people's secrets, alone in their houses as she often was. Blackmail would be a possibility. And blackmail, Paula was sure, could lead to murder if one was threatened with exposure. But why would she behave so despicably? Unless she resented those who employed her or she imagined they looked down on her, thinking of her as menial.

Contemplating, she decided that informing Jack wasn't a good option. "If the police confront Cynthia," Paula mused aloud, "it would be obvious to her that we're suspicious. That doesn't seem like a good move to me."

"Yeah, and we'd lose our cleaning lady."

"You're right. And I'm quite sure you and I don't want to spend our summer cleaning this huge house." Paula chuckled, with a grim overtone.

"Do you even know how?" Laurie raised her eyebrows.

"Laurie! Of course I know how."

"You don't need to get mad. How was I to know? You've never told me anything about your growing up. Were you always rich, Grandma?"

"No. And I'm not rich now and never expect to be. We were . . . always comfortable, however. But my parents believed that a woman's place was in the home. How I regret that now. And I never questioned their reasoning. So they expected me to do all those housewifey things. Cook, and clean, and shop. It's no wonder I dislike cooking now."

"You're a good cook."

"Of course. My mother saw to that. It's just that—that on reflection, I'd have liked to have had choices. And no one even thought about what I'd do if I was widowed, as I was.

"But, enough of that. We've gotten off the subject. Worse than having to clean, I'd have to face Lynn Pappas when she returns and explain why Cynthia was no longer available."

"That means, Grandma, that you or me has to ask Cynthia why she's driving a ratty old pickup instead of her fancy car."

"You're right. And it's going to be me. I do not want to place you in a vulnerable position again. Once was enough."

"Well, then, why don't you just manage to be going out the door when she does, and you can say, 'Oh! Why are you driving that ratty old pickup?' "

Paula grimaced. "I think I could be a mite more tactful than that, but, yes. That's a good idea. Let's see. I could decide suddenly that I need to go grocery shopping and ask her to move her car so I can get out of the garage."

"Yeah. That'd work. I'm pretty sure she's parked behind where you usually put yours."

"In the middle, you mean."

"Well, yeah. But, Grandma, we need to go to the store. I need some tampons."

"Oh. I'm sorry, Laurie. I never thought to ask you."

"That's okay, Grandma. I brought enough for a couple of months when I came. But you're not going to leave me out of this. I want to hear what she says. Let's *go!*"

A few minutes later, Laurie heard her grandmother speak loudly. "Cynthia," she said, "could I ask you to move your car? Sorry to interrupt, but Laurie and I have decided to go shopping and out to lunch."

Cynthia shut off the vacuum. She'd obviously been doing the living room. "Of course," she said. "I'll get my keys. You've managed to persuade her that her life won't end if she's seen in public?"

"It wasn't easy, but yes." She should have realized Cynthia would pick up on that, but the less said now, the better. "Laurie," Grandma called, "I'm ready. Let's go."

Laurie had spent the time while Grandma got herself ready putting makeup on her face. She usually didn't use any, wasn't worth the bother, but heck, she decided, squinting, it helped. Maybe with a little more time and something darker, she could quit scaring people who looked at her. She'd ask Grandma for advice.

"Come *on*, Laurie," Grandma called.

Oops! It wouldn't help if she was so slow that Cynthia had moved her car and gotten back in the house. She grabbed her purse and scooted out the door to the garage. Grandma already had the garage door open, and Cynthia had moved the pickup to the street. She climbed out, and headed up the sidewalk toward the house.

Grandma, who was standing nearby pretending to be interested in the hanging baskets of geraniums, said, "These are a mite dry. Would you mind watering them for me, Cynthia? It slipped my mind, with all that's happening."

"Sure, Paula," Cynthia said, hurrying up the walk.

"Oh!" Grandmother did a double take.

Much too obvious, Laurie thought, wincing.

"Whatever are you driving? Where's that beautiful car of yours?"

"Oh, I traded for this week with Albert," she said. "He wanted to impress some businessmen he's dealing with, and this one . . ." She chuckled. Sounded nervous, Laurie thought. "This one just wouldn't look right. I've tried to persuade him to upgrade, but he's very fond of it. Says it's perfect for the construction work he does. Good to see you're nerving yourself to get out and about, Laurie. That's the spirit. Well, I'll see you next week." She hustled into the house.

Laurie and Grandma looked at each other, and both giggled. This was really kind of fun. Grandma held a finger to her lips. "Shush! We mustn't blow it now."

"What do you think?" Laurie asked, after they were both safely in the car.

" 'Methinks the lady doth protest too much,' as Shakespeare said. Come on. We'd better get out of here."

It was a first step in getting Laurie out of the house, but only mildly successful, since she insisted they eat at a drive-through. The salad Paula had was decent, rather to her surprise, although eating behind the wheel of a car left something to be desired. It was the first time she'd ever done that.

Laurie's meal, however, a double hamburger and French fries, was disgusting. It almost turned Paula's stomach. She thought of commenting on the desirability of a more healthful diet, but refrained. She doubted that Laurie would listen anyway.

"I don't really want to go shopping." Laurie sounded pouty.

"Well, I was thinking," Paula said. "I'll bet they'd have something at a cosmetic counter that would help to cover your bruises. I seem to remember that the cosmetics are right at the entrance of that big department store at the mall, and we could hurry in and out."

"Do you think?" Laurie said, putting her hand to her face.

"I feel sure others have skin defects they want to cover, even black eyes. Certainly pimples and such. You're lucky for your age," Paula said. "I remember being tormented with a poor complexion."

"You?"

"Me." She found a parking space near the outside entrance, and soon the nice lady behind the counter was producing jars and tubes. She didn't even ask what had happened, which Paula thought was extremely tactful. They purchased the ones she recommended and headed back to the car.

"What now?" Laurie asked, as soon as they were inside. "How do we find out if Cynthia was telling the truth about the car?"

Paula sighed. "I guess I'd better call the detective. This is the kind of thing the police can follow up on better than we. Let's stop at the grocery first, though. There are a few things I'd like to get and you . . . ? I know, just tell me what you need."

"Thanks, Grandma."

When they got home, Paula put the groceries away before making the call. Finally, realizing she'd been procrastinating, she sighed, then punched in the number of the police station. She was not looking forward to this. "Is Detective Compagnio in, please?" she inquired.

"I'm sorry. He's out of the office," a woman's voice said.

"Oh. I see. Would you please ask him to call Paula Madigan at his convenience? He has my number."

"I can transfer you to his assistant. Just a moment."

"No," Paula said quickly.

"Someone in the office can take care of you, I'm sure," the smooth voice continued. "If you'd give me an idea . . ."

"I have some information for him, thank you, but I'd like to speak to him personally." Paula spoke firmly.

"I'll give him the message." The voice definitely sounded annoyed.

"Whew," Paula said when she hung up. "They must use that woman to grill suspects."

"Maybe she thought you *are* one," Laurie said.

Paula felt a gigantic yawn coming on. She tried to suppress it but was only moderately successful. "I don't know what's coming over me. I think I'll rest in my room for a while. Wake me if I'm asleep when the detective calls, will you?"

"Sure, Grandma. Guess I'll read. That *Ruby in the Mist* is great. I want to know how it ends." Laurie was already hurrying toward the living room. "Go take your nappy-nap," she said over her shoulder.

Umph, Paula thought. But she wasn't going to let a little snippiness stop her from what suddenly sounded like a lovely way to spend the afternoon.

She awoke with a start when Laurie flapped the bed coverings around her shoulders. "Wake up, Grandma," she said. "Boyfriend number two is here to see you."

Paula reared up. "Boyfriend . . . what?"

"I told you that detective had a thing for you. He's here. But you'd better brush your hair." Her grin was impudent.

Paula definitely needed to have a little talk with her granddaughter, but not now. She splashed some cold water on her face and ran a brush over her mussed hair. Plastering on a smile, and hoping she didn't look as if she'd been asleep, she hurried into the living room.

"Good afternoon, Detective," she said. "You certainly didn't need to come by. It wasn't that important."

He stood, holding out his hand. "Good afternoon to you, too. Sorry I was out when you phoned. I checked in from my car and decided it was just as quick to stop by on my way back to the station."

She took his hand but released it quickly. Out of the corner of her eye, she spotted Laurie settling down in one of the big chairs with her knitting, pretending to ignore them. She started to suggest Laurie leave, but then decided not to. After all, she had been part of the whole thing and Paula'd promised to share with her. Besides, after her outrageous assumption about Jack's motives, perhaps it behooved her to have someone else here.

A chaperon? She winced, but then said, "Laurie and I discovered something we thought you should know."

Jack frowned and opened his mouth. Paula held out a hand. "Wait. I know what you're going to say. But this was inadvertent. Laurie and I . . . well, we remembered that Cynthia Lamphear drives a big, silver car. It seemed totally impossible that she could be a murderer, but after we . . . Anyway, I suggested that Laurie go outside and check to see if there was anything familiar about the car. And, guess what? She wasn't driving it today. She's driving a, as Laurie put it, a ratty green pickup. So, we decided to ask . . ."

Jack sighed and ran his hand through his hair. "You decided to butt in instead of calling me."

"Well, yes, when you put it that way. If your office suddenly started questioning her about it, we figured she'd become suspicious, so we could at least find out her reason for driving a car I'm quite sure she'd normally be ashamed to be seen in."

His mouth twisted. "And?"

"She said that she and her husband had switched for the week because he wanted to impress some businessmen."

"So you decided to call me?"

"Yes. The police are obviously in so much better a position to check out the whereabouts of that car. We thought it best to keep you informed."

Did her tone sound too sanctimonious?

CHAPTER FOURTEEN

"I almost laughed out loud at the look on the detective's face when you said that, Grandma," Laurie said. "That was one pissed man."

"Laurie! Your language!" Paula had been meaning to speak to her about it but so far had restrained herself. But this . . . "You must not use words like that. Have you any idea how much you'd shock anyone my age? I mean, people don't . . ."

"People do, Grandma. Just like I've said, you must have grown up in a *very protected environment.* Coach Sorry says it all the time, and just the other day, Ellen said it when Mark spilled an entire box of cereal on the floor. I mean, should she have said, 'golly'? And the detective. Can you think of a better word for how he looked?"

"Well, annoyed?"

Laurie grimaced. "Come on. You, though, did you ever take acting lessons? I mean, 'Mrs. Innocence.' "

Paula opened her mouth to protest, but before she could stop it, she'd snorted, then dissolved in laughter. Laurie did, too, and then the two giggled as if they both were teenagers, Paula thought, instead of a teenager and one "protected" old lady.

The doorbell rang, and Paula covered her mouth with her hand. "I hope that isn't Jack." And they both dissolved again in barely repressed snickers. "You answer," Paula said, "and give me a chance to compose myself." She dashed off to the bedroom.

As she emerged from the bathroom after washing her face, she heard Laurie talking to someone in the living room. A woman, thank God. But who?

"I'm so glad you weren't hurt more seriously, but what a rotten thing for someone to do!"

Paula recognized Sally Gunderson's voice as she walked down the hall and into the living room. Sally was standing just inside, holding a foil-covered plate.

"Oh, hi, Paula," she said. "Hope this isn't a bad time. I just dropped by to see how things were going, and whether there's anything I can do. What an awful episode for you two. Here." She held out the plate. "Figured you weren't doing any baking these days, so I brought some chocolate chip cookies."

"How thoughtful." Off to the side, she noted Laurie sniffing appreciatively, then grinning. "And you're right. It has been a difficult time. But, as you can see, Laurie's doing well. We just hope . . . Well, this person has to be stopped, Sally."

"You used the singular. Then you're assuming that the murderer was the one who hit the kids?"

"Yes. Yes, I am. Oh, excuse me. Please sit down. My, the cookies smell good. Perhaps we should sample them?"

"Of course!"

"There's lemonade in the refrigerator, Laurie. Could I persuade you to do the honors?"

"Sure, Grandma." She took the cookies, then departed for the kitchen.

"What a lovely girl your granddaughter is." Sally smiled. "She'll be even lovelier when her bruises fade, of course."

Paula smiled in agreement, glad, though, that Laurie hadn't heard her. "They're improving every day, thank goodness. Laurie thought she could never appear in public again. And thank you, yes. I'm finding her quite delightful. I haven't spent as much time with her as I'd like, and I'm pleased with how she's turning out. And enjoying her company. Her mother, you know, is in Europe for the summer." No need to expand on that. Let her assume Jennifer was traveling in a more orthodox manner than she was.

"Missed you at golf last week, of course. Hope you'll be able to come again next week."

Paula nodded. "I'm planning to."

Paula only half listened as they chatted briefly about the activities of the community. Another part of her brain was whirling. Sally was one of the people she'd intended to pump. The woman had lived here a long time, she was bright, and she gave every sign of being truly concerned about Laurie's accident—no, not accident. Attempted murder. How could she best lead up to questioning the woman?

Laurie backed into the room carrying a tray. "I put the rest of the cookies in our cookie jar," she said, "so you can take your plate home." She held the tray out to Sally, who took one of the glasses, and then to Paula, before setting it down in front of her own chair. Where she'd be in the middle of the conversation, Paula noted. And where she could reach the cookies. She started out by taking two.

When there was a conversational lull, Paula commented, "It's so difficult to think of anyone in this community being capable of murder, isn't it? I mean, one expects such things in a bigger city—even some of our smaller communities these days. The murder rate is rising every year, according to the papers."

"You're right," Sally said, "but surely this . . . Well, surely when the police catch the person, they'll find it was someone who's mentally ill. I mean, cold-blooded murder just doesn't occur in a group such as ours." She reached for another cookie.

"Doesn't occur?" Paula was nonplused at her statement. Didn't the woman read the newspapers? "If only that were true, Sally. But just the other day—that shooting on Mercer Island.

Come on, it does happen all the time. If only we had an inkling about why. You've lived here a long time, and you seem to know everyone. Do you have any ideas about who could be so angry as to attempt to kill two young people?"

"No, I really don't. And I believe we should leave it to the police, not make assumptions about those who are innocent." Sally shut her lips firmly.

"I can't do that, Sally. After all, it was my granddaughter who was targeted." Said granddaughter was taking cookies three and four, she noted out of the corner of her eye. "But what about the anonymous letters people are receiving? Who could be so low as to snoop, and then send the hurtful things?"

"I can't imagine." Sally's hand closed in what appeared to be an inadvertent spasm. "Oh," she said, as she picked up crumbs. "I'm so clumsy. Do excuse me."

"Of course," Paula said as she handed her an extra napkin. She mustn't allow herself to be diverted. "You're right, though. It *is* difficult to imagine anyone we personally know involved in such a thing, isn't it?"

Sally nodded and took a sip of lemonade. Her glass definitely was quivering.

I must be striking a nerve, Paula thought. Was it because Sally was nervous about the letter she'd received and the fact that the community was finding out about her husband's affair? Or was there more to her nervousness?

Whatever, she wasn't going to allow the conversation to get away from her. "Have you had any thoughts about who could be writing the letters?" she asked.

Sally took a deep breath. "We always assumed it was Martha, of course. But I've heard rumors that other people have gotten letters since Martha was killed. Not that anyone will admit to it. And who can blame them? If someone did, everyone would assume they had something to hide."

Sally clearly was trying to exude innocence, with her eyes wide and guilt-free. Perhaps she was hoping Paula, being new, hadn't heard about the letter reporting her husband's infidelity. What a difficult situation the poor woman was in, having people gossip about her philandering husband. How long could that marriage hold together, she wondered.

"I've heard people think that it was Alice Ramsdale all along," Paula said, "but I don't know. It's so easy to jump on someone apparently no one likes. Poor woman."

"Poor woman?" Sally said, raising an eyebrow. "I mean, if she *is* the letter-writer . . ."

Paula sighed. "I'm beginning to wonder if that isn't too easy a solution. I don't know Alice, but . . . Somehow, if I were going to indulge in such behavior, I'd make a real effort to be pleasant to people so they wouldn't be suspicious."

"Humph!" Sally said. "I think you're being too nice. And maybe, most likely, you're smarter than whoever's doing this."

"Well . . . thank you, I think!" Paula chuckled, hoping her comment didn't sound too hollow. "Well, I've also heard that people are being blackmailed, although I don't know how anyone could possibly know unless it was happening to them. But if it's true, don't you find this disconcerting?"

Sally's eyes widened, and her hand really jerked, rattling the ice in her lemonade glass and threatening to spill it.

"If I knew of any such thing," she said, setting down the glass, "I would surely take it to the police. But now, I must be going. I have to . . . to set up next week's foursomes and do the chart. You said you'll be joining us, did you not?"

Laurie's eyes widened as her eyes met her grandmother's. "Yes," Paula confirmed. "Yes, I did say so. I'm so sorry you have to rush off."

"Thank you for the cookies, Mrs. Gunderson," Laurie said as Sally stood.

"You're welcome, Laurie. And . . . and I'm truly sorry you were hurt." Her expression was strained.

After Paula escorted their visitor to the door, she returned to the living room. "Well. What did we learn from that little episode?" she asked Laurie.

"That woman is scared. I'd say scared shitless, but you wouldn't like it, Grandma."

Paula grimaced. "No, I wouldn't. And yes, I agreed that she's scared. But why? What of? We know, if the information you heard is correct, that she received one of the letters. But why should talking about it . . . Well, of course it would be unpleasant to know that everyone's gossiping about her marriage."

"She ought to know that you can't keep something like that quiet. I mean, everybody at Kamiak Hills knows exactly what everyone else is doing, when they go to bed, and who they go to bed with. What can you expect? It's worse even than where I live in New York. Lots of the people in our building are gone all day, and we never get to know them. But here, everybody knows each other. She sure got jumpy when you mentioned blackmail, though."

"I noticed. She definitely did."

"I'll bet she's being blackmailed!"

"Could be," Paula said. "But what would be the point since everybody already seems to know about her husband's philandering?"

"Maybe she doesn't know everybody knows. Or else she got a letter or is being blackmailed about something else. Or maybe," Laurie said thoughtfully, "she's scared because she's the murderer, and she's afraid she's going to get caught?"

Laurie grinned. "And, Grandma? Does everyone who goes to visit someone here bring something to eat?"

Laurie studied her face in the mirror, grimacing as she opened

142

and shut her eyes. She still looked awful. But life was boring. She missed swimming practice. Josh had turned out to be more fun than she'd expected, but gosh, he was just a kid. Anyway, what good was she doing for their investigation by sitting in the house all day? She and Josh had learned lots more than her grandmother had, just from listening to the grownups sitting around the pool.

Could she nerve herself to go back?

Yes, she decided. That's what she'd do. She'd never see any of these kids again probably, after this summer. Grandma'd move back to her own house, so when she came to visit—she was sure Grandma would want her to—it'd be a whole 'nother bunch of kids. So they had to look at her battered face? Tough.

She went looking for Paula to tell her what she'd decided, and found her on the deck reading. A man was standing out on the grass about fifty feet away, hands on hips, glaring at his golf ball, and Grandma didn't even notice. Must be a good book. "Grandma," she said, pulling up a chair alongside her. "I've decided to go back to swim practice."

"Wonderful!" Grandma laid down her book. "I'm glad to hear that. You enjoyed the team so much."

"Yeah, I did. And besides, I'm not going to find out anybody's secrets while I sit here, and I figured I might as well be at the pool. The other kids can lump it if they think I look like a creature from outer space."

"Oh, no one will, I'm sure. They're good kids. Every time I run into one of them, they ask about you, and they really miss you. And, I hate to admit it, but you and Josh did overhear gossip that might be important. Just remember, as I said, don't ask questions. Just listen. We certainly do not want a repeat of the attack on you two."

Yeah, that was for sure. "I wonder," Laurie mused. "Do you think Josh'd like to go sit in the stands and watch? I know he's going nuts, and then he'd be around the grownups a lot longer than I will. I could drive him there in our cart."

Laurie felt a little squeamish about that, but she'd get over it, and it was a good excuse to get to drive the cart every day, if Grandma went along with her plan.

"Good idea. You won't even have to call the coach, I'm sure. Just show up. Why don't you run over now and ask Josh what he thinks about going with you?"

"I'll phone him. That'd be faster, and maybe we can still make the afternoon practice. I'll go call him now."

Josh was glad to hear from her, she could tell, even if he didn't say so. "Hey, man," she said, "I'm planning on going back to swim practice. You want to come along?"

"Ah, I don't know. It's pretty boring watching people not doing anything but going back and forth all over again."

"Even if you sit with all the old gossiping ladies? Paula's good with our listening in on them talking. She even suggested it—thinks we might hear something really useful."

"She told you that?" His voice squeaked, he was so surprised.

"Yeah. She figures the police aren't doing enough to find out who hit us, and she actually suggested we see what we can find out. She ordered me not to ask questions, but we can get around that. I figured if you sit there, you'll hear a lot more than I will. And, get this, she'll let me take the cart to haul you."

"Far out! You want to go tomorrow?"

"I was thinking now. Practice starts in half an hour. Why not? Are you doing anything?"

"Are you kidding? *Mom!*"

Laurie winced and held the phone away from her ear.

"Mom, Laurie's going back to swim practice, and Mrs. Madigan says she can take their cart. Can I go?"

Faintly, Laurie heard Ellen's voice in the background. It

sounded enthusiastic.

"Sure!" Josh said into the phone. "I'll be ready."

CHAPTER FIFTEEN

It did feel good to be in the water, Laurie thought, even though she could tell her muscles were going to ache tonight. Gramma'd been right. Some of the mothers hugged her. All the kids had been glad to see her, and nobody'd said anything about how she looked. Well, except for that creep, Lance, who swam with the nine- and ten-year-olds. He'd said, "Eeuu!" and held his nose. But his big brother had slugged him and told him to shut up.

Alan had been especially nice. He'd even put a hand on her shoulder and said, "Great to see you. Welcome back." He had sexy brown eyes.

Now, as practice wound down, she was looking forward to finding out if Josh had overheard anything worth reporting to Paula. Impatiently, she switched from leg to leg as Coach Sorry made them stand on the deck, dripping, while he talked about the meet some of them were going to compete in the next weekend. "I expect some winners," he said. "You're all really coming along." But finally he put his pen back on his clipboard and said, "Okay, that's it. See you tomorrow morning."

Josh had already hobbled his way over to the cart and was sitting in the passenger seat. He looked like he'd burst if he didn't talk to her soon. Had he learned something important?

But, no. "What a bunch of gossips," he started out saying. "Wow. Kathy's mother told everyone about how much Kathy's braces are going to cost. I mean, thousands of bucks! And Kathy hates them."

"Hates what? The braces or her parents?"

"Both, I think. And Carrie's mom said how much money they're saving on some cruise they're taking. It's only going to cost ten thousand bucks."

"Josh," Laurie said, "haven't you figured out that they're really bragging about their money, not complaining?"

"Huh? Are you kidding?" He looked at her wide-eyed.

She glanced at him in disgust. "Honestly, Josh!" He really was immature. "Come on, we don't care how much money they have, we just want to know who's up to something they shouldn't be. Didn't you hear anything worth reporting to Paula?"

He scratched his head. "Well, they sure don't like that Alice person. And Mrs. Wilson got one of those letters. They all jumped on that, wanted to know what it said, but she clammed up. Said it was none of their business, and besides, it hadn't been true. Alan's mom wanted to know if the person had wanted blackmail money, but Mrs. Wilson really got mad at that. 'Of course not,' she said. What'd they think she was? 'I may be indiscreet occasionally,' she said, but she'd never, ever done anything anyone could blackmail her for."

Laurie turned the key and started the cart. "Was that all?" she asked.

"Well, then somebody said somebody should have shot Alice instead, and then they got into an argument about that because somebody else said that was an evil thing to say, but then Mrs. Wilson said that Alice *was* evil."

"Wasn't there anything *useful?*" She steered the cart out onto the path, where two carts sat side by side as the women in them chatted. Finally, Laurie beeped the horn, just a short beep.

Both heads turned toward her. One woman looked annoyed.

The other grinned and waved. "Just a sec. Here comes Alan," she said.

Alan grinned and punched Laurie's shoulder as he passed by, then hopped into the driver's seat after his mom moved to the back. The cart took off, faster than Paula let Laurie drive. But that was probably okay. He was old enough to have a driver's license, and he probably didn't wander onto the grass like she did.

"Well they gossiped for a while about your cleaning lady," Josh said. "Lance's mom said Cynthia doesn't need the money, that she probably takes the jobs to annoy her husband. 'He makes plenty,' Mrs. Wilson said. 'Even enough to spoil that kid of hers by paying for her skating training in Colorado. *I* think she's thumbing her nose at the rest of us.' "

" 'How's that?' someone asked. I forget who. 'Well, by pretending she's doing something worthwhile, not being just a *lady* of *leisure.*'

" 'Like us?' somebody else asked. 'I don't know about the rest of you, but Hugh and I worked hard to get where we are.' "

Laurie pulled up in back of the Cogsdill house as Josh said, "They all mumbled that they'd worked hard, too, but some of them have been rich all their lives, my Mom says."

Laurie rubbed her chin. "Nothing sounds like it'll help us, does it? Do you want to give up and stay home?"

"Heck, no! Just because I didn't learn anything today doesn't mean I won't. I don't have anything else to do, and it was kind've fun, listening like that. Nobody paid any attention to me. Besides, I'm still mad at whoever smashed into us, aren't you?"

"Of course."

Josh swung his legs out of the cart and grabbed his crutches. As he started to hobble toward the house, he asked, "You're going to pick me up in the morning?"

"Sure. I'll be here. Hey, you're getting pretty good at getting around on those things, aren't you?"

"Yeah," he agreed over his shoulder. "But I'll be awfully glad to get off of 'em. Guess I might get a walking cast next week. That'll sure be an improvement."

"Far out!" Laurie waved, then swung the cart toward their house and into its parking place. Carefully, she plugged it in and locked the door behind her, feeling guilty as she did so. Maybe if she'd remembered to do it that other night . . . Well, probably not. The detective had thought whoever the murderer was would have found another cart somewhere. But still . . .

Laurie hurried up the steps to the deck. She'd hoped to have something useful to tell Paula, but no. Not today anyway. But she wasn't going to quit, and Josh felt the same. Whoever had hit them was probably the murderer, but what made her the maddest was that the person behind the wheel had ruined their summer and hadn't even cared enough to stop. If she could do anything about it, whoever it was wasn't going to get away with it.

Paula did join the women for golf on Tuesday, as she'd told Sally she would. Not to her surprise, she found herself partnered with a woman she'd never met before named Chris. Not Sally. Obviously the woman preferred to avoid her after their awkward conversation the previous week, although she did wave in a friendly manner as the two carts passed in front of the clubhouse.

The day was warm, would possibly be unpleasantly so later. It was, after all, almost August. Not unexpectedly, she'd found that the Pappas house had an efficient air-conditioning system, so hot days wouldn't be a problem. Actually, the deck could be quite pleasant even on hot days, as it often had a breeze from the north.

149

As she waited to putt on the ninth hole, she scrutinized the Pappas house, with its red-and-white striped deck furniture, and the Cogsdill home, although in this spot it was partially shielded by trees. Anyone sitting on either deck would be obvious to the golfers, no more so than any of the other houses along the course, but they all lacked privacy. If she'd been choosing a home in Kamiak Hills, she'd have chosen one in a different location.

Her game had been a little sloppy today, she mused as she entered her score on the chart in the clubhouse after they finished play. No doubt her handicap would go up for next week. Strange. Some would rather have it high so they had a better chance of winning, but with her it was a matter of pride to lower it.

As she walked back through the clubhouse, she glanced through the double French doors of the dining room, noting that the room was crowded. Alice Ramsdale, however, sat by herself at a table in the far corner, beneath an almost full-grown palm tree. Craning her neck, Paula could see that Alice was just being served. What an opportunity! She had pondered on how best to become better acquainted with the woman who everyone was blaming for the anonymous notes. What better chance could she have?

She wended her way through the tables, smiling and nodding at various acquaintances. Pasting a smile on her face as she approached Alice, she said pleasantly, "Good afternoon. I see you're eating alone, and it's so crowded in here. I haven't had a chance to get to know you and I thought perhaps we could share . . . ?"

Alice beamed up at her. "Please do join me," she said. "I know you're staying in the Pappas house. And . . ." Wiping the smile off her face, she added, "We both were there when Martha Abingsford's body was found. I heard about the unfortunate accident your granddaughter was in. I'm so glad that the two kids weren't killed."

"Thank you." Alice's expression showed genuine anguish, Paula thought. Difficult to do if she had been the perpetrator. But on the other hand, no one was walking around Kamiak Hills with a guilt-plastered face. Placing her purse on a third chair, Paula seated herself. The waitress was prompt, handing her a menu almost immediately. The clubhouse staff justifiably prided itself on service.

"Um, I believe I'll have the whiskey chicken wrap," Paula said, "and iced tea."

"I noticed you playing today. Was this your first time back after . . . ?" Alice hesitated, but her eyebrows lifted inquiringly.

"Yes, I haven't played since the accident. But my granddaughter Laurie is recovering nicely and has returned to the swim team, so I figured it was time for me to get back to my own activities."

"And do you like living in our *friendly* community?"

Paula blinked. Had she imagined that sarcastic tone? "I do," she answered. "Yes. I was just thinking, as I walked through the dining room, what a nice place this is. I've been here such a short time, and I'm beginning to feel comfortable."

"Oh, yes. On the surface, everyone's your friend. But do you get invited to their homes? Are you included in their little gatherings?"

"Well, just a few," Paula answered. "But I've been here such a short time."

Alice placed a hand on hers. "Don't be fooled," she said. "It's all on the surface. They have cliques, ones that do not have room for outsiders. You'll find out if you're here long."

"Oh? Well, I'm sorry to hear that." Paula made her answer deliberately noncommittal, all the while wanting desperately to remove her hand. She really didn't like personal touching, especially from someone she didn't know well and wasn't sure yet whether she liked. The woman's behavior when they'd found the body in the bunker of the fourth hole had been abysmal.

Fortunately, Alice did lift her hand, if only to pick up her fork. "You'll excuse me if I start eating?" she asked.

"Oh, of course. I'm sorry. I should have suggested you do," Paula said. "It's so nice of you to share your table."

"I've lived here since Kamiak Hills opened," Alice said, "but I really can't name anyone I consider a close friend. Oh, they're happy to have me work on tournaments and projects. I *am* efficient. Everyone recognizes that. As they should. But am I invited into their homes?" She stabbed a chunk of chicken from her salad. "Of course, I was working those early years," she continued. "I'm a nurse, you know."

"Yes. I remember your saying that out on the course that . . . that day."

"Yes. That infamous day." The twist of her lips surely was meant to be a smile but didn't quite make it. She chewed silently.

Paula's mind groped for words. Anything. "Are you still nursing? That must be such a gratifying vocation. And I'll bet you were a good one."

Now Alice did smile. "Yes. I *am* a good nurse. And people still ask me to take private duty assignments. They know they can count on me. It's been a way to get to know people also. Superficially, anyway." Again, she chewed silently.

What a sad woman, Paula thought. She did feel sorry for her. "Tell me," Paula ventured, remembering the quiet man, presumably her husband, who had accompanied her on the course that day, "does your husband have friends here? I mean, are people unfriendly towards him also?"

Alice looked at her, eyebrows raised.

"I'm sorry," Paula said. "That was presumptuous. I just wondered . . . I'm sorry I asked."

"You mean does Edward have friends? Are you kidding? Edward? He's so . . . so docile. Not exactly good company. No. He's like me. Plays golf with the men. But otherwise, we pretty much go our own way."

Docile? Was that a true description of the man Paula had seen on the course? Or, more likely, was he cowed? Now Paula felt sorry for both of them.

Could she help this woman? *You're not a social worker,* she chided herself. But, perhaps she could present Alice a gift of friendship. She had time to spare now that Laurie was getting better. She could easily fit in doing something with Alice. And, along the way, if she learned anything that would help their investigation, that'd be a plus. Alice probably knew more about everybody in Kamiak Hills than anyone else did, except maybe for Cynthia, and she could be of help in the investigation. Unknowingly, of course.

And, of course, she could be the murderer. Paula must never forget that.

"Alice," she said impulsively, "we're evidently both being treated as outsiders here. Perhaps we could do something together? Uh, how about lunch at the Pappas house with me, as a starter?"

Confusion, pleasure and suspicion competed across Alice's face, but pleasure won. "How nice," she said. "I'd like that very much."

"What would be a good day for you?" Paula asked. "I'm pretty much free. I'm sticking around more than usual. Don't want to leave Laurie alone, don't you know? Silly perhaps. I think she's intelligent enough to stay out of trouble but I just . . ." She sighed. "I worry."

"Of course you do." Alice's hand reached out again, and Paula gritted her teeth as it reached toward her. Fortunately, the woman merely patted her hand, then removed her own.

"Um," she said, "how about Friday? That'd be a good day for me."

Paula thought quickly. Friday was Cynthia's day to clean, but she left at noon. That might work out well. The house would be ready, and all she'd have to do was prepare the food ahead of time. "Friday's good," she said. "Why don't you come about eleven, and we can have something cool to drink on the deck first?"

"Excellent! I'll really look forward to it."

Her smile this time was genuine. It changed her expression immensely, Paula thought. With the unhappy lines smoothed out, she appeared almost pretty.

"But now," Alice said after glancing at her watch, "would you excuse me? I have an appointment at one-thirty."

"Of course. I'll look forward to seeing you Friday."

Paula watched as the woman threaded her way through the tables to the exit. Heads turned, watching her and then glancing with up-lifted eyebrows at Paula. She smiled back sweetly. Let them wonder. Perhaps there was a smidgen of truth to Alice's derogatory comments. Paula was genuinely pleased with herself. It always felt good to do something nice for someone.

Chapter Sixteen

"Excellent!" Laurie said when Paula told her about inviting Alice to lunch. "Josh and I haven't been much use, but I'll bet that woman knows everythin*g*, and I mean *everything* about everybody. But nobody likes her. How'd you ever stand eating with her today, anyway?"

"It was interesting, Laurie. I actually felt sorry for her. Can you imagine living somewhere and never being accepted? Never being invited to people's homes?"

"Well, it's her own fault." Gramma was such a *nice* person. She probably would trust a con man or an identity thief. She needed someone, just in a different way than Laurie's mom did. How'd she ever gotten along all these years? Well, of course it was probably that husband of hers. Her grandfather. That was hard to take in. Mom had never, ever, talked about him, and you'd think Paula might have brought a picture of him, but no. She was going to have to ask Paula about him someday.

"Sure," Gramma said. "But how many people do analyze their own behavior and figure out something like that? I intend to be very nice to her, and I'm hoping, well . . ."

"That she'll tell all?"

"Well, that, too, of course, but really I just felt that maybe I could help her."

Laurie shrugged, wondering what Gramma was planning. Well, if she wanted to be nice, Laurie could be nice, too. "Okay. I'll smile and be goody-goody to her."

"Oh, I hadn't planned that you'd be there, Laurie. I think she'll be much more forthcoming if she's alone with me."

Laurie frowned. "I thought we were going to investigate together. You said I'm a good listener. Come *on*, Paula."

Gramma scrunched her lips together the way she did when she didn't like something Laurie said. But then she gave in. "Tell you what. How about if you join us while we're eating? I invited her for eleven. Thought we'd have a drink out on the deck first."

"Smart, Gramma. Put lots of alcohol in her drink. She'll talk more. Everybody does."

Paula laughed. "I hadn't thought of that, but it's not a bad idea. What if you just show up about noon, eat with us, then excuse yourself? How's that for a compromise?"

"Great. I'm kind'a looking forward to it. I know who she is, but I've never heard her talk. Is she really as obnoxious as everyone says?"

"Sometimes, I'm sorry to say. But maybe not always. We'll find out, won't we?"

"I'm having a guest for lunch today," Paula said. Cynthia was scrubbing pieces of the stove as Paula ate breakfast. Unnecessarily, Paula thought, but it wasn't her place to say anything. As little cooking as she did, the stove hardly needed an overhaul.

"Oh?" Cynthia said, right eyebrow raised.

"We'll stay out of your way. We're going to have a drink out on the deck first, and I'll put my casserole in the oven to be ready at noon."

Cynthia waited, clearly expecting to be enlightened as to who was coming. Perversely, Paula smiled sweetly, then took another sip of coffee. Let her wait.

When the doorbell rang at eleven, Paula was ready. She'd set the table, concocted a salad, and the artichoke and chicken casserole, her favorite, was doing its thing in the oven. As she hurried down the hall, she heard the muted roar of the vacuum.

Alice stood on the porch, looking a tad apprehensive, Paula thought. "Do come in," she invited with a friendly smile.

"Thank you." Alice stepped over the threshold. She looked especially nice, having probably just been to the hairdresser, Paula surmised. Her almost black hair had been styled in a softer, more flattering do, albeit sprayed into submission. She wore a dress, not a usual sight in the community, and it was flattering, a soft green print that fell gracefully. "Thought maybe you'd enjoy these," she said as she held out a pot of lavender African violets.

"Beautiful! And how thoughtful of you. Thank you. I'll put them on the kitchen table, where we can enjoy them at every meal."

As they stepped into the hall, the sound of the vacuum ceased. Within an instant, Cynthia appeared from Laurie's bedroom, the vacuum preceding her. "Oh," she said, after she shut her mouth. "Oh, hello, Alice."

All the preparation had almost been worth it just to see the expression on Cynthia's face. Paula put her hand to her mouth to hide her reaction.

"Good morning, Cynthia." The smile on Alice's face was genuine, although maybe a touch . . . triumphant? A silence descended on them until Paula broke it by turning toward her visitor and asking, "Perhaps you'd like to see the house? If we aren't interrupting you, Cynthia?"

"Oh. Not at all. I still have to do your granddaughter's room, and then I'll be on my way." She opened the door to Laurie's bedroom. Carioca bolted out, looking annoyed, and saying so in her inimitable manner. "Oh, that Laurie. She's always forgetting that those cats need to get to their food and litter. Shoo," she said to Mum-mum, who had stopped to wash her face in the doorway.

"What beautiful Siamese." Alice stooped to pet Mum-mum, who stiffened and glared. "Oh. Well, it doesn't like strangers, I guess." She straightened. "I *would* enjoy a tour. As I told you, I've never been inside here. I understand it's lovely."

"Indeed it is. Although much too large, in my opinion. I have no idea why they chose to have five bedrooms. Let's go this way," Paula suggested, as Cynthia, stiff-necked, turned her back and retreated into Laurie's bedroom.

Alice was unnervingly silent as Paula led her through the house until they reached the kitchen. "The place *is* nice," she said, sounding begrudging. "I certainly wouldn't care to have those white carpets, though. I myself have hardwood. Much warmer. And you're right about the five bedrooms." Her glance took in the kitchen. "So many cupboards, too. Like the bedrooms, why so many? Are they all full?"

"I wouldn't know," Paula said. "I've never looked into most of them. Can anyone ever have too many?" To her amazement, Alice proceeded to open several, inspecting the contents. One contained cut glass, another held a meat-slicer and several chafing dishes. A third was filled with an array of alcohols.

"I knew the Pappases entertained large groups. I heard about their parties, even if I was never invited." Alice's tone was self-pitying.

Paula cleared her throat, then raised her eyebrows questioningly. "Obviously, we can choose almost anything to drink. I myself thought lemonade with a shot of vodka would hit the spot on a warm day such as this."

"Sounds good to me. I'm not much for fancy drinks, anyway."

"Fine." Paula fixed the drinks, smiling to herself as she made sure which glass now contained a double shot of alcohol. "I've enjoyed the deck so much," she commented, picking up the tray with the glasses and heading for the door. "It *is* an especially nice day, isn't it?" Paula half expected Alice to find at least one cloud in the pristine blue sky. A gray one, no doubt.

The two women settled on the matching red-striped chaises with a table in between. "Tell me," Alice asked after taking up her glass and sipping, "how did you happen to end up house sitting for the Pappases? Is this something you do regularly?"

"Oh, no. My husband died suddenly, on the golf course at home, don't you know. I was . . . I was unprepared, I guess, for living alone. Well, at least in that house where we'd lived so long."

"Oh, my dear," Alice said. "How horrible." Her face reflected her feelings. "I am *so* sorry. Are the Pappases good friends of yours? How fortunate for them that you were available."

"Oh, no, I'd never met them. But we had a mutual friend who knew about their impending trip, and she thought it would be good for me . . ." To Paula's amazement, she found herself pouring out the whole story, even touching on the fact that she had not been used to making decisions. Alice was a skilled questioner, she concluded. No wonder she learned so much about people. And she truly gave an appearance of being sympathetic. Was that all an act? So people would confide? But why, then, had she turned so many people off?

And she needed to remember that her intent was to learn more about Alice, not the other way around. "I've decided not to return to my old house," she said. "I'm putting it up for sale the next time I make a trip down there. I'd considered moving here, to Kamiak Hills. But perhaps that's not such a good idea, from what you tell me. Even aside from the murders and the attack on the kids, I'm finding that there seem to be so many people hiding all sorts of . . . well, not such nice behavior. I guess I was naïve, but it does seem to be a place with too many secrets."

A man who wore pants that definitely tended toward pink strode across the grass toward them, golf club in hand. He looked vaguely familiar; probably someone she'd seen at the clubhouse. When he glanced up at them, Alice waved and called, "Hi, Mike. How are you?"

He glanced up, startled. "Uh . . . well, hello, Alice. I'm fine. Except for this rotten shot! Uh, how're you?"

"Good, good."

He raised an eyebrow, then shook his head and turned to face his errant ball. Paula wondered if the expression on his face reflected the shot he needed to make or was a reaction to seeing Alice being entertained in the Pappas house.

"Mike Garrison," Alice said. "I nursed him while he was recovering from testicular cancer. Nasty disease."

Alice did indeed know people's most intimate affairs. And she didn't hesitate to spread her knowledge. That alone might turn off a lot of people.

Alice's glass was almost empty, Paula noted, and as she watched, her guest drained the last of it. Paula swung her legs to the side of the chaise and stood. "Let me have your glass," she said, "and I'll refresh both of ours. The ice melts so fast on a day like this."

The house was silent. Apparently Cynthia had finished and left. Laurie'd be showing up for lunch soon. It was time to get to the point.

That, however, was not easy. Prying went against everything that Paula had been trained to do as a child and young woman. As they chatted about golf and other unimportant subjects, her mind scrabbled for the best way to get the conversation on track. *Be blunt,* she decided. Alice had already drunk half of her second glass. She ought to be well-oiled.

"I *am* concerned," Paula finally said, "about these anonymous letters everyone seems to be receiving. Anonymous letters don't

160

seem conducive to a well-ordered society." *Pompous,* she thought, as she carefully watched Alice peripherally. A sly look whisked across her face. *The gossip's true,* Paula thought, instantly convinced that Alice was indeed the letter writer. "Why, do you suppose, anybody'd choose to stir things up that way?" Paula asked.

"Oh," Alice said, "perhaps she—assuming it is indeed a woman—thinks people ought to be stirred up a little. They can be so sanctimonious and self-righteous, don't you know? Maybe they should suffer a little, like the people they've harmed. Don't you agree?"

"Uh . . . not exactly. But what about the gossip there's a blackmailer at work? Isn't that the likely reason for the letters?"

"Certainly not." Now Alice's expression was indignant. As she reached for her glass, she almost knocked it over.

Good, Paula thought. The alcohol was taking effect. "You don't think the two things are connected? Writing anonymous letters and blackmailing people?"

"Absolutely not," Alice said. "I mean, letters are about trivial things, but blackmail? I know about a number of transgressions that people could be blackmailed for, but I wouldn't . . ."

Paula eyed her silently, unable to think of a response. She set down her glass, and stared at her guest. "What sorts of transgressions, Alice? I . . ." Then she almost bit her tongue. Had she pressed too hard?

Alice smiled conspiratorially. "I'm sure I can count on your discretion, Paula. I'll give you one example. Ben Griffin. You know, the man who was in your foursome the day of Martha's murder?"

"The one who's wife was just murdered?"

"Well, yes. But would you ever guess he has AIDS? I know that he's gone to great lengths to hide it. As a banker, I'm sure he felt it would be a disaster if people knew. I don't know how he got it, but just the suggestion . . ." She waggled her fingers. Her expression was rueful.

"But . . . but . . . Alice, how did you happen to find that out if he's so secretive? If I might ask."

"I was at their house one day for a meeting organizing the best-ball tournament. I'm a nurse, remember? I used their bathroom before I left, and all it took was a glance at the medicine in the bathroom cabinet. Medicine that was prescribed by Seattle doctors. I never told anyone, of course. But he knew I knew. I could tell."

"Oh, dear," Paula said, thinking that Alice had explored the bathroom cabinets just as she had those in the Pappas kitchen. "Don't you think you should tell the police? I mean his wife was murdered . . . Detective Compagnio really should know that it's conceivable that Ben was being blackmailed. And if you know about anyone else . . . I've developed a lot of respect for the detective. I feel sure he'd be discreet. And I know he'd appreciate your insights." Was she piling it on too high?

"I'm concerned about Laurie and Josh, Alice. I personally feel, and Detective Compagnio agrees, that they must have inadvertently stumbled on a secret that someone was willing to kill for. Just because the kids are recovering from their injuries doesn't mean that the murderer won't go after them again. If you have any idea whatsoever what this whole thing could be about, I implore you to get in touch with him. He won't tell anyone you've talked to him, I'm sure."

Alice fidgeted nervously. "I don't . . ."

"Please. You're a nurse. You have to be compassionate to be the good one you have a reputation for being. Think about how you'd feel if either of those kids was killed." The thought suddenly occurred to her. "Do you have children of your own?"

Tears welled in Alice's eyes. "We had one," she said. "A little girl. She had a birth defect, and . . ."

"Oh, I'm so sorry for bringing it up," Paula said, feeling terribly guilty. Perhaps that alone accounted for some of Alice's strange behavior. "Let's talk about something more pleasant."

Alice shook her head. "That's okay. It was a long time ago. But you're right. I'd feel truly horrible if the murderer attacked the kids again. I—I will think about going to the detective. But yes, let's change the subject. Tell me more about yourself," she suggested. "Are you a bridge player? Are you into jogging?"

Back to collecting information, Paula thought, but she obliged to the best of her ability. She didn't have anything to hide. Well, that wasn't strictly so. Probably most people had foibles they preferred not to talk about. She'd never discussed her marriage with anyone. As she talked about the life she'd had before Fred's death, it became even more evident to her how she'd been manipulated into being a subservient wife.

Alice picked up on it. "These activities you were involved in . . . uh, they all sound like you were acting as a secretary to your husband. Didn't you have any hobbies of your own?"

"That's very perceptive of you, Alice. You're entirely right. I didn't realize it until after his death. I've never talked about it to anyone before."

Alice smiled. "I hope you've done so because we're becoming friends. I'd like that very much."

"How nice to think we are." As she spoke, Paula did feel guilty. She'd invited Alice here for selfish reasons. Maybe they should become friends. She had another secret of course, one that she'd never shared with others: her estrangement from Jennifer. Now that they were back in touch, she was going to need to gradually introduce her only child into conversations. Not too many people even knew she existed. "My daughter Jennifer," she began. "Laurie's mother, well, she lives in New York and . . ."

The sliding door opened, and Laurie popped out. "Hi, Mrs.

Ramsford. Hi, Gramma. It smells dee-licious in the kitchen and I'm starved. Is lunch ready?"

CHAPTER SEVENTEEN

"Was it a waste of time?" Laurie rinsed the plate she was holding, loaded it into the dishwasher, then reached for another while Paula took care of the leftover food. There was enough casserole for lunch tomorrow, Paula surmised. Alice had thanked them profusely, then left ten minutes before.

"All I heard was stuff," Laurie said. "I mean, what did it matter what you did with yourself back at your old house? Some of it was interesting, though. That's the first time I've ever heard you talk about my grandfather, ever. How come? I've been wondering. He sounded pretty bossy. Mrs. Ramsford, though, she sounded okay. Almost like you were friends. But . . ."

Paula sighed. She hadn't realized Laurie'd been eavesdropping, but she should have guessed. And her granddaughter did tend to run on at the mouth sometimes. She shut the refrigerator door. "You managed to have three questions in that little discourse. No, I haven't talked about Fred much. Yes, he was bossy. And yes, Alice did not sound obnoxious. If it weren't for the fact that I became convinced that she writes the anonymous letters . . ."

"Oh. You did find out something."

"I did. There's no question in my mind that she's the letter writer. But also, I doubt very much that she's the blackmailer. Alice is a strange woman. Has a code of ethics of her own, I decided. I may have accomplished something, though. She admitted that she's aware of some people's secrets that could be blackmailable, if there is such a word, and I think . . . I hope . . . I convinced her to go to Detective Compagnio with what she knows. If the detective knows who he might question, and those people will cooperate, then I would think there'd be a better chance of uncovering the murderer. Let's hope so."

"But she didn't tell you what any of those secrets were?"

Paula hesitated. It was good that Laurie had missed the discussion about Ben Griffin. That's how stories did get spread in a community. Each person telling one. Laurie very likely would feel that Ben's illness was something to share with Josh. She didn't like to lie, but this time she would.

"No," she said, glad that Laurie's back was turned.

"Bummer. Are you going to call the detective?"

"Not yet. I'll give Alice's conscience a chance to work. I really think I persuaded her to talk to him. I'll wait until Monday, I think, and give him a call then."

Saturday, the Wilsons took a group including Laurie and Josh to watch a major soccer tournament. When the phone rang, Paula answered on the second ring. She still didn't get that many calls, so when one came while Laurie wasn't home, she always answered quickly. It wasn't that she really expected more bad news concerning her granddaughter, but an underlying unease kept her alert.

"Oh, Paula!" Ellen Cogsdill's anguished tone made Paula stiffen. "Have you heard the news?"

"No. What this time?"

"There's been another murder! This time they found the body propped against the flag on the second . . . Oh, is anyone ever going to want to play . . . Oh my goodness. What a terrible . . ."

"Ellen!" Paula knew her tone was sharp. Couldn't her neighbor ever get to the point? "Ellen," she said again, slowly,

"Who? Who was murdered this time?"

"Why, Alice Ramsford! That's who! The first people on the course this morning couldn't believe . . . I mean, Alice! No one liked her, but most people thought she was the one . . ."

"I'm truly sorry to hear that. Ellen, I'm going to have to cut this short. I had Alice to lunch just yesterday, and she told me some things that I need to pass on to the detective. Can I call you back later?"

"You actually had Alice to lunch and . . . Oh, my goodness, I can't believe . . . Did you . . . ?"

Paula interrupted, "I'll talk to you later, Ellen. I must get off the phone now."

Ellen was still making sputtering noises when Paula hung up. She hated to be rude, but obviously, reaching the detective was crucial. She punched in the number of the police department. "I need to speak to Detective Compagnio," she told the person who answered the phone. "I have vital information to share with him." Laurie sat down at one of the kitchen chairs and listened to Paula's end of the conversation.

"He isn't here," the woman said. "I'm quite sure he's going to be busy all morning, perhaps all day."

"I understand that Alice Ramsford has been murdered. My information concerns her. Please tell the detective that I had lunch with her yesterday, and she had indicated that she'd go to him with knowledge that she had."

"I'll pass this on to the detective as soon as he comes in." The woman on the other end of the line sounded more interested now. "Who is this, please?"

Paula gave her name, then hung up. She should have guessed he'd be tied up. He must thoroughly dread new calls from Kamiak Hills. Oh, if only she'd insisted Alice go to the police immediately or had called them herself, Alice would probably still be alive.

That poor husband of hers. One more resident here who'd received bad news. The place seemed jinxed. What sort of villainous person was willing to cold-bloodedly kill so many people? Whoever it was must appear normal. And manage to go about life in a manner that didn't arouse suspicion. Most likely, it was someone she'd met or seen at the clubhouse or on the course.

And, oh my goodness, this was the second time that she'd failed to call the police when she should have. She cringed, thinking of what Detective Compagnio was going to say when he got a chance. She had, she realized, reverted to the old Paula Madigan who hadn't liked to make decisions, who in the past had always deferred to a man to do so.

She lifted her head when she heard the sound of a car stopping in front of the house and then the slam of the car door as Laurie burst through the front door. "Gramma!" she shouted. "Have you heard? There's been another murder. Mrs. Ramsford!"

"Yes. I heard. Ellen just called me. I feel terrible."

"Why? Well, nobody should get murdered, but you think she was the one who was writing those anonymous letters. Isn't that, well, sort of asking for it?"

"No doubt," Paula said. "But I do think underlying, that she was a decent . . . Well, at any rate she didn't deserve to die. What an ignoble way to be found. Someone must have truly hated her. I'm just picturing . . . Well, never mind." The vision in Paula's brain was of the body of her guest of Friday, propped against the pole, legs splayed, with her lovely green dress bunched around her hips. Perhaps that wasn't the way she was found, but the image simply would not go away.

"You're kind of pale, Gramma. Why don't you sit down? I'll get you some water."

Paula did feel wobbly. She sat. "Thank you," she said as

Laurie handed her the glass.

"You use a lot of big words, Gramma. What's 'ig . . . ignoble' mean?"

"Oh. I think it means not noble, common, but I'm envisioning maybe undignified?"

Laurie's lips moved as she practiced the word. Good. A hard way for a teenager to increase her vocabulary, but that's how life was sometimes.

Oh, how she wished the phone would ring, and it would be the detective. Or maybe not. He'd chew her out from top to bottom, and she deserved it. She just wanted to get it over with and perhaps help the investigation with what she'd learned on Friday.

Paula hovered around the phone all day, but it was late afternoon, after five o'clock, actually, when the detective called. Without preamble, he said, "I understand you have information for me."

"I do. And I am so sorry. I had Alice Ramsford here for lunch yesterday, and . . ."

He interrupted. "I'm surprised. I didn't think she was in your circle. Am I to surmise that you, in spite of my warnings, are still poking around where you shouldn't?"

Paula's back stiffened. He really could be insufferable. "Do you want to hear what I found out? Or do you not?"

The deep rumble of the detective's laugh sounded over the phone. "You're not going to change, are you? I should have guessed."

"I won't change until that murderer is caught, you're right. Then I can retreat into minding my own business the way I used to."

Now she heard a deep sigh. "Okay. Out with it. What did you hear?"

"Well, first of all, I became convinced that she is—was the

writer of the anonymous letters. I also decided that she likely was not the blackmailer that everybody says has been threatening people."

"And?"

"I have no way to be sure that she wasn't the blackmailer, but she did know about at least one of the people who was open to blackmail. She also indicated that she knew about others. She wasn't the least bit shy about poking into cupboards and closets. I was astounded at her guts, actually. I'm pretty sure I had persuaded her to take her information to you. I pressured her, reminding her that Laurie and Josh were likely still in danger."

"And who was the one person she told you about?"

"Ben Griffin. The banker. It seems he has AIDS and does not want the community to know. She found out by looking in his medicine cabinet." Oh-oh, she thought suddenly, looking at Laurie who was sprawled sideways in the nearest armchair. She hadn't planned for Laurie to know that fact. Well, she'd have a word with her when she hung up.

"Ah, yes. Ben Griffin," the detective said.

"You sound like you already knew."

He ignored her statement. "Did she name anyone else?"

"Unfortunately, no. But she said there were others . . ." Paula's stomach sank. "I guess I really didn't learn anything that would help, did I? Since it sounds like you already know about Ben. I am so very sorry, Detective. Again, my best of intentions went awry. If only . . ."

"There're lots of 'if onlys' in the world, Paula," he said somberly. "Neither of us knows if she would have come to me in time, if at all. I'd have liked to talk to the woman, of course. And Paula, I did ask you to call me Jack."

"Well then, Jack, it just occurred to me. Since you know about Ben's secret, couldn't you . . ." She held her breath. He was the policeman. She was an outsider, an amateur. He'd likely be furious if she continued what she'd been going to say.

The phone line hummed as neither of them spoke. Finally, Jack asked, "Couldn't I what?"

"Well, since you know about Ben's illness, couldn't you probe a little, find out if he is indeed being blackmailed, and by whom?" She swallowed. He'd probably never speak to her again. She was truly butting in where she didn't belong.

This time the silence was prolonged. Finally, Paula said contritely, "I'm sorry. That was truly presumptuous of me."

"Yes, it was. And it assumes that I don't know my business." He sighed before continuing. "I really shouldn't tell you this, and I'll deny I ever did if it comes out, but that thought did occur to us. And we did talk to Mr. Griffin. He wasn't being blackmailed."

"Oh."

"But his wife was. She's the one who cared if her neighbors found out."

"Oh, my goodness. And she was the one murdered! What *is* going on, Jack? That's really scary."

"Yes, it is. Don't remember ever dealing with a situation like this. I appreciate your coming forward with the information you found out, but I must reiterate that you are not, and I emphasize *not* to butt into our investigation. Not only could you screw things up, but you could learn something that would put you into real danger. I don't want that to happen, Paula. Do I have your promise not to interfere?"

"You know I won't make a promise I can't keep. But to be honest, this was probably a one-shot deal. I don't really know very many people here in the Hills," she said. "If I do think of something, I'll call you first. How's that?"

"Better than nothing. I have one question. Did anyone else know that there was a chance she was going to talk to me?"

171

"Well, yes. Laurie. And she may have told Josh." Laurie was obviously straining her ears to try to hear the detective. "Laurie, how about it? Did you tell Josh or anyone else that Alice was going to go to the detective?"

"Well, sure. I told Josh. But he wouldn't have told anybody."

"You probably heard her answer, Jack. We'll check with Josh and let you know. I sincerely hope he didn't tell his mother." She knew her voice sounded contrite.

"Don't worry," Jack said. "What's done is done. Just let me know if you find out anything, okay?"

"Absolutely. And . . . again, I apologize."

"Apology accepted."

"Hi, Laurie," Josh's mother greeted her when she arrived at their kitchen door. "The kids are in the family room watching *Animal Planet*. Go on in."

"Thanks, Ellen," Laurie said. Paula had wanted her to call their neighbor Mrs. Cogsdill, but that hadn't lasted long. Must be a thing with Gramma's generation because the first time she'd tried to call Josh's mother that, she'd laughed and said, "Don't be formal. I'm not used to it. Just call me Ellen."

Josh was sprawled in front of the TV with his brother and sister watching a grizzly bear scoop a huge salmon out of river rapids and flip it onto the bank. It was pretty fascinating. She waited for a second, until the bear starting eating the fish. It was still wiggling. Ugh.

"Hey, Josh," she said. "I need to talk to you."

"Huh?" He lifted his head.

"Come on, let's go outside."

"Okay." With a last look at the screen, he clambered to his feet and grabbed his crutches. "It's a rerun anyway." Mark and Susan didn't appear to even notice Laurie'd come in or that Josh was leaving.

"What's up?" he asked as soon as they got out on the deck.

"Gramma just talked to Detective Compagnio. She told him all about Alice's visit. He was real interested that she'd been going to go talk to him but not very happy that Gramma had waited to tell him until it was too late." She was itching to tell him about that banker, but she'd promised not to. Josh wouldn't tell anyone, she was sure, but . . . "He wanted to know if anyone else knew she was going to talk to him, and Gramma told him that I'd told you. And he wanted to know if there was any chance you'd told anyone else."

Josh made a face. "Of course not. I promised. Anyway, I don't like to bring the subject up with Mom. She'd . . ."

"She'd freak out?"

"Yeah. You know Mom. She's bad enough about letting me out of her sight without reminding her about our getting hit."

"Gramma said it was really funny when Alice arrived. She hadn't told Cynthia who was coming to lunch, and I guess she about dropped her teeth."

"Cynthia was there? Was it her day to clean?"

"Yeah, but . . ." Their eyes met. "Ohmigosh," Laurie said. "She was gone when I got home, but do you suppose . . . ? I'll bet Gramma never thought about that, that she might have stayed and snuck around and listened to what was going on. Come on! Let's go talk to Gramma."

Josh opened the door a crack and poked his head inside. "I'll be right back," he said to his mom.

"Josh, I'm ready to dish up dinner. Where are you going, for heaven's sake?"

"We thought about something we've got to tell Mrs. Madigan."

"Josh, can't it wait until . . . ?"

He pulled the door shut. His mother made a face but didn't try to stop him.

"I should've thought about Cynthia," Laurie said as they scurried across the grass between the houses. Josh could do about anything on those crutches, Laurie thought. Except he couldn't get into the pool until the cast came off. What a bummer on these hot days.

"Mrs. Madigan," Josh shouted as Laurie slung the sliding door to one side, "we've thought of something important!"

Paula looked up, surprised. "What's that, Josh?"

"It's about Cynthia. Laurie says she was here part of the time while you were talking to Alice. What if she hung around and eavesdropped? What if she knew you'd persuaded Alice to talk to the detective. What if . . ."

Paula's face was almost funny. Her jaw dropped, and her eyes popped. "What if she's the murderer? Oh, my goodness! By the time I was putting the pressure on, I'd assumed she'd finished cleaning and left. She'd said she was going as soon as she finished Laurie's room, which never takes her more than about ten minutes. We were talking softly, anyway."

"And we never did get to look at that car that she says her husband's driving now," Laurie reminded her.

"Kids, you are a wonder. I guess I wasn't cut out to be a detective. I'll call Jack right this minute."

"I'd better go," Josh said reluctantly, "or Mom'll kill me. Let me know what you find out, okay?"

"You bet!" Gramma said. "Laurie can call you as soon as I talk to the detective."

Chapter Eighteen

It took a while to track down the detective. Paula left messages, then waited impatiently. When the phone rang in the early evening, Detective Compagnio sounded surprised but pleased to have heard from her. "Just got back from a movie with my grandkids," he said. "What's up?"

Paula was startled. It had never occurred to her that he had descendants, most likely because he hadn't mentioned offspring at the time she was so distressed about Laurie. "Oh." She groped for words. "Well, the kids came up with a suggestion that I thought I should pass on as soon as possible. It occurred to them that Cynthia Lamphear could possibly have overheard my discussion with Alice." She went on to explain the circumstances.

"And," she reminded him, "there's still the question of her car. It seems so . . . so tidy that it hasn't been available for Laurie to look at to see if it possibly aroused a memory of the accident."

"Indeed," the detective said. "I do appreciate your calling. I'll get right on it."

"You will let me know?" Paula asked.

He hesitated. "Unorthodox. But I guess I owe you that much, don't I?"

"I would think so," Paula said, smiling to herself.

She hoped to hear from him quickly, but as the evening wore on without the phone ringing, she became restless. Finally, at eleven o'clock, she gave up and went to bed. The next day, she found herself simply puttering and discovered it was difficult to resist calling the police station. More than once she caught herself heading toward the phone, but then managed to restrain herself.

Finally, late Monday evening, Jack phoned. "Sorry not to get back to you sooner," he apologized, "but we were unable to reach Mrs. Lamphear. Or her husband. It's impossible that she murdered Mrs. Ramsford. She and her husband flew to Colorado to visit their daughter, who's training there for ice skating, as you probably know.

"They just got back. Their flight arrived at six P.M., and there's no doubt they were on it. We confirmed that they stayed at the hotel whose name they gave us, on Friday and Saturday nights. Which means, of course . . ."

"Which means she couldn't have done it." Paula felt deflated. It wasn't that she wanted to see her housekeeper declared a murderer; she just wanted *somebody* to be unmasked. This couldn't go on. The community was in turmoil. She'd spoken to several people on Sunday: the Wilsons, Ellen, and even Coach Soriano. She'd gone to swimming practice today with Laurie, partly because she wanted to see how much she'd improved, and it was considerable, but also simply because she hated to have her out of the house alone. She wasn't the only one who felt that way. Many more mothers than usual had come, and the buzz had been about nothing much else besides the question of who, possibly, could be the culprit.

The detective repeated her statement. "No, she couldn't have done it."

"Well, where does that leave us?" Paula asked.

"As I've told you before, Paula, it doesn't leave *you* anywhere." His tone was curt. "We have leads. I can't share them, of course. But please, please, for Laurie's safety and yours, stay out of it."

"Humph." Paula was exasperated and completely flummoxed. What more *could* she do? "This whole thing is destroying this community," she said to Jack.

He sighed. "We're well aware of that. The higher-ups let us know, as if we couldn't figure it out on our own. We'll get 'em," he said. "He or she is an amateur. And amateurs generally make mistakes. If Laurie were my granddaughter, however, I would double my efforts to see that she is not alone, except in your locked house. We're doing all we can."

Humbled, Paula said, "I know you are. I appreciate it. I just wish that I could help."

She hung up slowly as she thought. So far, her efforts to uncover information had, if anything, only led to further disaster. She would never forgive herself for probably putting Alice Ramsford in danger. She'd wanted to help the woman and had thought she could. Instead, her meddling had backfired. Should she totally quit her snooping?

Jack no doubt would do everything in his power to find the murderer, but there was no escaping the fact that Laurie and Josh were still in danger. The police's best efforts had so far failed. No, Paula couldn't quit.

Since Cynthia had been cleared, it might be worthwhile to question her. Not accusingly, of course, but simply because she most likely knew more of what was going on in the community than almost anyone else, what with her multitude of cleaning jobs. Surely, Paula could tactfully probe as to her knowledge.

In the meantime, everywhere she went—swimming practice, the grocery store—she began to look at cars. Jack had been right. There were a lot of grey or silver-colored cars in the Hills. She tried to surreptitiously inspect each of them for damage. Probably hopeless, she knew. By now, most likely whoever had plowed into the kids would have had the car repaired. Could she tell, if she looked closely, that a front end had been freshly repainted?

Several times she drew strange looks. Once a woman had set her groceries on the hood, stared at her with an unfriendly glare, and asked, "Looking for something?"

Should she explain? No, Paula decided, as she groped for an excuse. "Looked so much like a car that belongs to a friend of mine I haven't seen for a while, that I . . . well, obviously, it isn't hers." The woman raised an eyebrow, then unlocked her car and loaded her sacks as Paula slunk away.

She told Laurie what she'd been doing and urged her to do the same. "We might get lucky," she said, "and you'll see one that triggers your memory of the accident." She sighed. "I hate to revive unpleasant memories, but oh, I wish we could find who did this to you."

To her surprise, Laurie gave her a hug. "Don't feel bad, Gramma. I've been doing the same thing. But I just can't remember what it was about that car I feel like I ought to remember."

Paula knew she'd been procrastinating. But it had been brought home to her by Laurie, who'd asked, "Where's the doc these days? Are you mad at him about whatever was in that letter you got?"

"No, of course not. It was simply gossip, and he had a perfectly good explanation. And, no, I'm still not going to tell you what it was about."

"Well, he did bring me a card and that beautiful bunch of roses the day after I got home from the hospital. You shouldn't make him mad, Gramma. He's pretty good looking for somebody as old as . . ."

Paula shot her a look.

"You know what I mean. He's not young, for gosh sakes.

Anyway, he's rich, and you're not getting any younger."

"Laurie!" Paula was shocked. "I am *not* looking for a husband. I had one, remember?"

"You don't act like you miss him much. Maybe you can do better this . . ."

"Laurie! That is absolutely enough! The men in my life are not your business. Or the lack of them, as the case may be. I don't want to hear any more on the subject."

"Well, Mom seems to think she has to have a man around."

"Your mom always did have some peculiar ideas, I'm sorry to say. We didn't see eye to eye then, and we probably never will. Wash your hands. Dinner will be ready in ten minutes."

As she set the food on the table, Paula fumed. Laurie could be infuriating at times. But, Paula had to admit, she'd truly been remiss about David. She had been tied up with Laurie's care, she told herself, but strictly speaking, that wasn't why she hadn't called him. She'd been more disturbed about his wife's death than she'd admitted to herself, and that wasn't fair to him. She needed to make amends. But not while Laurie was within earshot.

The next morning was his half day off, if she remembered correctly, so after Laurie left for the pool, she dialed his home number, hoping he wasn't using the morning for errands. But no, the answering machine picked up.

Impatiently, she spoke into the phone. "Hi, David. This is Paula Madigan. Thought I'd call and . . ."

"Hello!" David's melodious voice interrupted. "Just got in the door. Good to hear from you, Paula."

"It's been too long," she apologized. "I'm sorry, but . . ."

"You've been swamped with care for Laurie. I know. I understand. I'd have liked to help, but, well, I wanted to be sure I'd be welcome."

"Of course you're welcome," Paula said quickly. "I thought

179

I'd made it perfectly clear the last time—that day at the lake," she finished lamely.

"What's been going on?" he asked. "I won't ask if there's any news about who hit them. My patients keep me informed," he said dryly, "and I assume it would be common knowledge if the police had found out. But how's Laurie doing? Emotionally as well as physically?"

"Good," she said. "The young are so resilient. She's actually back at swim practice and has been for a while. I persuaded her that no one was going to be upset at the way her face looked, and I was right. They were really glad to have her back."

"I have an idea. Laurie told me, that day when I dropped by with the roses, that you'd promised you'd take her to Mount Rainier when she recovered. Just read that the flowers are at their peak. How about if the three of us make a trip up to Paradise Sunday?"

"Oh, David, what a wonderful suggestion! It's a long way for one day, and I admit I wasn't looking forward to the Seattle traffic. My husband usually . . . well, actually, he always drove on our longer trips. What's the weatherman say?"

"More perfect weather."

"That sounds so good. Is the Inn open again? Last I knew, they were renovating it. I do hope they didn't spoil it. It was so special."

"Yes, it is. And we won't notice most of the changes. The biggest thing they did was retro-fit it for earthquake protection, I understand."

"Good. I'd suggested going there because, on our way up here from the airport, Laurie was so fascinated with the mountain. I think she was envisioning climbing it someday herself."

David chuckled. "I did climb it. When I was in college."

"I'm impressed. She'll want to know all about your experience."

"It's actually not that difficult a climb, if you're in shape, of course. A lot of plodding."

"Well, she'll think you've done something special. How about if I bring lunch?"

"I was thinking it'd be good to eat at the Inn. My treat."

"Oh, we'll both look forward to it. Sunday it is."

When Cynthia came on Friday, Paula again arranged to be in the kitchen while she was working there. "Wasn't this past weekend the one you were going to visit your daughter?" she asked, disingenuously. "Did you have a good visit?"

"Yes, we did," Cynthia said. "She's making so much progress. The Junior Nationals are coming up, and her coaches expect her to do well. It's conceivable that she'll qualify for the adult Nationals. We're *so* excited."

"Oh, that's good," Paula said, twiddling her fingers as she tried to work up her nerve to question her housekeeper. "I've been thinking. The police don't seem to be getting anywhere at all in finding the person who hit the kids. I'm afraid, since they weren't killed or hurt more seriously, that they're putting it on a back burner." She sighed. "You know so many people," she said, "what with all your activities and the houses you clean. May I ask, have you seen or heard anything at all that arouses your suspicions? Everybody seems so sure that people are being blackmailed."

Cynthia shrugged. "Of course I haven't. Nobody's going to tell me anything. You think somebody's going to announce that they're being blackmailed? Come on. Leave it to the police, Paula," she said. "It's their business, and they're equipped to investigate. You're not. As I told your granddaughter, asking questions can be dangerous."

"That's what Detective Compagnio keeps telling me," Paula

muttered, disappointed. Didn't Cynthia care that the murderer was still undiscovered?

CHAPTER NINETEEN

How on earth had August arrived so fast? Paula'd been leafing through the book *Altruistic Armadillos* she'd brought home from the library for Laurie. It was truly fascinating, but she found that she wasn't really concentrating as she waited for Laurie to arrive home from practice. Sighing, she shut the book and laid it on the table beside her.

The Pappases would be returning from their trip in just three and a half weeks. What on earth was she going to do? And why had she so shunted that fact out of her brain? Perhaps she'd had a good excuse for putting off decisions because of the stresses of the summer, but now it was crunch time.

One thing she knew. She had to sell her house in Bellevue. She needed to go there immediately, settle on a real estate agent and list her house. She had no pangs of regret at the thought. Mostly she was glad that she'd left the place in good order; nothing much would need to be done to make it available for showing. But even if a miracle occurred and an eager buyer showed up on her doorstep the first day, there was no way the house would sell, be appraised, and close before it was time for her to leave here.

She'd been alone long enough after Fred's death to find that she quite liked to live by herself. Any place, actually, would do. But that was before the arrival of Laurie. Now, it was . . . it was depressing to think of saying goodbye to her granddaughter and returning to a solitary existence. Especially knowing what sort of life Laurie would be returning to.

She swallowed and thought. What if . . . what if Laurie did *not* return to New York? What if Laurie stayed here, with a grandmother who adored her? The more she thought of it, the more excited she became.

She wouldn't hit Laurie with the idea right away but would lead up to it gradually. If she was at all interested, she could help her grandmother choose a new home, one suitable for both of them, one in a district with outstanding schools, one . . .

Whoa, she thought. She was getting ahead of herself. For one thing, there was Jennifer. Laurie obviously loved her mother, and for all Paula knew, she might be counting the days until they were both home in New York. Would it be fair to either to suggest Laurie stay in Washington? There were more issues than just the usual mother-daughter bond. For instance, Laurie had indicated that she'd done a lot of the managing of her household. Jennifer probably leaned on her.

On the other hand, Jennifer had rather strongly expressed the desire to "get on with her life." She might be relieved to no longer have the responsibility of raising a teenager. Given her last minute arrangements for sending Laurie to Washington for the summer, it appeared that Jennifer was as . . . as flighty, if that was the word, as she'd always been.

Suggesting her granddaughter remain here could be touchy, though, because if it weren't handled right, Laurie could feel rejected. Thirteen was not a good age for that to happen. Was she wrong to even consider suggesting Laurie stay?

"Gramma!"

Startled, Paula looked up to see Laurie at the top of the steps leading to the lawn below the deck.

"How come you didn't hear me the first time?"

Paula smiled. "I was thinking deep thoughts. Mulling over what a short time we have left in this house and that I'd better do something about it."

"Yeah, I'd figured that out."

Did Laurie look a touch sad? Yes, Paula decided. She refrained from smiling too obviously. She'd need to go about this slowly. "I was thinking that I need to make a trip to my old house and put it up for sale. Should have done it long ago."

"Where're you going to go, then?"

Paula sighed. "That's the question. I suppose that's why I've neglected to take action sooner. I certainly would not want to live at Kamiak Hills if they haven't caught the murderer, that's for sure. Maybe Cedar Harbor? It looked like a nice town when we went there for dinner. Might be worth exploring."

"Yeah, but you do have some friends here. Ellen and Doc and the detective. Do you know anybody up there?"

A mature comment, Paula thought. "Cedar Harbor isn't that far away. Also, I've always thought Edmonds looked nice. Maybe a condo on the water . . . I don't know, Laurie. This is the first time I've really sat down and thought about it. What I do plan to do, though, is go home and make arrangements to sell the house. I'm thinking I'll go tomorrow. I have nothing else planned. That is, if Ellen would . . ."

"Take me with you," Laurie interrupted. "I mean, I want to see where you lived so long, and I want to see where Mom grew up. It doesn't matter if I don't go to practice. Everybody misses some of the time."

"Well . . . I don't see why not," Paula said. "I'd enjoy your company."

Laurie beamed.

Laurie craned her neck as the sign on the freeway indicated that the next several exits were into Bellevue. It had only taken them about an hour to get here.

Paula said, "I forget sometimes what a big city this has

become. When Fred and I married, and we bought our house here, it was still more like a small town. Now I swear it has as many high-rises as Seattle. And look at this awful traffic." She slammed on the brakes as a Jaguar cut in front of her to exit. "If I had a car like that, I'd drive more sensibly."

Gramma *did* drive more sensibly. Always. If I had a car as cool at that one, Laurie thought, I probably wouldn't drive "sensibly" either. They followed the Jag off the freeway, and then turned left to head east.

"I made a call this morning before you were up to a real estate agent who I remembered sold a house in the next block quickly and efficiently." She glanced at her watch. "She'll meet us soon, so I won't take you on the scenic route."

"Is there a scenic route?" Laurie asked, glancing at the walls of cement.

"Oh, my, yes. There are some very lovely sections, with horse trails and parks and mansions. I mean, billionaires live along the lake front. Anyway, for Bellevue, my house is really quite ordinary."

A few minutes later as they drove into a driveway and parked, Laurie said, "Ordinary?"

Gramma almost looked guilty. She shrugged. "I knew it might appear impressive to you, but I'll show you impressive before we leave town." As they walked up the driveway, she studied the yard. "Well, the landscapers kept everything in good shape. Although they've trimmed the shrubbery more vigorously than I like. All those little round balls. Personally, I prefer a much more casual look." She shrugged. "What I like doesn't matter anymore."

She deactivated the alarm system, unlocked the front door, and gestured to Laurie to step inside.

"Wow," Laurie said, looking upwards at the open two-story entry hall.

Gramma peered outside. "Oh. Here comes the real estate lady. Why don't you look around, Laurie? Your mother's bedroom was the first on the left upstairs."

"Okay. I will." Slowly, she walked up the steps. How weird it was going to be to actually stand in the room her mother grew up in. She was only four years older than Laurie, nearer three, when she'd left this house and ran away. What an awful thought. Laurie couldn't imagine hating her parents enough to do that. Well, knowing Grandma, it had to be Mom's grandfather that she hated. She wished somebody'd tell her the whole story sometime.

Laurie realized she was actually shaking as she opened the bedroom door. It was almost like a ghost would be inside. Not a ghost—her mother was alive—but she definitely had a strange feeling as she stepped into the room.

Maybe it was because the room had to look like it had the last time her mother was in it. Like a . . . like a shrine, maybe. She walked over to the bulletin board above a desk. Pictures, lots of them. Kids, not much older than she was. There were several of one boy. Dark hair, and soulful eyes like her mother had mentioned. Maybe that's who she was thinking of whenever she'd said it.

And several newspaper articles. Peering closely, she was surprised to see her mother's name on the by-line. Jennifer Madigan. The articles were from a school paper, she could tell, reading them. One was about a school assembly, and several were about sports events. Mom said sometimes that she'd like to be a writer someday, but Laurie hadn't paid much attention. She'd heard the phrase "writers write," and Mom didn't.

The bedspread was lavender, and several pillows were stacked against the headboard. She ran a finger across the desk. No dust. Somebody had to come in here once in a while to take care of it. Gramma, she supposed, although maybe this summer while she was house-sitting, it was somebody she paid to do it.

Feeling guilty, she slid the closet door open. Clothes still hung there, ones that were way out of date. Gol. Had Mom actually worn *that?* Laurie opened a couple of drawers. They still had clothes in them, too. It was creepy, but sad, too, that the room had sat waiting all those years for Mom.

Voices sounded as Gramma and the real estate person walked up the stairs. Laurie shut the drawer she was looking at and hurriedly slid the closet door shut. Then she stepped into the hall.

"It's a lovely home," the lady was saying. "Should be easy to sell at the price we're talking about. Sure you don't want to ask more?"

"No," Gramma said. "Just want to move it as quickly as possible. "Oh, hi, Laurie. You found your—mother's room." She looked embarrassed.

"Yeah. Yeah, I did."

"It's in excellent condition," the lady said as she looked into another bedroom. "Are you wanting to move your things before I advertise it?"

"No. If you don't think it will deter lookers. I could put it all in storage. I'll have to anyway, as I don't know yet where I'm going. I think I told you I'm house-sitting up in Kamiak Hills."

The woman raised an eyebrow. "No problem. That won't be necessary. Happens often, when a seller is transferred or something."

Questions were boiling inside Laurie, but she decided to wait until later, maybe on the way home, to ask them.

The real estate lady took them out to lunch in a classy restaurant. Laurie'd never eaten in one like it before. White cloths covered the tables, and the waiter was dressed like he was going somewhere important, like a wedding. Laurie'd never had anyone pull out the chair and then push it in as she sat. She tried not to look impressed, but it was hard, especially when the waiter shook out the huge white napkin and spread it on her lap. There was even a woman sitting on a platform like a little stage and playing a violin.

Gramma had to order for her because there wasn't anything on the menu she'd ever heard of. Laurie wasn't sure about the salad when it came, all alone except for the rolls. It was almost too pretty to eat, but there really wasn't much to it. When their main courses came, the food on the plates looked skimpy. With what their lunches had cost, she'd have thought there'd be enough food to take home a doggy bag. Although . . . somehow she suspected people didn't ask for one in a fancy place like this.

Gramma and the lady talked about Bellevue and how it'd grown, and the price of real estate and things like that. Laurie really wasn't interested except when they talked about how much they were going to ask for the house. It was more money than she could ever imagine. She and her mother could live the rest of their lives on that.

They stopped at the woman's office where Gramma signed papers, and then the lady dropped them off at the house. "Now what?" Laurie asked, after they walked in the door and Gramma just stood there, sort of looking around. Maybe she minded leaving more than she'd thought she would.

"There are a few items I should take," she finally said. "The things in the safe . . ."

"Safe?" Laurie knew her voice squeaked. "In a house?"

Gramma shrugged. "Just a little one. Most people have one for important papers and jewelry and such. It's fireproof, so everything should survive in the unlikely event the house burned. I'll clear it out now."

Laurie toddled along behind her grandmother, who went into what must have been the master bedroom. The room was sort of blah, Laurie thought. A huge bed, covered with a beige quilted spread, some sheer curtains over the windows so you couldn't look outside, and beige drapes that could be pulled over it at night, she assumed. Not a room anyone would want to spend much time in.

The safe was behind a picture of a sailboat on what was probably Puget Sound. Grandma laid it on the bed, then turned back to take several small boxes out of the safe. Laurie studied the picture. She liked it. You could almost feel the breeze ruffling up the water, and the boat leaned sideways as it stirred up a wake. In the background were some of the mountains Laurie had seen across the sound. Behind her, Gramma shut the safe and then reached for the picture.

"Aren't you going to keep it?" Laurie asked.

Startled, Gramma raised here eyebrows. "You like it? You could certainly have it for your own if you want."

"Yes. I would. It would . . . remind me of Washington when I get back home."

Why did Gramma look so disappointed? She handed the picture to Laurie, then picked up the several boxes she'd taken from the safe, leaving it open.

Gramma put a few more things in the car. Her golf clubs. Two suitcases she'd filled with clothes. "I'll need these," she'd said, "when the weather turns in September. This should tide me over until I actually have a place to move in. Climb in. I'll take you on a quick tour. We need to get out of town before the rush hour. It's really horrendous here."

Gramma'd been right. Bellevue did have a lot of houses that were bigger and fancier than hers. Laurie didn't like them. Why would anyone want a huge ugly house? The ones near the horse trails were nice, though. That'd be neat. She'd never thought about wanting a horse like some of her friends did, but watching several girls heading out on the trail made her think that it could be fun.

On the way home, Laurie nerved herself to ask some questions. "Uh . . . Gramma, why don't you or my mother ever talk about why she left home? And your . . . Mom's father. Was he that awful?"

Gramma was quiet for a long time, and Laurie was afraid she wasn't going to answer. Finally, though, she did.

"I suppose you should know. You're old enough. What happened, basically, is that your mother and your grandfather never did get along. I swear it was from the moment she was born. I can still picture her scrunched-up red face as she bellowed when he held her. He'd thrust her at me with a disgusted look. And never once, of course, did the thought ever cross his mind that he could change a diaper.

"Jennifer was always . . . very independent. Fred, however, had grown up in a household where the men made all the decisions and nobody questioned the 'head of the household.' "

Laurie could hear the quotes around the phrase.

"Neither did I. I've changed a lot this summer, Laurie. It's been good for me."

"Well, what made you change?"

Gramma's fingers drummed the steering wheel, and Laurie sat, holding her breath, hoping she'd keep talking.

Finally she did, and when she did, she talked fast. "I thought Jennifer had never contacted us again after she left. As it turns out . . . your mother *had* written. Fred never told me. I knew nothing about what had happened to Jennifer until she called that day in June. It seems that Fred intercepted all her letters. When I found out, especially when I found out about you and that he'd denied me the opportunity to hold you, to enjoy having a granddaughter, that I . . . Well, I shouldn't say it, but I now hate the man. I regret every year I spent with him."

"Gol, Grandma," Laurie said. "Is that why you never changed

Mom's room in all those years?"

Grandma nodded. "I kept hoping she'd come home."

CHAPTER TWENTY

Narrowing down her search for a new home was not going to be simple, Paula realized as she worked her way through the newspaper real-estate ads as well as those in several booklets she'd picked up. This was, after all, the only time in her life she'd been in this position. She'd toured houses with Fred when they were picking the one they'd ended up living in for their entire marriage. But choose? She didn't recall even being consulted. She'd merely tagged along, one step behind her domineering husband.

She did enjoy the deck on the backside of the Pappas home, where she'd again settled on a striped chaise under the umbrella while Laurie was at afternoon swim practice. The deck made it possible to be outdoors so much more during the warm days of summer. In Bellevue, she'd have likely been in the study. She'd definitely add that to the list of desired features she presented to the real estate agents.

The house should have character, she determined, and not be a clone of those in its neighborhood. Perhaps, she thought, waterfront would be nice. Expensive, of course, but what else did she have to spend the substantial funds she'd been left after Fred's death? She'd always enjoyed the trips they'd taken with friends on their yachts and several vacations she remembered, especially Rosario Beach Lodge on Orcas Island and Kalaloch on the ocean. How much more pleasant it would be to face the water instead of the busy and sometimes obtrusive golf course.

It might be fun, albeit nerve-wracking, to pick a new home that suited her and no one else. Except, possibly, one that would also be suitable for Laurie, should that work out. Her heart thumped at the thought.

Edmonds appeared to be the most expensive of the three places she'd mentioned as possibilities to Laurie. But that didn't matter, she again reminded herself. Next week she'd look into the school situation at all three towns, just in case. Newspaper ads were now showing back-to-school items to entice kids and remind their parents that shopping expeditions were in order. What fun it would be to outfit Laurie.

"Gramma!" Laurie shouted as she steered the golf cart into its parking place. "We've got news!"

Startled, Paula dropped the newspaper and lifted her head. Laurie's face was flushed and she was grinning as she hurried onto the deck. Josh hobbled as close behind her as he could manage on his crutches. "You're not going to believe this! They know who killed Babs Griffin!"

"You're kidding! How'd they . . . ?"

"It was Cynthia who figured it out!"

Paula was stunned. How could this be, after what the cleaning lady had said just last week. And she hadn't given an inkling yesterday that anything was up. "Well, who was it? And how? I mean, how did she figure it out?"

"It was Babs's husband! Cynthia was there cleaning, and she noticed that Babs's favorite club was missing from her bag. A jumbo driver. And somebody'd put another one in that didn't match. Cynthia thought it was suspicious that Edward hadn't noticed and called the police since Babs was killed by having her head bashed in. When the police got there and started asking questions, he broke down crying. He didn't mean to do it, he told them. She'd just ridiculed him one time too many. Josh heard one of the ladies at the pool say . . ." Laurie smirked as she spoke. ". . . that she'd insulted him about his love-making. She said that his you-know-what was too small!"

"Laurie!" Gramma was horrified. "That's—not something to discuss in front of . . . Good heavens! Didn't they think about the fact that Josh was sitting there? Whatever were they . . ."

Josh shrugged. "I always sit a couple of rows behind them, and they don't even notice me anymore, I guess. They sounded like a bunch of crows. You know."

"Yes, but . . ." Paula winced as she pictured Josh and Laurie discussing the length of a neighbor's penis. The world had changed more than she could ever have imagined.

"But . . . but . . ." she sputtered, "does that mean he was the one who hit you two?"

"I don't know. Guess you'll have to ask your boyfriend."

"Laurie, I don't have a boyfriend! I've told you that."

Laurie shrugged. "Tell that to the detective," she said. "I've seen the way he looks at you. He and the doc, too, when he gets a chance. I know what guys look like when they want to get into somebody's pants, Gramma. There've been enough of them hanging around Mom."

"Stop it. You're being gross, Laurie. I don't want to hear language like that, especially from a thirteen-year-old who isn't dry behind her ears."

Laurie sniffed and tossed her head. "Just thought you'd like to know what's going on. Come on, Josh, let's go tell your mother."

Would Jack call? Paula wondered. From what she'd heard about police work, he must be swamped with all the details of arresting someone, dealing with lawyers and filling out paperwork. She wouldn't bother him, she decided.

As she hoped, though, he phoned in late afternoon. "You've heard about the arrest?" he inquired.

"I imagine everyone between here and Seattle has. Laurie's hovering in front of the TV, assuming it will be on the news."

"I'm sure it will be. The newspaper ghouls were on our backs within, I swear, minutes. I shouldn't say that. It's their job, of course, and this is especially newsworthy for having occurred in a neighborhood like yours. I was wondering if I might drop by this evening and update you."

"Oh, that's so good of you," Paula said. "I know. If you're able to get away, why don't you join us for dinner? I have a nice roast in the oven and baked potatoes . . ."

"That sounds so much better than the fast food I'd have stopped for. I couldn't make it before six-thirty, but if that's okay . . . ?"

"Certainly. We'll expect you."

The local news was coming on as Paula entered the living room. She didn't speak, just stood behind Laurie with her hand on her shoulder as both watched the two commentators, somber-faced, relating the story. "Police appear to have solved the series of murders in the upscale neighborhood of Kamiak Hills north of Seattle with an arrest today. We take you to the scene."

Laurie was staring avidly, and Paula, to her chagrin, found herself doing so also. A buxom young woman with a microphone in her hand stood in front of the Griffin house. "Police today made an arrest at the home behind us of Edward Griffin, a Seattle banker." Her voice sounded shocked that anyone with a position such as his could be a murderer. "Residents who have been appalled at the series of golf-course murders here will surely sleep better tonight knowing he has been apprehended."

Why, Paula wondered, did the news channels think that a picture of an empty house was newsworthy? Still, she had to admit, there was something sad about its facade. "As well as the three victims actually found on the golf course, a hit-and-run that seriously injured two local teenagers is thought to be related."

The television switched back to the main studio. Laurie sniffed. "They could have given our names."

"They did when it happened."

"Gramma! You didn't tell me. You could have taped it!"

"Laurie, I had many things on my plate without worrying about something like that. Like if you were going to survive."

She tossed her head. "Probably be the only time I'll ever be mentioned on TV."

"I hope so. Unless you do something wonderful."

Laurie's face brightened. "Like write a famous book? Or maybe I'll be acting in a movie?"

Paula put her hand to her forehead. Oh, Lordy, Lordy.

Then she remembered what she'd come in to say. "Jack's going to join us for dinner. I do hope you'll be a little more circumspect with your language than you were earlier, Laurie. Just listen to what he has to say. I'm grateful, I have to admit, that he's taking the time to update us."

"I'll behave," Laurie said. "I promise."

The detective was beat. He looked a lot older, somehow, Laurie thought as she opened the door. Bags under his eyes; saggy jowls. "Come on in," she said, stepping back. "Grandma's just slicing the roast, and her hands are all goopy."

"Nice of you to have me," he said. He held out his own empty hands. "Wanted to bring something, but I was running so late . . ."

"That's okay," Laurie said. "Grandma won't care. She's just excited to hear about you arresting that banker. I never met him, but everybody kind of feels sorry for him. Guess his wife could really get to him, the way she criticized him and all."

"Laurie," Grandma said as she came down the hall, wiping

her hands on a towel, "don't keep the detective waiting in the doorway. Good evening, Jack. Thanks for coming."

"Oh. Sorry." Laurie stepped back. "Come on in."

Now his face lightened as he stepped forward. He definitely had a thing for Gramma. It was kind of cute, actually.

"Sorry I'm late. Thought of picking up some wine, but I figured you wouldn't want to spoil the dinner waiting for me."

"Absolutely." She took his hand. "It's so good of you to come."

"What didja find out about the other murders?" Laurie asked. "Did he . . . ?"

"Laurie! Let Jack have a break for a bit before you question him. How about we have dinner first? We set it up in the kitchen. No formality tonight."

"That's great," the detective said.

"Would you care for a glass of wine while I finish preparations? I have a nice Chardonnay."

"Sounds wonderful. Just one. Otherwise, I think I'd fall asleep on your sofa."

Laurie wondered how Gramma could stand to wait all that time to find out the details, but she helped by pouring the wine. She'd already set the table, and it looked nice. She'd used the good china and glassware, and put the violets Alice had given them in the center.

"Haven't been keeping regular hours while this is going on," he said. "I must be getting old. Long days didn't used to get to me like this."

"Of course you're not old. But you're not twenty anymore, either. How did you happen to get into police work, anyway?" Gramma asked.

"Pretty much the usual way for someone my age," he said. "Vietnam, where I ended up in military police." He swallowed some wine. "My wife didn't much like the man who came home, and she left me."

"Oh, I'm sorry to . . ."

He waved away Gramma's sympathy. "It was for the best. And a long time ago. Anyway, I'd had some college before I got drafted, so I went back with a major in police science. When I graduated, there was an opening here, and . . ." He shrugged. "Could have ended up in worse places. At least it's not inner city. I'd had enough violence in the war." He sipped some more wine. "Never expected a series of crimes like you've been having here."

"No, I'm sure you didn't."

Laurie ate fast, hoping Gramma and Jack would, too. But they didn't. They chatted about their families and where they'd gone to school and all that stuff. Finally, though, Gramma suggested, "Shall we have our coffee in the living room?" and then things got moving.

After they got settled, Gramma said, "It must feel good to find the murderer. I never expected Cynthia to be the one who'd help you solve it. She was so adamant that we all should stay out of it."

"There's a difference between butting in and informing the police when one has useful information," he said.

Sounded like he was criticizing Gramma for the times she hadn't, but she didn't seem to notice.

"And she handled it correctly. Came to us and let us confront him, rather than accusing him herself. Might have been a drastically different outcome had she done that. Yes, we're grateful to Mrs. Lamphear. But . . ." He frowned.

"But what?" Gramma asked.

"There is one more thing I wanted to tell you," the detective said. "Were you aware that the Griffins had only one car, and it's a red sedan?"

"Well, that tears it," Gramma said.

They were all quiet for a minute, thinking. The detective hadn't come right out and said it, so Laurie did. "What you're telling us is I still have to look over my shoulder every time I go out, and Gramma won't want me to go anyplace alone. You're saying the murderer's still out there someplace, somebody who might kill again. Maybe me. Maybe Josh."

The detective nodded. "You've got it. That's exactly what I'm saying, although we haven't notified the newspapers. It'll probably be necessary, though. That's up to the chief. Yeah, Laurie. We don't know of anyone else specifically who might be in danger, but you and Josh need to be extremely vigilant. Whoever it is must continue to wonder if one of you is going to remember something that will lead us to him. Or her.

"And," he added, "we can't even be positive that the hit-and-run driver *was* the murderer. You kids may have gotten too close to someone else's secret."

"Oh," Grandma said. "I hadn't thought of that. Oh, I so wish you two had paid attention to all the warnings people gave you about the dangers of snooping."

"So do I, Grandma. So do I."

CHAPTER TWENTY-ONE

"Oh, wow! Are those really trees?" Laurie had her nose pressed against the glass in the back seat of David's car, Paula saw as she glanced over her shoulder.

They'd entered Mount Rainier National Park just moments before. The trees *were* impressive, even though she'd seen them many times before. "They're pretty special, aren't they?" she replied. "But there are even bigger ones in other national parks. Spruce in the Olympics, and redwoods down in Northern California. Someday I'd like to show them to you."

David's eyes twinkled as he looked at her. It *was* fun traveling with someone Laurie's age who grew excited at things that Washingtonians took for granted.

"How old are they?" Laurie asked.

"Oh, I think, something like a thousand years. When we go into the Visitor Center at Paradise, you can ask a ranger."

They passed through Longmire, park headquarters, but didn't stop. They couldn't see everything in a one-day trip. "Let's take the Stevens Canyon-Cayuse Pass route home, shall we?" David suggested.

"Good idea."

They'd entered the switchbacks that led to Paradise and finally pulled into the parking lot. It was full, not unexpected on a Sunday in August. But Paula let David worry about finding a place to park, and after about ten minutes of circling they got lucky and were able to slip into a spot being vacated by a car.

Laurie was quiet now as she unbuckled her seat belt and stepped out onto the asphalt. She stared upward. It was clear she was speechless for the moment.

Paula understood. The mountain really was special. "Believe it or not," she said, "the summit's still almost ten thousand feet above us. And we're actually a mile high here."

Laurie didn't answer, and Paula turned to see that she'd headed over to a group who were obviously preparing to make the climb. The four men and a woman were surrounded with gear and were stuffing sleeping bags into packs, filling water bottles at a nearby fountain, and pulling on cumbersome boots. She and David followed.

"What're those for?" Laurie asked, pointing.

"These?" one of the men answered. "Oh, they're called crampons. We put them on over our boots to get a good grip when we're on the ice."

The man probably had kids at home, Paula surmised as he patiently pointed out the route they'd take up the mountain and showed Laurie his ice axe. "We'll stay at Camp Muir tonight." He chuckled. "If you can call it a night, when we'll be on our way by two A.M."

"Oh, wow," Laurie said.

"There's a telescope at the Visitor Center," he said. "You can follow the climbers who are on the mountain today."

"Thank you," Paula said. "We will." They watched as the group loaded their enormous packs and headed over to the trail. She took a deep breath, then exhaled. "I'd forgotten how wonderful the air smells here. It's so . . . fresh and pure."

"And thin."

She chuckled. "That, too. You were right, David, the flowers *are* at their best."

"Who planted them?" Laurie asked.

David and Paula both laughed. "Lots of people ask that," David said. "But you could say God planted 'em. Let's walk up the trail a ways. Those red ones," he said, pointing, "are called Indian paint brush and the blue are lupine. If we went high enough to hit snow patches, there'd probably still be alpine or avalanche lilies popping right through the snow."

A female ranger leading a small group of people came down the trail toward them. She was dressed in a dark-greenish uniform, badge on breast, and her Smokey Bear hat sat squarely on her curly dark hair. "Maybe I'll be a ranger," Laurie said, turning to watch the group as they descended.

"You could be," Paula answered, smiling. "Or, while you're in college, you could come up here in the summer and work for the Park Company, either in a restaurant or the souvenir shop. Some of my friends did that, and one actually married a ranger." She herself had briefly considered the possibility of a summer at the mountain, but her parents had curtailed any thought of that immediately. How much she'd missed in life, she mused.

A piercing whistle drew their attention to a nearby gigantic boulder, where a large, fat brown rodent with prominent front teeth sprawled. As they watched, it slithered down and hustled toward them. Laurie clutched at Paula, until it stopped, sat up, and begged.

"Oh! Do we have something to give it? What is it?" Laurie asked.

"A marmot," David answered. "Whistling marmot, folks call it. They communicate with each other that way. Probably telling their friends, 'Here come some suckers!' And no, we wouldn't feed it even if we had something. The rangers say it's a bad idea. Animals who're fed can lose the ability to fend for themselves.

"Speaking of food, are we ready for lunch?" David asked.

"Yeah, I'm starved," Laurie answered. "Let's eat!"

Paula chuckled. She had to admit that she, too, was ready to eat.

"Oh, man," Laurie said as they entered the Paradise Inn through its French doors. "They made this thing out of whole logs. You could roast a cow in that fireplace!"

"They mostly dismantled it to retro-fit for earthquakes. You wouldn't know it had been redone," David said. "I read that they actually numbered the stones in the fireplace before they took it apart, rock by rock, so it would be exactly the same when they finished the work. The building's on the National Historic Register."

They had to wait a bit but finally were seated in the dining room and then enjoyed a fabulous meal. "This was a real treat," Paula said, after they finished. She put a hand on his. "Thanks so much, David, for suggesting this trip, and for the lunch."

David beamed. "My pleasure." After paying, he escorted them out through the French doors. "Shall we go over to the Visitor Center now?" he suggested.

"Sure," Laurie said. "I want to watch the climbers."

They had to wait their turn, but finally Laurie was able to press her eye to the telescope. "They're going awfully slow," she said.

"You would, too, if you were up there. The air's really thin," David explained. "You can't go fast when you don't have enough oxygen."

Didn't look like fun, was Paula's opinion when she took her turn. Standing on top of the mountain must make the climb worthwhile.

"What do they do when they have to go to the bathroom?" Laurie asked.

David laughed. "I don't think you really want to know."

Paula was tired by the time they loaded themselves into the car to return home. Laurie managed to stay awake through

Stevens Canyon, but then fell asleep. That's what the fresh mountain air did to people, Paula thought.

She was almost dozing herself when David spoke. "It's awfully late to ask you, but are you free tomorrow evening, by chance? I've decided to go to a party at an associate's home that I'd planned to skip. But I'm thinking it would be fun if you were with me. I know you've been sticking around Laurie, but I thought maybe now that an arrest has been made . . ."

"Well, actually . . ." As far as she knew, the police had not publicly announced that they weren't satisfied the attacks had been solved. Jack had been really forthcoming when he'd shared information with her. But then it occurred to her that Laurie had plans to go to a soccer game tomorrow evening with the Cogsdills. "Yes, I'd love to go with you, David."

"How would you like to go look at a few houses with me today?" Paula asked Laurie at breakfast.

"Sure. When?"

"As soon as you get home from the pool. Don't dally. I thought we'd hit Cedar Harbor first. We can have lunch in that great restaurant." She hesitated. She'd planned the expedition as she lay in bed the night before. It would be a full day, but rewarding, she hoped. "I'm going to a party with David this evening, and—"

"Cool," Laurie interrupted.

"Well, yes. I guess it is. It's going to be a busy day, though. I'll probably be leaving with David for the party a bit before you get home this afternoon. I don't like to leave you alone, but since you're going to that soccer match this evening, I figured it'd be okay."

"I *am* capable of taking care of myself."

"I know that, Laurie. It's just that . . . I still worry. Until they catch the person who hit you and Josh . . ." She sighed. "I've said that so many times. It's getting really old."

"Yeah, I know. I haven't forgotten. I won't do anything you wouldn't want me to, Grandma," Laurie said with that impudent grin she used so often.

Cocky, Paula thought. Perhaps too much so?

Cedar Harbor, with its small-town atmosphere, looked appealing as a future home. There was a mix of condos, middle-class homes, and a few McMansions. Not many, which was good. Yards were well-tended and businesses that lined the main street appeared to be thriving, even though there was a mall out on the freeway. A happy family carrying buckets and beach paraphernalia appeared at the head of steps leading from the pier at the end of the main street as Laurie and Paula walked into the Cedar Harbor Inn for an early lunch. They were seated immediately and were lucky enough to be given a window booth. Gulls floated over the water, occasionally swooping down for a tidbit. The time went by quickly, and Paula almost felt guilty as she hustled Laurie along.

The agency Paula had chosen at random turned out to be only a half block away. The realtor, Betty Anderson, greeted them with a warm smile when they walked in. She was attractive, well-dressed, and, it quickly became apparent, knowledgeable.

"I'd like you to meet my granddaughter Laurie. She's visiting me for the summer," Paula said.

"Hi. Great to meet you." Betty held out her hand.

"Uh . . . great to meet you, too," Laurie responded, taking the proffered hand.

Good. Paula'd had the impression Laurie's manners had been improving over the summer, and her action did confirm that.

"You'll be living alone, then?" Betty asked.

"Um, probably," Paula said, with a sideways glance at Laurie, whose face didn't indicate a reaction to the question. She must have heard it. What was she thinking?

"Well, I've made a list," Betty said. "We'll take a quick look at the four or five I think would most likely suit you." And then she went on to describe them at a greater length than Paula thought advisable, given their time table.

Glancing at her watch, Paula said, "Shouldn't we just go see them? I'm sure I'll be able to narrow the choice down."

"Oh. Certainly. As I said, they vary in price a good deal, and . . ."

Paula interrupted, "I think we'd better go. Price isn't a consideration. I'll have no trouble with financing." The woman really was garrulous.

Betty perked up when she heard that. She would, no doubt, be in line for a substantial commission should Paula choose a home in Cedar Harbor. "Certainly," she said, picking up her purse. "We'll go to the nearest one . . ." She kept talking as she led them out to her car.

The first two houses Betty showed them were okay; nice actually, but uninspiring. Laurie began to lag behind, and as they came to the third, she glanced at it quickly, then said, "I'll wait here."

Paula felt like doing the same, but she dutifully followed Betty through the front door. That was enough. A flight of stairs led to the upper story, and the layout was traditional, with the living room looking out on the rather busy street. "No, I can see right away that this wouldn't do."

It was discouraging, she thought as they drove away. Next week they'd try Edmonds. Betty must be discouraged, too, as she was no longer talking. "Tell me more about the community," Paula suggested, trying to be pleasant.

"Oh, it's a delightful place to live," Betty said. "Everything anyone could need. Several churches, an active historical society. They're working on funding a museum that can also serve local functions. We love the fact that we have small-town America but can reach Seattle easily for events there. And we do have a new police chief. Everyone's so pleased at his appointment."

An odd thing to mention, Paula thought. Betty had avoided looking at her as she said it. "How so?" Paula asked.

"Well, since you've lived locally, you may recall hearing about the two murders that occurred recently, including the death of our long-standing police chief. But serious crime is extremely rare, I assure you," the woman said quickly and firmly. "However, you did say you've been spending the summer at Kamiak Hills? So you know how these rare events can occur, even in a good community?"

"Indeed I do," Paula said, hoping Laurie wasn't listening. "But let's talk about . . ."

"We sure do," Laurie said. "I was in the hospital after that hit-and-run, and . . ."

"Oh, you poor dear," Betty said, her expression horrified as she swung her head toward Laurie.

"Uh . . ." Paula said as the car swerved.

"Oh. Sorry. Well, there's one more place I hope you have time to look at. I know your schedule is tight, but I've saved what I think is best for last."

Paula glanced at her watch. "A quick look."

Sally turned into a lane that led through a forest of maples and second-growth firs. "Oh," Paula said as the house came into view. It was what people called Northwest style, built of cedar and with a roof that peaked over what she assumed was the living room.

"Let's go this way," Sally said, leading them around the house and onto an expansive deck. She did her thing with the lock, and they stepped inside. Large windows faced Puget Sound, where a green-and-white ferry plowed through the water on its way to Seattle. Mount Constance and the Brothers, with a few puffy clouds near their summits, dominated the skyline across the Sound. Turning, Paula saw that the house really wasn't large; the kitchen and dining area were separated from the living room by low dividers

"The only thing is," Sally said, "it's medium bluff. Doesn't have a way to reach the beach at present. Could be done, though. Either stairs or an elevator. And of course, we have access in several places, including the downtown dock."

Paula again glanced at her watch. Too bad they didn't have more time. "We do need to hurry. Can we just take a quick look? Laurie?"

She realized Laurie had gone ahead down the hall to the left and bedroom wing. She found her standing in the doorway of the first. "Oh, wow," she said. "Even the bedrooms have a view. It would be so neat . . ." She flushed and stopped talking.

"Yes. It would. But we really do need to go today."

Betty was uncharacteristically quiet until they'd almost reached the agency and Paula's Toyota. "Well, that's probably the best I have to offer, but I can review the listings and get back to you."

Paula smiled. "Why don't you work up some details on the last house for me, and I'll call you next week. I have a few other things I want to look into."

Betty brightened. "Oh. Well, certainly."

Paula was quite taken with the place, but first she'd like to check the schools and possibly broach the subject of Laurie staying with her. That was going to be difficult. She didn't have much practice in dealing with issues.

Paula found herself picturing life in the house in Cedar Harbor as she carefully wrote a note to Laurie with instructions for the evening. The place would suit her, she was becoming increasingly sure. It was a good size for a person living alone. Even if Laurie did move in with her—and she was hopeful that that would occur—Laurie was only five years from leaving for college, so Paula would inevitably be alone again soon.

Stop getting distracted, she told herself. She needed to concentrate on her writing. The Cogsdills would no doubt have been willing to include Laurie for dinner tonight, but they'd fed her and transported her enough that Paula had begun to feel like she was taking advantage. Laurie had to come home to change after swimming, and she might as well feed herself, then join Josh and his family for the evening. Paula finished the note with the admonishment, "KEEP THE DOOR LOCKED," then went to prepare for her evening out.

Her rose-colored silk dress, she decided. She always felt almost pretty when she wore it. When David arrived to pick her up, her decision was validated by the look on his face. She turned her head, trying to hide the blush that enveloped her.

She'd done everything she could to prepare for the evening, both for herself and for Laurie, but still, as she locked the door behind her, she shivered in trepidation. When would she be able to get over this nervous stirring of her innards? When they caught the murderer; that was when, or, barring that, when they moved away. Or maybe, maybe she never would again be confident that the world was a safe place for Laurie.

While they were looking at the house today, she'd gotten the definite impression that Laurie *would* like to stay with her. If that should work out, Paula thought, would she be able to overcome her fears and not overwhelm Laurie with her caution?

Josh reported on the gossip of the mothers at swimming practice as Laurie steered the cart homeward. "I was bored out of my mind. They were so totally excited because the murderer had been caught, those that came. Guess the rest thought it was safe to stay home now. I sure had a tough time not telling them what you found out last night from the detective. That was heck'a cool of him to tell you."

"Yeah, it was. Hey, you better pull that crutch inside." Josh wasn't paying attention. A tree, the first of a row of those skinny tall ones, loomed ahead on the right.

"Oh. Yeah." He jerked the crutch into the cart. "The doc says I can get off them next week."

"Great."

They pulled up in back of the Cogsdill house. "You still don't remember what it was you thought you should from that night when we were hit, do you?"

"No, I don't. And it really bugs me." Laurie chewed her lip. "Jack says Cynthia can't be the murderer, and I'm glad, I guess. I mean, she's an okay lady and it'd be really hard to think of her killing someone. But I've looked at every silver-colored car I'm anywhere near. Except Cynthia's. Why would she never drive that car everybody says she's so proud of?" Laurie thought for a moment, then added, "Doesn't make sense."

Josh hopped out and put his crutches under his armpits.

"Do you know where she lives?" Laurie asked.

"Sure," he said, giving her the eye. "It's one street over from us, and up about a block. It has green shutters."

"Gramma and I should drive by there once in a while. Maybe we could get a chance to see the car some time."

"What difference does it make?" Josh asked. "The police have cleared her."

Laurie couldn't exactly put into words why she was still bothered that Cynthia seemed to be hiding the car. Why? What possible reason could she have?

"I don't know," she answered. "What if . . ." The thought came to her suddenly. "What if the police made a mistake?"

"Ah, come on, Laurie. They don't goof things like that."

Laurie shrugged

Josh looked at her skeptically. "You're not thinking of doing anything dumb, are you?"

"Do I ever?"

He raised his eyebrows.

"Josh!" his mom called from their deck. "You've got a phone call. It's Mark Severan."

"Okay, be right in." He raised himself onto his crutches and hurried up the stairs, then called over his shoulder, "See ya in a little while."

He really was amazing on those things, Laurie thought as she steered the cart toward the Pappas house and slowed. But then, after glancing over her shoulder to be sure Josh hadn't lingered outside, she kept going, swinging around the far side of the house. She'd had an idea.

Yeah, Josh might think it was being dumb . . . but why shouldn't she just check Cynthia's house? She might even get lucky and find that car parked in front. Driving over there should be okay. It was still broad daylight, and she waved at a woman who was getting out of her car two houses farther on. Other people were fussing in their yards. She crossed the street, then headed up the next one.

There, on a little hill, was a stucco house just like all the rest of them here at Kamiak, with a tile roof and geraniums. Seemed like most everybody had the same flowers. If this was where she lived, she'd have planted something else. She didn't know what. Something a different color, anyway. Maybe that was why Cynthia had picked green for her shutters; she didn't want to be like everyone else.

The house looked empty as she drove up to it; she didn't know why. She could see into the front room, and there were no lights on, no flicker from the TV. No car in front of the house.

The garage must be in back, like some of the places around here. She drove on past the house, then turned at the next corner. Yes! There was an alley. She steered into it, counting the houses on her left. Cynthia's would be the third.

Shrubby bushes lined the alley behind most of the yards. She slowed, peering through the leaves. This *was* the right house. The only one with green shutters. She eyed the bushes, hesitated for just a few seconds, then eased the cart next to them and parked, with the cart scrunched next to the largest shrub. Pulling a branch aside, she could see the garage. And the garage had a window.

Her heart was pounding, like when Coach Sorry had them sprint in the pool. No one would see her here. The houses on the other side of the alley all had shrubs lining the alley, too.

Slowly, Laurie slid over and climbed out of the passenger side of the cart. Parting the shrubs, she eased through the gap, wincing when a branch scratched her, then tiptoed toward the garage. That was silly, she knew. It just felt . . . safer. Even the garage had green shutters, she noticed.

Leaning toward the window, she put up her hands to shut out the daylight behind her. Her heart jumped. Cynthia's car *was* there. It was a really big one, though, but like every other car, it . . .

"Oh my Gawd." Her gaze had reached the front end. She knew, instantly, that this was *the* car, the one that had hit her and Josh. It was that star-shaped thingie on the front of the hood. That's what had been buried in her memory and had made her think of flashing stars. The streetlights shining on it that awful time must have caused her to have all those nightmares. She had to tell Gramma . . .

She whipped around—and there, standing with arms folded, was Cynthia.

"See something interesting?" she asked.

Chapter Twenty-Two

Laurie cringed but tried to hide it as her mind whirled. How was she going to get out of this? What could she say so that Cynthia wouldn't know she'd recognized the car? Stalling, she put her hand to her breast and said, "Oh! You scared me. I . . . I just wanted to get a look at your car. It was . . . I mean, I knew you . . . Why aren't you driving your car these days, Cynthia?" She attempted a smile, but she knew the effort was feeble.

"What business is it or yours, girlie?"

Laurie hated to be called that. "Well. I guess you didn't know that I think—I thought the car that hit us, Josh and me, was silver colored, and . . ." She shrugged.

"And? You wanted to look at mine?"

"Well, sure. Wouldn't you?" She gulped. "But obviously, it wasn't yours. I mean, I thought—think I'll know if I see the car that it was. But it isn't. I mean . . ." She knew she was babbling. "I'm sorry, Cynthia. I shouldn't have snuck into your yard. I'm glad . . . I'm glad it wasn't your car." She had to swallow rising vomit to get that lie out. Would it work?

Cynthia stared at her, no longer smiling. Then she said, "I'll have to have words with your grandmother about this. It just won't do."

"I know. I mean, I'm really, *really* sorry!"

"Get along with you." Cynthia flapped her hand toward the hidden cart. "Go home. I'll be talking to Paula in the morning."

Laurie scooted, but stopped and turned. "Howd'ja know I

was here?" she asked curiously.

"I saw you go by in your cart from my kitchen window. You were staring at the house." She shrugged. "Thought I'd keep an eye on what you were up to. And it was a good thing I did. Your grandmother is not going to be happy with you, Laurie."

"I know. I'm sorry," she said once again. Then she ducked through the bushes. Had she said it too many times?

Laurie pushed the cart to its limits. Could she get home before Gramma left for her party? She whizzed around the corner, if you could call it whizzing in a cart, and was back at the Pappas house as fast as she could make it. Stopping in front, she ran to the front door. It was locked. She rang the doorbell. "Please, God, don't let her be gone," she prayed.

No one answered, neither Gramma nor God. She was crying now, but she managed to get back into the cart and drive it around to park it in its cubbyhole, plug it in, and lock the door behind it.

Taking the hide-away key from its nail under the deck, she went into the kitchen. Still hopeful, she called, "Gramma?" No answer.

Then she saw the note. *"Dear Laurie, There's soup in the pan on the stove, and buttered baguettes in the microwave. Heat for twenty secs. And there's pie in the refrig. I won't be late. Just be sure to lock up the house when you leave with the Cogsdills. Have a good time at the soccer match! Love, Gramma. P.S. Carioca hasn't come in, so I didn't put the cat's food out or Mum-mum would have eaten it all. Hopefully, Carioca will show up before you leave. Lock the cat door, so we know they're both taken care of, please."*

Laurie gulped. Why couldn't Gramma have been home? Now what should she do? "I need you, Gramma," she wailed.

Should she call Jack? He'd be home, wherever that was. Would he believe her? Should she tell Josh and Ellen? She wanted Gramma here. She wanted Gramma to take over!

Would anyone believe her?

And Josh. The last thing he'd said was, "Don't do anything dumb." And she had. She should have waited. Gramma was going to be mad at her and so would Ellen, and . . .

She looked down at herself. Her suit was almost dry, but the first thing she'd better do was get dressed. Hurriedly, she rinsed off in the shower and put on her blue shorts and her red t-shirt. She wasn't hungry, that was for sure. The thought of food almost made her throw up. Well, she decided, maybe the pie. She should eat something.

She was just scraping the plate when a car horn sounded in front. It would only be a couple of hours, maybe three, before she'd be home and so would Gramma. She'd wait. She'd let Gramma handle what to do.

She shoved her plate and fork into the dishwasher and grabbed her purse. Locking the front door behind her, she hurried to the van.

"Hop in," Ellen said. "The matches will be starting in fifteen minutes."

The party was being held in honor of the new director of the medical clinic. Paula felt completely at home the minute she walked in the door. God knew she'd attended many similar gatherings. The home had a fantastic view of the Sound, and now, as she stood there, the sun began its descent behind the craggy Olympic Mountains. Brilliant oranges, reds and golds glowed from behind the peaks. Lights twinkled like stars in the darkened hills below. David's arm slid around her back, and his hand cupped her elbow. She smiled up at him.

"Having a good time?" he asked.

"Wonderful." That, perhaps, was an exaggeration. After all, she'd never met any of the people there before. They were all pleasant, and some more than that. One woman in particular had intrigued her. She and her husband, it turned out, were both physicians. Initially, Paula felt the pang of jealousy that hit her sometimes when she encountered a woman who'd really done something with her life, but she pushed it aside. After Stephanie—that was the young doctor's name—had related a few stories of her residency and her practice, Paula was quite sure medicine would not have been her choice. How difficult it must be to deal with people who were in great pain or, worse yet, those who had incurable diseases. And the hours, and the interruptions!

The gathering reminded her of the dozens, maybe hundreds, she'd attended with Fred. Polished people, often fascinating, with the accoutrements of the wealthy. Scrumptious homes like the one she was in, as well as vacation places at the ocean, or Aspen or Vail.

"Thanks for bringing me, David," she said, smiling up at him. His extraordinary good looks stood out in a room full of handsome people.

"Can I get you another drink?" he asked.

"Oh, no. The wine we had with dinner was enough for me. Uh, I wonder if we shouldn't think of leaving," she suggested. "Laurie should be getting home about now."

"You're worrying, aren't you?"

"Yes, I am. Silly, I guess, but . . ."

"She's a good kid."

"You're right. But David, she's only thirteen. I can remember doing some pretty dumb things when I was that age. I was very careful, though, that my parents never found out. Didn't you do anything when you were a teenager that could have had bad consequences?"

He laughed. "Yeah, I remember a few. Mostly involving fast cars and parties. You're right about being stupid when you're a teenager. On more than one occasion those episodes could have had dire consequences—and we were completely oblivious to that possibility. But I don't see Laurie into that sort of thing. Not yet, anyway. And probably never. I'm impressed with your granddaughter, Paula."

"Thank you." Rationally, she agreed with him. But still . . . "I can't help it, David. I just have this feeling of foreboding."

He set down his glass on a side table. "I understand. I can't blame you, after what you've been through. And you won't be comfortable until you find her all tucked into bed. I'll get your coat."

They said their goodbyes and left, walking down the street until they reached David's BMW. He unlocked the doors with his remote, opened hers, then bowed and gestured. "For you, milady."

"I appreciate this, David. I'm probably being silly, but I *am* anxious."

Laurie was exhausted. Even if she hadn't had the scene with Cynthia, she'd be tired. She still got that way sometimes, ever since the accident. It had been a long day, with two swimming practices, the traipsing around through all those houses, and now the soccer match. It'd been a good game, but their team lost. "If only the Severan twin, whichever one it was, hadn't missed that penalty shot," she said.

"Yeah," Josh agreed. "Mark. He never misses usually. Everybody'll give him hell."

"That's not nice, Josh," Ellen said. "You could tell he felt awful."

"Yeah, I know. I didn't say *I'd* give him hell."

Ellen sighed. "Well, when we get to the pizza place, you be especially nice to him."

"Yeah, Mom."

Laurie yawned. "Uh, Ellen. Would it be okay if I skipped the party? I'm really pooped. Could you maybe swing by and drop me at our house?"

"Certainly, Laurie. I sometimes forget you're still recuperating because you're doing so well and all. Of course, we'll drop you."

Laurie didn't tell her why she really wanted to go home. Maybe Gramma would be there, and if she wasn't, she'd be home soon. She'd promised she wouldn't be late.

The door was locked, and no one answered when she rang. "Damn," she muttered. Well, at least this time she'd tucked her own set of keys in her purse. She unlocked the door, waved to Ellen, who waited until she was sure Laurie was inside, then shut and locked the door behind her.

Their route took them through the main shopping area. And, Paula realized suddenly, past the pizza place where the gang so often stopped after matches. She peered toward the parking lot. *Yes!* There was the Cogsdill van, or at least one that looked just like it. "Pull over," she suggested. "It looks like the kids are here. We can pick up Laurie."

"Will she think you're checking up on her?" David asked with a raised eyebrow.

"Well, I am, and I don't care," Paula said. "She'll just have to get used to it until they catch the murderer."

"Oh-kay." He pulled into the parking lot.

The soccer bunch was easy to spot as they walked through the door. Noisy. Pushy. Exuberant. Nobody seemed to mind the kids' bad manners. The staff and other patrons were undoubtedly used to such gatherings. She eyed the group, then waved when she spotted Ellen and her husband Stan.

"There they are," she said to David. "Let's . . . Except," she said anxiously, "I don't see Laurie. There's Josh, and the Cogsdill kids, and those twins Josh hangs out with . . ."

Her voice rose. "Where's Laurie?"

He took her arm. "Come on, we'll ask. No doubt there's an explanation."

The house was strangely silent. Usually, the cats sensed her arrival and came to greet her. Carioca hadn't come in before she left, but they should both be bellowing now for their food. She checked her bedroom, their favorite place to snooze. No cats. She slung her purse onto the bed.

"Mum-mum? Carioca? Where *are* you?" she called.

Nothing but silence. They never missed a meal. Their chubby shapes showed that. Why weren't they here demanding to be fed?

Finally, she opened the back door and called, "Mum-mum? Carioca?"

And then she listened. Did she hear a cat somewhere? Yes. She did. And it was two cats, no doubt about that. Bellowing with the distinctive sound of Siamese. There weren't any other Siamese living around them; at least none that were allowed outside.

Why *were* they outside and unfed and screaming? Shutting the door behind her, she headed out onto the golf course.

The half moonlight barely lighted her way but didn't make walking easy. Thank goodness there wasn't anything to trip over except the boundary markers, and she knew where they were. She crept along toward the sound of the cats, past the row of trees. The ninth green lay just ahead. She could see something on the green, something box-shaped.

It was a cat carrier! Two of them! And the cats were inside. "I'm coming, Mum-mum. I'm coming, Carioca," she called. Their mournful howls of complaint grew even louder when they heard her voice.

Suddenly, she was desperately afraid. What was going on?

She glanced behind her. The Cogsdill house had a dim light on, but she knew the family was at the pizza place. The house on the other side of the Pappases' was completely dark. They'd been gone all summer, visiting their daughter in Massachusetts, Gramma had told her. That's why nobody'd heard the awful noise the cats were making. She opened her mouth to scream anyway. Maybe somebody'd . . .

It was then that Cynthia Lamphear stepped out of the night. "I told you it was dangerous to play detective," she said, the whites of her eyes flashing.

In spite of her fear, Laurie's back stiffened. It might have been dangerous—well, obviously it had been—but she'd been successful, when nobody else had, not even the police. But what good was that going to do her now? What did Cynthia plan to do?

Cynthia stepped toward her. She carried a gun, Laurie saw. She gulped.

What on earth could she do?

Chapter Twenty-Three

The Pappas house was completely dark as Paula and the doctor drove up. "See? Probably sound asleep, like Ellen said." Silently, David took her elbow and escorted her onto the porch. After she unlocked the front door, he followed her into the house.

Tiptoeing now, Paula hurried to Laurie's room, peeked inside, and then flipped the light switch. "Oh," she cried, "she's *not* here! I knew it! And there's her purse on the bed. And David, where are the cats? I knew it was too quiet in here. She was going to lock them in the house, and they'd have been here, bellowing by now. Laurie!" she yelled. "Are you here?" An ominous stillness greeted her cry.

"Call the police," David ordered, "while I double-check the rest of the house."

Paula's fumbling fingers weren't cooperating. She had to dial three times before she got it right. "Please. This is Paula Madigan. You know, I'm staying at the Pappas house in Kamiak Hills, and . . ."

"Yes, Mrs. Madigan. What can I do for you?"

"Detective Compagnio's the one who's dealing with the murders here." Oh, if only she didn't have to explain everything! Maybe she should have just dialed nine-one-one. "Oh, help! I've just arrived home and my granddaughter's missing. She's the one who was injured by the hit-and-run . . ."

"We'll send someone immediately," the voice answered. "And I'll call the detective."

"Thanks! Thanks so much." Paula banged the receiver down. She knew at once from his expression that David had found nothing. Together, they hurried into the kitchen. She slid the door to the deck open.

"David! Listen!" From the direction of the golf course, the unmistakable cries of distressed Siamese reverberated. "What on earth's going on? I'll bet Laurie's out there. But why are the cats screaming?"

David put his finger to his mouth. "Shh!"

Paula was already out the door. She nodded, although she doubted if he could see her.

David took the lead as they silently crept towards the ninth green.

Get Cynthia talking, Laurie thought suddenly. Their cleaning lady had always liked to talk, and if Laurie could only stall long enough, Gramma should get home. Would she realize something was wrong and that Laurie wasn't with the Cogsdills?

If she looked around, she would. She'd see Laurie's purse where she'd tossed it on the bed. She'd realize the cats were gone, too. And if she opened the door, she'd hear the bellowing coming from the ninth green. That's what she'd do, she decided. Talk, and ask questions, and stall, and hope.

"Seeing your daughter skate must have been really cool. Did she win while you were there in Colorado?" she asked.

Cynthia blinked. She must have been surprised at how calm Laurie seemed. That was good. She'd keep hiding her fear.

"No, we didn't get to see Serita compete, but she won the last competition she was in," Cynthia said. "It wasn't on the national level, but everybody was pleased. But never mind. Now . . ."

"Uh . . ." Laurie edged sideways. She had to get Cynthia turned so that she wasn't facing the Pappas house and wouldn't see lights when Gramma came home. "Does she ever skate with a partner?"

"She tried that once, briefly, but decided to put that off for the time being and concentrate on singles."

Laurie's teeth were chattering. She'd never had that happen, except when she was freezing cold. She clenched her jaws, then slid her feet sideways again. Talk, talk, talk. That was what she needed to do. "Uh . . . Why? Why did you try to kill Josh and me?"

"Isn't that obvious?" Cynthia's voice was cross. "You two children playing detective were dangerous. You were asking too many questions and getting too close to the answers. I tried to warn you, remember? I didn't want to have to hurt you."

"That means you did murder what's-her-name," Laurie said.

"Martha? Or Alice? What choice did I have? They were both threatening to go to the police. I couldn't let that happen. It was so stupid. Martha wasn't paying me that much to cover up for her. All she'd done was shoplift. Silly thing to murder for, but I didn't have a choice."

The woman was crazy! Why hadn't they ever realized there was something wrong with her?

"But Alice . . . The Inspector said you couldn't have killed her. How did you . . . ?"

"How'd I fool him? It was easy. The policeman who called never asked what time we *flew* to Colorado, only what time we returned. We'd booked a red-eye. It was cheaper. I didn't know at the time that Alice had become a problem that had to be eliminated. It worked out perfectly." Her voice was smug.

A dim light glowed at the house. Yes! Laurie moved several more inches as inconspicuously as she could. "But why weren't the bodies found at their homes?" she asked.

In the faint light from the moon, she sensed that Cynthia shrugged. "I clean those houses," she said. "Can you imagine what I'd have faced if I'd killed them there? The police make such a mess. Fingerprint powder, dirty footprints. I like order, as you ought to know. So I lured them outside."

Laurie's jaw dropped. Was the woman serious?

Cynthia gestured with the gun. "Let the cats out," she said. "They've accomplished my purpose."

"Uh . . ." Laurie said. "What was that?" she asked as she reached Mum-Mum's carrier.

"To get you out here, of course. Isn't that obvious? Same reason. Can you imagine bloodstains on that white carpet?"

Laurie gulped. She had a sudden vision of her own body sprawled in the living room, a red stain spreading beneath it. If she let the cats out, they'd streak for home, and Paula wouldn't have a clue what was going on. She pretended to struggle with the latch as she scooched sideways once more.

Come on, Gramma, she pleaded silently. *Open the door!*

"Hurry it up," Cynthia ordered.

"I'm trying," Laurie said. "The catch on this cage always sticks."

The light came on in the kitchen and then . . . and then the sliding door opened. Figuring she'd taken as long as she could, Laurie opened the door. Mum-Mum, after a low growl that turned into a shriek, streaked for home. She'd been the louder of the two, Laurie realized. She should have let Carioca out first. Again, she pretended to have trouble with the catch but could only stall so long.

Finally, she opened the second crate's door, and Carioca, who was a little more timid, hesitated. "Hurry it up, Carioca," Laurie said, as loud as she could. Two figures slid out from the kitchen, and headed silently toward them. The one in front didn't look quite right to be Gramma. The doc, probably? Hooray!

Then she stood. She had to get Cynthia talking again.

"But," Laurie asked, "why'd you put them on the golf course?" *Other than the fact that you're stark, raving mad,* she thought. "I mean, it must have been a lot of trouble to bury Martha in the sand trap. And Alice . . ."

"Just thumbing my nose at all the rich biddies who live here. Kamiak Hills, huh! If I'd had a quarter of the money most of them have, paying for Serita's training wouldn't have been a problem."

"But you live here, too."

"So what? I told you. Money! Serita's training! We bought our house early on . . . We had enough, except for . . . It takes a lot to seriously train for the . . . Just the costumes alone . . . Some mothers make them, but . . . And the coaches, paying for the rink time, the travel . . . Now, with the economy . . ."

Cynthia sounded like she was falling apart. That made Laurie even more nervous. Was this a good thing? Or was it bad? She edged a bit more, just to be safe. Gramma and the doc must have heard the cats. A cloud moved across the quarter moon, and the night became even darker. She couldn't see the figures anymore, but staring would not be a good idea. Purposefully, she focused on Cynthia's face. "Uh . . . we hadn't found out anything important. Just gossip. You know what the people around here are like. I thought in New York where I lived that I knew everything that was going on. But here . . ."

Cynthia shook her head. "I don't care what they do in New York. You *were* getting close, weren't you?" Her tone was sarcastic. "And you recognized my car this afternoon."

"Uh . . . Why no, Cynthia. I . . . I didn't." Did she sound like she was telling the truth? Probably not, she thought. It was pretty hard to make her voice sound sincere when she was shaking so much.

Cynthia smiled grimly. "I don't think you're being truthful, although I don't know why you recognized it." Her voice verged on whiny. "My husband had just finished fixing the damage. He restored the car in the first place, you know. His hobby. It's a classic."

As if that mattered, Laurie thought.

"No one would have known it had been . . . Except you. Well, enough talking," Cynthia said. "I'm truly sorry, but it *is* your own fault. If you'd just listened to me and minded your own business, I wouldn't be forced to do this." She raised the gun.

Was that a shadow right behind Cynthia? Laurie's heart thumped.

"I'd put that gun down if I were you."

It *was* the doc.

Cynthia's head spun around, and then instantly she moved. She grabbed Laurie, pressing the gun against her head, hard.

"Uurk!" Laurie'd thought she'd been scared before, but never had she been as petrified as she was now. She felt like she'd quit breathing entirely. Warm moisture told her she'd wet her pants. Shit! Not that it made any difference. The woman was nuts. She wouldn't care if she shot Laurie, even though she'd never get away with it. But that wouldn't do Laurie any good.

Gramma had arrived, and now she pleaded, "Oh, Cynthia, don't!"

"You can't kill all three of us," David pointed out, his voice calm.

"Oh? Why not?" Cynthia answered. "There's plenty of bullets in the gun."

"The police are on their way," David said. "You couldn't move the bodies . . ."

Laurie almost fainted. Bodies! Hers, Gramma's, the doc's.

"Cynthia, please! Please don't hurt Laurie," Paula begged. "Think about your daughter. Remember Serita. They're . . .

They're almost exactly the same age. They have their lives ahead of them."

Laurie felt Cynthia shudder, and the muzzle pressed against the side of her head wavered. Had Gramma said the right thing to stop her?

Yes! Cynthia's arm dropped. She tossed the gun toward David's feet.

"I didn't want to kill anyone," she said.

Chapter Twenty-Four

Paula threw her arms around the sobbing Laurie.

"Oh, Gramma, I'm *so* glad to see you! I'm *so* glad you got here!"

"Hush, hush," Paula said, patting her granddaughter on her back. "It's all over. We can stop worrying. You're safe now."

Laurie's head bobbed. "I know. You and the doc . . . Oh, you got here just in time."

Cynthia had collapsed in a heap, Paula could see as she looked over her granddaughter's shoulder. Her arms were wrapped around her knees, with her head buried between them.

David put the gun down carefully, far from Cynthia, and slid one arm around Paula. The other encompassed Laurie. "You'll have a lot to tell us. How on earth . . . ?"

Paula shook her head. "Let it wait."

"It was her car," Laurie said, between snuffles. "I recognized that thingie on the hood, and she caught me. Oh, Gramma, I was so dumb."

"Here comes the backup," David said. Paula looked up to see two people carrying flashlights hurrying toward them.

"Gramma," Laurie whispered into her ear, "I've got to take a shower before I talk to anyone. I . . . I . . . peed . . ."

"No problem." Poor Laurie, Paula thought. It was understandable that she'd had an accident because of her deep fear, but she'd really feel humiliated if anyone else found out.

"I'm going to take Laurie right to the house," she told David.

"Will you talk to the police?"

"Certainly." He stepped back.

Paula didn't recognize the two officers who approached her, but she stopped long enough to tell them, "We found Laurie, and your murderer. Dr. Cordiner is back there on the ninth green with her. He'll explain everything, but I want to get Laurie inside. She's been really stressed."

"Certainly, ma'am," the first man said, pausing beside them as the other continued, "We'll handle things out here. Take care of the girl. The inspector should be here shortly."

Paula thanked him and caught up with her granddaughter, who'd scurried toward the house.

Laurie ran the water as hot as she could stand. She felt . . . contaminated. She should be feeling really great now that it was all over, but so far, it wasn't working.

She'd heard the doorbell ring. Probably the inspector, she figured. She wasn't looking forward to talking to him. She'd been so foolish. He'd warned her, too, and she'd almost gotten killed because she hadn't paid attention. Almost got Gramma killed, too, and the doc.

Finally, though, the hot water began to run out. She dried slowly and thoroughly, dressed in the clean clothes she'd brought into the bathroom with her, and wrapped her wet hair in a fresh towel.

The inspector stood as she entered the living room. "Good evening, Laurie," he said. "Glad it all turned out okay. Your grandmother has brought me up on what she knows, but . . ."

"But, yeah. She doesn't know how really dumb I was."

He didn't answer, just raised an eyebrow, then sat down and opened a notebook. Beside him on the couch, Gramma stirred, then said, "Well?"

Laurie sighed as she settled in a chair. Might as well get it over with. "This afternoon, when Josh and I got back from swimming practice, I . . . I asked him if he knew where Cynthia lived. It'd been bugging me because we'd never had a chance to look at her car, and that just didn't make sense. So Josh told me to go over a street and look for the house with green shutters."

"You mean he condoned what you were going to do?" Gramma looked liked she'd throttle Josh when she got a chance. And that wasn't fair.

"No! He actually . . . Well, the last thing he said, was, 'Don't do anything dumb.' "

"And you did anyway? Laurie, I'm appalled, I'm . . ."

The inspector laid a hand on Gramma's knee. "Let's hear what happened."

Rumbling noises from Gramma sounded like a volcano that was getting ready to erupt.

"It *was* daylight, and there were people out working in their yards . . ."

"Humph!"

Laurie had never seen her grandmother so perturbed before. Here, she'd been hoping—well, sort of—that Gramma was going to ask her to stay here with her, maybe in that cool house in Cedar Harbor. She'd felt a little guilty at the idea. She'd be deserting her mom, but she could spend vacations with her. And maybe now that her grandfather was dead, her mom'd like to come back here to Washington. It'd sure beat that stuffy apartment in New York. Maybe Gramma hadn't meant she wanted Laurie to stay with her, but it had sounded like that was what she was hinting. Laurie sure hoped she hadn't blown it.

Glancing sideways at Paula, the inspector said, "Laurie, please tell us exactly what happened tonight. Every detail."

"Well . . ." Laurie wiggled, trying to get comfortable. "I meant to just drive the cart by her house, you know. I thought her car might be outside. But the house looked like nobody was home, so I decided to drive on around into the alley. I crawled through some bushes and looked through the window of the garage, and . . ." She gulped.

"And what?"

"And she caught me. She came up behind me. I thought I fooled her when I told her I didn't recognize the car, but I guess I'm not a very good liar. It was a shock. That thingie on the hood . . . I knew the minute I saw it that the star-shaped thing was what I'd been trying to remember."

"What did she do?"

"She pretended that she believed me. She said she was going to complain to you, and that I'd be in real trouble. I guess I am, aren't I?"

The inspector actually smiled. He had a nice smile. He didn't look like he was mad at her. "I wouldn't put it like that. You found the murderer for us. Personally, I think you deserve a medal for all you've gone through. But you did put your grandmother through a lot, also. Now tell me, how did you all end up out on the golf course?"

"Well, the cats weren't home when Ellen dropped me off after the soccer game. And they should have been. So, after I'd hunted everywhere, I opened the door to the deck, and I heard them screaming. I just had to see what was going on. When I saw they were in their cat carriers I got scared, but it was too late."

Nobody said anything while the inspector wrote in his notebook. Grandma was still glaring, though.

"Everything she did was so convoluted . . ." he said. "Did she give you any inkling why she'd murdered those women and lured you out onto the golf course?"

"Yes. I was so freaked out. She's totally crazy. She actually said she didn't have any choice about killing them because she couldn't let them go to the police. She seemed to think I'd agree . . . And, Jack, you told us she couldn't be the murderer."

"I'm aware of that."

"She said . . . she said that no one asked what time they flew to Colorado, that they were on a red-eye—"

"Uh-oh," Gramma said, glancing sideways at Jack. "I suspect heads will roll."

He nodded, his expression grim.

"Yours?" Gramma asked, looking sympathetic.

"Only because it was my ultimate responsibility. I wasn't the one who made the call. Let's hear the rest of the story."

He obviously was anxious to change the subject. Laurie proceeded to repeat the entire conversation she'd had with Cynthia. She started to shake again. Gramma noticed and came over to stand beside her.

"Remember, it's behind you," she said, rubbing her shoulders. "And you can be credited with solving the mystery."

"Yeah, but I could've gotten you and the doc killed!"

"But you didn't. So it's time to move on."

"Your grandmother's right, Laurie. We're grateful. Very much so. No one knows how many more people she would have decided to kill." Glancing at Paula, he asked, "Speaking of Dr. Cordiner. How did he get involved in the situation?"

"Well, I'd been to a party in Edmonds with him."

The inspector looked at Gramma sideways with a peculiar expression.

"But I was nervous the whole time. He was good enough to hustle me home and then come into the house to check on Laurie." She swallowed. "I'll never forget . . ." She reached down and hugged Laurie, tight.

"I'm sure you won't. But, changing the subject, the Pappases will be returning soon, I understand. And you'll be . . . ?"

"Yes, we'll be leaving shortly. Right now I'm feeling I'll be glad to see Kamiak Hills in my rear-view mirror. I won't be returning to Bellevue, however. I have my place there up for sale. I've been looking at other houses. I found a place rather quickly that I'm seriously considering. It's up in Cedar Harbor."

"Good choice," Jack said. "My son lives there. He's in law enforcement, too. Works in Edmonds. He's considering applying for an open position there at the Harbor, now that they have a new police chief."

"The real estate agent mentioned that there'd been a problem."

"You could say that. The problem, however, personified by the police chief, ended with his murder. It's a long story."

"I'd like to know more about the town. Perhaps I can ask you some questions? Later? I know this isn't the time."

"Sure." He shut his notebook.

A knock at the sliding door in back sounded, and the detective stood. "Probably one of my men," he said. Gramma followed him.

As they approached the slider, Laurie could see a uniformed officer and the doc. Paula opened the glass, and he stepped inside, holding out his hand.

"Inspector," he said.

"Doctor," Jack replied. Weird, Laurie thought. She could almost see bad vibes shooting between them. What was that about?

Suddenly, Laurie felt totally worn out. Bed sounded like heaven. Without saying anything, she headed to her room.

Jack stepped onto the deck and joined the officer. "We'll be out here a while. Glad it's over. Take care of your granddaughter. She's a great kid."

"Thank you, and goodnight, Jack."

David slid the door shut. "How's Laurie doing?"

"Feeling contrite. She really took some horrible chances . . .

But there's no point in making her feel worse. She was able to pull herself together and give the inspector a report. She seems to feel especially bad that she put you and me in jeopardy."

He nodded. "I feel sure that she's gained a lot of maturity from this experience. Thought I'd just check with you and then be off."

"Thank you, David." She stretched wearily. "Thanks for your help."

The living room was empty as they walked through. Laurie'd clearly headed to bed. Paula tried to hide a yawn herself but failed. David looked at her with that empathetic expression she was sure he used on patients. Always the doctor, she assumed. At the front door, he gave her a quick hug, then left.

Gramma had finished breakfast when Laurie walked into the kitchen the next morning. Her cereal bowl was empty and pushed to one side. Looking glum, she was hunched over a mug of coffee. Glancing at the clock, Laurie could see it was almost ten. Wow, she'd almost slept the clock around.

"Good morning, Gramma." She opened the refrigerator and took out the container of orange juice.

"Good morning," Gramma answered, looking up. "And how are you?"

"I'm good." Laurie was surprised to find that she really did feel upbeat. She'd slept soundly. No bad dreams, like she'd been having so often since the accident. She'd probably never, ever, be able to forget that scene on the ninth green. But, wow, what a story it would make someday when a teacher wanted her to write an essay about a "life experience"! She chuckled.

"You really are," Paula said, looking surprised but much more cheerful herself.

"Yeah, it's over, and I didn't have any nightmares. I can quit looking over my shoulder and wondering who wants to kill me."

"I'm sure you'll be pleased to know that you made the news this morning, and they did give your name this time. Tonight we can set it up to tape. That is, if you really want to rehash the whole thing later."

"Sure. I mean, it's the most important thing that ever happened to me." She drank the juice, then set the glass down while Gramma watched, smiling. "What are we going to do today?" she asked.

"Well, I hadn't made any plans. Seemed like it'd be a good idea to take it easy. And I wanted to see how you were. But first thing, Laurie, I think it's time we had a little talk."

"Oh?" Laurie said warily. "What about?"

"Specifically, your plans. Laurie, I think maybe you've sensed what I've been thinking, but it's time to bring it into the open. How would you like . . . Would you consider staying with me this winter and going to school here?" Gramma's voice trembled, but she looked determined.

Laurie's heart thumped. *Yes!* She'd been right that her grandmother'd been thinking along those lines. She chewed her lip, and then said, "I have thought about it. I'd feel guilty, sort of, leaving Mom. But you know, I'm not sure she wouldn't be glad, deep down. I mean, she knows that's a dump where we live, and the school isn't so hot. Besides, she's always talking about getting on with her life now that I'm so grown up."

"But would she be able to manage without you?"

"I don't know. But she survived all those years when I was just a kid. And I can't plan things for her forever. Don't you think, maybe, it's time she learned to organize things herself?"

Gramma beamed. "That's a very mature comment, Laurie. Yes. I do think so. And as long as you do everything for her, she never will."

Her grandmother sipped some more coffee. "In that case, shall we inspect that house in Cedar Harbor more thoroughly tomorrow? We didn't even see all the rooms. Or should we look further?"

"It was great. I think it'd be perfect for us." Laurie frowned. "Are you sure you can afford it?"

"Completely. And Laurie, I'm thinking that I can help your mother out financially, too, now that we're back in touch."

"Oh, that would be so great! I love Mom. I'll miss her, but I'd . . . I'd been hoping you'd ask me to stay. And I figure I can visit her for vacations and maybe . . . maybe she'll decide to move back here. Wouldn't that be so cool?"

Jack called shortly after noon. "How're things going?" he asked.

"Really good," Paula answered. "I've been discussing Laurie spending the winter with me. And we're going to look at that house in Cedar Harbor tomorrow. I do still have one or two more questions . . ."

"Actually, that's why I called. Obviously I didn't have time last night for chatting. I was wondering if I could stop by this afternoon."

"Of course, Jack. That would be terrific. I'd ask you for lunch, but we're so off schedule. How would about two work for you?"

"Ideal. I'll be there."

Paula prepared a plate of finger sandwiches. She'd be thinking food again about the time the inspector got here, she imagined, and she knew how Jack liked to eat. She also prepared a plate of fruit. Laurie had announced that she was going over to Josh's while Paula's boyfriend was here. "Give you a chance to be alone," she'd said with a glint in her eye.

"He's not my boyfriend. I've told you that before."

"Uh-huh," Laurie said. She waggled her fingers goodbye and left when she'd finished breakfast.

Jack's eyes lighted up when he saw the food Paula had prepared. *The way to a man's heart . . .* she thought. But then, what was she thinking? He'd been friendly, but wasn't that all? Was she interested in any man's heart?

He opened the conversation by asking, "Was there anything special you wondered about in Cedar Harbor?"

"Well, yes. I finally nerved myself to bring up the question of Laurie staying here with me this winter."

"And?"

"And she's going to! I'm so excited, Jack. I know it'll most likely be just for the four years she's in high school . . . Which leads me to the one thing I haven't had a chance to investigate. How are the schools in Cedar Harbor?"

"The best. That's one reason my son and his wife chose to live there."

"I'm so glad to hear that. I'm expecting at this point that I'll buy the house we looked at there. It would be perfect for us, and yet not too big when she's gone." She described the view, the yard and the house with enthusiasm.

"Do you realize you called the place 'my house?' Sounds like you've made up your mind."

"Did I?" She laughed. "I didn't realize it. I guess my subconscious was trying to step in. Help yourself to more food," she suggested, realizing his plate was empty. "This is really lunch for me." She refilled her own plate.

"Thank you." He replenished his plate, then chewed thoughtfully for a few minutes. "And that leads me to a question also. One that's awkward at best. Um, I'm wondering about your . . . well, your relationship with Cordiner."

Paula glanced up, confused. "My relationship . . ." Good heavens, was he implying . . .

"I don't want to interfere, but, well, I'm wondering . . ." He wouldn't quite meet her eyes. "I'm wondering if, now that we're no longer involved in a case together, whether perhaps I could visit, after you get moved?"

"Why, Jack!" She smiled. The inspector was definitely blushing. "The only 'relationship' I have with the doctor is friendship." She knew immediately that that was true. He might want more—there were certainly hints in that direction—but that wasn't in the cards. "I'd like that very much."

A giggle sounded from behind the closed kitchen door.

Paula looked at him, then covered her mouth with her hand to suppress laughter.

His eyes twinkled as he reached across to take her hand.

ABOUT THE AUTHOR

Highlights of **Norma Tadlock Johnson**'s life include traveling through Europe in a Volkswagon camper, volunteering at an Olympic Winter Games, climbing Mount Rainier, and snorkeling with sting rays and turtles.

In addition to the cozy mysteries she is now writing, Johnson has published middle-grade novels, romantic suspense, four romances co-written with her daughter, Janice Kay Johnson, and a nonfiction about the mountain troops of World War II.